Also by Mark Teppo

The Potemkin Mosaic
Rudolph! He Is the Reason for the Season
Lightbreaker
Heartland
The Doom That Came to the Coffee Shop
In the Mansion of Madness
Beyond the Walls of Sanity
Solitaire

THE FOREWORLD SAGA

The Mongoliad (co-authored with Erik Bear, Greg Bear,
Joseph Brassey, Nicole Galland, Cooper
Moo, & Neal Stephenson)
Katabasis (co-authored with Joseph Brassey,
Cooper Moo, & Angus Trim)

The Lion in Chains (co-authored with Angus Trim)
Cimarronin (co-authored with Ellis Amdur,
Charles C. Mann, & Neal Stephenson)

Sinner
Dreamer
Seer
The Beast of Calatrava

LONGSPUR

MARK TEPPO

51325 Books

This book was printed in the United States of America. It is a product of Firebird Creative (Clackamas, OR).

I'll get the horses . . .

Book Design by Firebird Creative

First **51325 Books** edition: July 2022

http://www.markteppo.com

This one is for the patient ones. They know who they are.

LONGSPUR

1872
KANSAS

1

West—past the mountains and on the far side of the great and lazy river—the prairie began. It was so vast that it took the wind months to get across it. Early travelers from the east, when confronted by this endless sea of grass likened it to the ocean their grandfathers had crossed. There were no roads across this land. Maps were hand-drawn and jealously guarded. There were no mountains to guide weary travelers. There was only the grass and the wind.

Some thought to follow the river, but it went north, as if it was frightened to strike out across the flat prairie. It did turn north eventually, but trappers and explorers told stories of impossible canyons and impassable forests. No, the way west was across the prairie, in much the same way that their grandfathers had set their prows to chase the sun. West, west, always west. Eventually, they had to reach the other side.

At night, alone upon the plains, you rode under the gravid belly of the night, bloated with stars. At night, the grass sighed and whispered. Other sounds—your plaintive cries, the blowing of your horse, the creak of wagon wheels—were swallowed by the prairie.

At night, the grasslands gave birth to strange things . . .

He started awake, and his desperate chest-heaving gasp broke the delirium blooming in his brain. He came rushing back from a place that he thought he should know, but which he could not place. His heart pounded in his chest, a thunderous rhythm like a thousand hooves, and his face and arms were covered in sweat. He tried to speak, but his tongue knew no words, and the only sound he could manage was a strangled murmur.

The stars winked at him. *There is no sun*, they whispered. *There is only us and the shadows.* But such comfort was no comfort at all, and he wanted to turn away from their false light. His limbs were heavy, and he struggled to move. He was not bound. It was only a camp blanket tangled around his legs. He fought his way free, and the uneven ground banged against his elbows and shoulders.

The dying embers of a fire lay on his left, and he found solace in the fading glow of the coals. Beyond the fire, he sensed the presence of several horses—he couldn't remember how many they had. Two or three, at least. Regardless of their number, they were reminders of who he was and where he was.

There was a shape beside the fire, an outline that wasn't as dark as the night. A shape he did not know, and as he became aware of it, it looked at him. He caught sight of a tiny gleam that might have been starlight reflected from watchful eyes. He thought he heard the sound of someone crying, but when he sat up and leaned forward, the shape vanished.

All that was left was a whisper. *What falls, rises.* The voice sounded like the speaker was standing right behind him, but when he whirled around, there was nothing there but darkness.

What dies will live again. The voice fled as he struggled to stand, as he struggled to wake up.

This wasn't the first time he had been visited like this in a dream. Other dreams frightened him more: dreams of ghastly battlefields, littered with hundreds of dead—blue and gray, alike; dreams where he had seen the faces of those he had killed; dreams where he had returned to Silverglen and found nothing but broken and gnawed bones. This dream always left him unsettled, as if there was something inside him that could not scrubbed away. A stain. A blemish. A mark that would always come back.

When he woke again, coffee was bubbling in the cast iron pot balanced on a pair of rocks next to the fire. The dark drape of night had been replaced by a rippling sheet of pale blue cloth, streaked with gossamer strands of white clouds. A pair of birds called to one another nearby, and he heard the soft noise of a horse blowing out through its nose as it ate.

Elm sat up slowly, his body stiff from a night of sleeping on the hard ground. His ribs ached—a memory of a recent injury—and when he ran a hand across his face, he encountered the bristly touch of a week or so's worth of stubble. He kept rubbing—using both hands now—and the rough scrape of his beard invigorated both his face and his hands.

Rock crunched beneath a booted foot, and he looked to his right, squinting into the glare of the morning sun.

The man was a black shape, outlined by the sun, and it was only when he reached the fire and crouched by the bubbling pot, that his features became visible. He had the eyes of a hawk and the face of a woolly sheep who was overdue for a shearing. He was a lanky fellow, unbent by his apparent age, and his rough fingers were nimble as they pulled the cast iron pot away from the fire.

The man deftly poured coffee into a pair of tin mugs. He set one mug down and raised the other to his own lips. He sipped noisily, as if he could not readily measure the distance between his lip and the rim of the cup through his thick beard. His eyes were hard—they had seen too much to be any other way—but there was still compassion in that face—mostly in the wrinkles and lines across his forehead and cheeks.

He had been a federal judge once—a respected keeper of the law in Baton Rouge—but his court was now encompassed by the open sky and the endless prairie.

"Civility should not be expected nor given until a man has had coffee or whiskey," the Judge said. He tilted his cup toward the sky. "And we're out of whiskey."

"We had some last night," Elm said.

"That was before you started thrashing and moaning," the Judge replied. "Kept me up half the night."

"And the other half?"

The Judge shrugged. "Coffee is all that is left."

"How far are we from a soft bed and a feather pillow?" Elm asked. He reached for the mug and found the coffee hot and strong. The last threads of the dream fled after the first sip.

"Too far," the Judge groused.

They were, by Elm's reckoning, still in Kansas. They had passed through Independence several days prior. The name of the town had soured the Judge. He had not been particularly keen on the disheveled appearance of the buildings that leaned against one another, and the locals were—in his words—an uncivil and unkempt lot prone to knifing one another as readily as they spit. Beyond Independence lay the great grass sea that stretched God knows how far to the west. Here Be Monsters would be how cartographers marked these blank spots, but there were no true monsters. There was only immense herds of shaggy buffalo that ranged freely and widely across the grass sea, and following behind them were a countless number of native tribes.

When the tribes came into contact with the new settlers and farmers who were trying to shape the earth to their own futile designs, there was, more often than not, bloodshed. There was always a border to protect: the Great Plains, Texas, Mexico. After the War, there were men who still wanted to fight for their country, and the West embraced those men with open arms.

They decided to avoid the well-traveled route taken by settlers, and for awhile, they followed the Santa Fe railroad as it coursed south and west. Eventually, they lost track of the rails and neither felt any urge to find them again. The landscape was uneventful—miles and miles of buffalo grass, the occasional stand of beaverwood and dogwood, tiny streams which the horses had splashed through without any effort, and the infrequent rocky outcropping from which they could survey the endless grass.

At night, there were so many stars that they made a river coursing across Heaven. Many times, when he dreamed, Elm imagined himself on that river, starlight flowing beneath the hull of his boat. Often there was someone in the boat with him, but he could never see their face. It wasn't always the same person, though it was never the Judge. That much he knew.

The Judge had opened his eyes to how truly strange the world was. It was as if Elm had lived his entire life believing that the world was flat—like a coin—and when the Judge plucked it from his hand and spun it, he realized it was more like an apple. While such knowledge broadened Elm's mind, with that knowledge came an awareness of darker things. Things which neither he nor the Judge could explain. *All things have a shadow*, the Judge would say, *just as all shadows come from something real.*

This wasn't as comforting as the Judge made it out to be.

Laelaps came over and licked Elm's hand. He was a black mutt with white spots on his muzzle and left ear. The dog had followed him out of Thrush, and he had spent several days telling it to go home, but the dog hadn't listened. Finally, Elm had crouched down to the dog's level and stared the mutt in the face. *You can stay*, Elm had said, *but you have to have a name.*

The dog wagged his tail so enthusiastically his entire body shook.

That night, Elm saw a shooting star. It passed through a constellation he had learned from Bostán, a young Romani boy whose curiosity was as boundless as the dog's earnestness. *That is Canis Major*, he said to the dog who was curled up next to him. *Zeus gave Europa a gift, a hound that never failed to catch its prey. He called the dog 'Laelaps.'*

It's a good name, the Judge had said. And that was that.

Another constellation that Bostán had pointed out to him was Canis Minor—the little hound. *In some of the stories, this wasn't a hound, but a fox,* Orchilí—Bostán's aunt and guardian—*had told him. It was called the Teumessian fox and it couldn't be caught.*

But if the hound always catches its prey? Elm's confusion made her laugh.

It is a paradox, she explained. *Two separate things that are both true, even though they can't be true at the same time.*

She hadn't stayed, but he could still hear her voice in his head. The world was a paradox; all things were true and eternal, yet nothing lasted forever.

Elm offered some of his coffee to the dog. Laelaps ignored the cup and licked the back of Elm's hand. Only the left. Never the right. Never the hand that pulled the trigger, as if he knew what Elm had done during the War.

2

The trading post was a pair of weather-stained buildings braced by a ragged band of cottonwoods. A crooked finger of smoke rose from an equally crooked chimney, and a half dozen chickens pecked nonchalantly across the dry ground in front of the house, as if they knew they weren't going to find any food but—being chickens—didn't have anything better to do. A paddock, designated by a series of posts more ancient than the Judge, constrained a sway-backed donkey who also appeared to have little else to do but stand near a scrub of pale grass. Maybe it was going to eat; maybe it wasn't. There was no rush.

Laelaps barked at the chickens, and when they didn't react with feather-flinging panic, he charged. They scattered in an cacophony of outraged clucking, and the dog gave a happy bark, delighted to have disturbed the bucolic setting. He wandered over to the house and raised a leg.

"Well done, dog," the Judge said. Elm wasn't sure which of the dog's actions the Judge was admiring. "A conundrum, don't you think?" the Judge offered. "Can a business be partially abandoned and still be a going concern?"

The porch leaned to the left, canted by time and indifference. Two posts at the front flanked a series of three steps. A stack of buffalo hides spread like moss on tree bark across a crooked railing. They were growing across the porch, and some had leapt from the railing and were attempting to escape across the yard. They hadn't gotten very far.

Elm let his gaze wander around the rest of the property. A small shed peeked around the corner of the house. It wasn't large enough to be a barn for horses; more likely, it was used to store dry goods. A slopping overhang on the far side sheltered poorly stacked firewood. Finally, there was a narrow privy that looked like someone had stood a coffin on end.

Laelaps barked, and Elm's hand dropped to the butt of his revolver.

The house groaned as if it was giving birth, and the front door creaked open. A bear—no, it was a man wrapped in bearskins—stumbled out. It was hard to tell where the hair on his head ended and his beard began—it would take at least an hour with a stiff brush to be sure.

"Good day and good travels to you, dusty men of the road," the bearded bear-skinned man shouted. A bone-rattling cough followed his greeting, and Elm thought the man's coughing fit was going to send him tumbling face-first off the porch, but the trader survived both his phlegmatic obstruction and the short descent with a loose-limbed familiarity. The chickens darted out of his way as he stumbled across the yard. "Well met," he said. "Well met, indeed."

He thrust out a hand, but since Elm and the Judge were both astride their horses, he turned the gesture into a loose wave that encompassed the property.

The Judge's mustache twitched as he got a whiff of the man. "I always like a man who offers pleasantries to strangers," he said.

The fat man's beard rippled, and Elm caught a brief glimpse of ragged teeth. "No one is a stranger here," he said.

"And where might 'here' be, friend?" the Judge asked.

"Twenty miles this side of the asscrack of the world," the man said. He brayed with laughter, delighted at the opportunity to indulge in what was undoubtedly a regular witticism.

The Judge looked at Elm. "I told you we should have taken that left at the river."

Elm shrugged. "You wanted to see the sights."

"Ah, wandering spirits." The trader nodded sagely as if he privy to a great secret.

The Judge brightened. "Speaking of spirits," he started.

The man clapped his hands together, and a puff of dust rose from the impact. "You are in luck, my friend," the man said. "I have whiskey." He clucked his tongue and let his gaze roam between Elm and the Judge. "Reasonably priced too," he added, a sudden—but not altogether surprising—shrewdness developing in his tone. "For gentlemen such as yourselves."

"Ah, a trader with a nose for bargaining. One of the oldest—and surest—signs of civilization." The Judge smiled. "My companion here worried we had forsaken it entirely."

"Have no fear, good sirs." The trader bowed in Elm's direction. "My humble store has everything you could possibly want." He gestured toward the house. "Perhaps more." He waggled his eyebrows. "Reasonably priced."

As Elm and the Judge dismounted, the bear-skinned man started to point at the trough, but his fingers thought better of the motion and danced in the air instead. "There's, ah, I'm sorry. I wasn't expecting visitors today." The trader laughed apologetically. His eyes were large and round, like a pair of bird eggs in a nest of twigs. "There's a well. Behind the house."

"I'll find it," Elm said.

As the trader and the Judge went into the house, Elm brought both horses over to the hitching rail. Both horses spared the brackish water in the trough barely a glance and turned to nosing for clumps of grass at the base of the porch.

"I don't blame you," Elm said, patting the flank of his horse.

He wandered around the side of the house and paused near the shed. He thought he had seen a flicker of movement through the partially open door. When the movement wasn't repeated, he walked cautiously to the shed and pushed the door open with his foot.

Shelves. And more buffalo hides. Elm examined the disarray, which was even more chaotic than the mess on the porch. He caught sight of a pale shape protruding from beneath one of the hides. It wasn't as dirty as the hides, nor as hairy. Elm eyed the foot for a moment, and then decided to leave it alone. He shut the shed door, but he didn't drop the latch. Whoever was hiding under the hides was small—either a woman or a child—and he wasn't going to lock them in.

As he drew a pail of water from the rock-lined well behind the house, Elm wondered why a man as gregarious as the trader would need to hide someone in his shed. Unless the trader didn't know about the person in the shed, but Elm discarded that possibility as unlikely. As he carried water to the trough, he let his gaze roam around the property again. Behind the house was a stand of cottonwood and a few pine trees. Beyond the yard was the dusty suggestion of a trail that had brought him and the Judge to the trading post. There was another clump of trees about a hundred yards away from the house. The rest of the terrain was open and exposed.

Beyond the cottonwoods, the ground rose to a narrow ridge, but it wasn't much of a bump in the landscape. A storm would barely have to lift its skirts as it crested the ridge. Along the top, there were a few rocks and a thin cleft where a pair of stones leaned toward one another.

A nagging thought tickled at the back of his head—a prickling sensation he hadn't been able to shake all morning. It wasn't the dream—he could barely remember, anyway—it was the stillness of the landscape. They had seen little in the way of game and heard less from birds. There were many stories about the great grass sea that stretched from the Mississippi to the Rocky Mountains, but the stories failed to encompass the desolate nature of the land. It had its own beauty—he was not blind to the majesty of watching a storm roll across a sea of undulating grass—but he was not accustomed to such . . . emptiness.

It was a rare man who could face such emptiness and not be inclined to fill it with something. The Judge talked—that was his way of dealing with all the open space—and Elm grew thoughtful. Did that make them a perfect complement for each other as they road west? Elm wasn't convinced, but the Judge's chatter kept him from getting too lost in his own thoughts, which had been troubling of late.

He glanced at the ridge again, mentally grasping at the frayed strands of his dream. What shadow lay in that darkness?

The Judge couldn't decide if the torpid effluvium around the trader came from the bearskins or from the man's own unwashed state. The man talked incessantly, but the Judge had long since stopped listening, in much the same way he had mentally distanced himself from the olfactory delight clinging to the trader like a dank fog. *How long had it been since this man has had a decent bath?* the Judge wondered, and then he considered his own remove from a tub of heated water. *Not quite a week,* he decided, which was socially outstanding in comparison to the hygienic distress suffered by the trader.

The Judge followed the trader into the crooked house, albeit with a twinge of reluctance. Inside, there would be no place for that smell to go, and when the door swung shut, the Judge suffered a spasm of panic. A grime-encrusted window allowed some light, offering a sliver of solace for his apprehension.

"Where did you say you was headed?"

The trader's words pulled the Judge away from the window. "I didn't say," the Judge said as he peered around for the trader.

There were shelves along one wall, piled with a haphazard assortments of dry goods and mining supplies. Shovels and picks leaned drunkenly against the wall. A trunk overflowed with fancy dresses more suited to plantation dinner parties or going to the theater in Chicago or New York. A nearby table was covered with an assortment of knives, revolvers, and rifles. There were buffalo hides everywhere. They were piled beneath the window. They were piled under the table. They were piled in stacks tall enough to hide behind.

There was movement in the gloom. "Where are you headed?"

"West," the Judge said, opting to give the man some kind of answer, in the hope that it might shut him up.

"Lot of ground to cover," the trader said. He made it sound like a question.

"It is," the Judge said.

A shape staggered around a pile of buffalo hides. "You Pinkertons?"

"What?" The Judge was taken aback by the question.

"Out of Chicago," the trader said. "That detective agency?"

The Judge frowned. It was difficult to get a sense of the trader's mood, and the way the man kept disappearing wasn't helping. "You get many Pinkertons out here?" he asked.

The trader appeared again. The Judge was reminded of the ground rodent who would dart in and out of their holes in the ground. "Why would we?" the trader asked suspiciously.

The Judge shrugged. "You're the one who asked," he said.

The trader bobbed up and down. "I did," he said, and as if embarrassed by this admission, he disappeared behind a stack of buffalo hides. He reappeared a few moments later, several feet to the left. "Heading west, are you?" he said, as if the previous minute of conversation hadn't happened.

"Aye," the Judge said. "We are."

"You'll need provisions. Supplies. I got what you need," the trader said. "Coffee. Tea. Whiskey. Bullets. Blankets. I got it all."

"Just need enough for a week or so." the Judge said.

"Just a week or so," the man echoed. The Judge heard noises like a badger rummaging in a tangle of brush.

"How about biscuits?" The question came from the Judge's right. "I got corn. And flour. Got a recipe here. Straight out of a fancy cookbook. How about preserves? Got a few jars. Canned last year." A pause, followed by a fumbling sound and a sucking noise. "Yep. Still good."

"Let's start with some whiskey," the Judge said, pushing aside the mental image created by those noises.

The Judge idly inspected a stack of books on the counter. Most were family Bibles, sold off when homesteaders found themselves caught between starvation and the comforting word of God. Halfway down, he found a small book made from cheap paper. A dime novel, one of those tawdry twaddles meant to entertain the unread and uneducated. He angled the book toward the window to get a better glimpse at the nonsensical illustration that undoubtedly graced the novel's cover. *Ferret Finnegan*, he read. Finnegan was a trapper of some renown, and this volume purported to be the certainly tall tale of Finnegan's encounter with the Black Bear of Mishkewanke. *Twice the height of a man and three times as fierce as an entire regiment!* the cover copy exclaimed.

He noticed the author's name and snorted loudly.

"Ah, a man of discerning taste and education." The trader put a pair of glasses on the counter and uncorked a dark brown bottle. "You familiar with that?" he asked as he poured a measure of whiskey into each glass.

"What? The Bible?" The Judge picked up the closest tumbler of whiskey.

"No. Vance. The guy who wrote Ferret Finnegan. Meriweather Vance."

The Judge drank the measure of whiskey in one swallow. He put the glass down and picked up the other one as if it was meant for him as well. "I'm not familiar with his work," he said, his tone brusque.

"He can spin quite the story," the trader said. He frowned as the Judge raised the second glass. "I met him once," he said.

"Who? Finnegan?"

"No, the writer." The man nudged the book with this thumb. "This is a true story," he said.

"Do tell," the Judge said. He tapped the now-empty glass in his hand against the counter, signaling its dismal state.

"Well, Ferret's not a real person, mind you," the trader said, oblivious to the Judge's hint. "But the writer fellow based him on a real person. He's Irish—like me, in fact—but more like that Scrumpo fellow. You know the one? He could shoot the eye out of a rabbit at a hundred paces. You know, he was—"

"Bumppo," the Judge said. "Natty Bumppo."

The trader shook his head. "No, no. That's not it. Scrumpo? Scrabumpo? Something like that. Anyway, I told Vance about the bear"—his fingers plucked at the heavy bearskin covering his rotund frame—"this one. Black bear. Shot it myself. A head taller than me. Teeth longer than my fingers."

"Is that so?"

The trader poured a measure of whiskey into the glass nearest to him, and he kept his hand on the glass as he poured. "Course, Vance makes the story better, which you'd expect, seeing as he's this famous writer and all."

"One would hope so," the Judge said. He sighed loudly, but his theatrical expression wasn't convincing enough for the trader to pour him another glass.

"You sure you're heading west?" the trader asked.

"That's the way the sun goes, isn't it?"

"Not much out that way until you reach Denver." The trader narrowed his eyes. "Take you more than a week."

"A week's worth of supplies is all we can carry," the Judge said, getting ahead of the trader's urge to sell more goods.

The trader nodded. "Wichita's only a couple of days," he said. "I hear there's a decent revue going on. Some bird who can really sing. Quite the looker too."

"Well, there you go," the Judge said. "We're looking to hear a decent songbird or two." Using two fingers, he plucked the novel from the stack on the counter. "That a shit box I saw?" he asked.

The trader frowned. "It ain't for public use."

"No? Where I am supposed to do my personal business then? In the corner?"

"Somewhere else," the trader said. "Not on my land."

The Judge tapped the edge of the book on the stack of Bibles.

"Now, that's not very gracious of you," he said. "Here I am, offering solid coin, and I can't even use the shitter."

"I ain't seen any money yet," the trader pointed out.

"You haven't been looking," the Judge said. He tapped the book again, and this time the man looked down. His eyes widened at the sight of the gold coin on the stack of Bibles. The man's hand darted for the coin, but the Judge was faster.

"Flour," the Judge said. He dangled the coin in front of the trader's face. "Bacon, if you have it. Corn. I'll take a jar of those preserves—an unopened jar, mind you. Some bullets too. My man outside will tell you what we require. And however much whiskey the rest will buy."

The trader licked his lips as he reached for the coin. "I might have a coupe of bottles . . ." he started.

The Judge closed his hand, and the coin was suddenly gone. "And I'm going to use the commode."

The trader made a noise in his chest, a noise not unlike the sound a bear makes when it has been awakened from a thoroughly pleasant nap. The rumbling grew louder, and the Judge opened his hand, revealing the gold coin once again.

"You supply your own paper," the trader snarled. He snatched at the coin before the Judge could make it disappear again.

The Judge flicked the corner of Vance's novel. "Oh, I've got that taken care of."

"That man needs to be dipped in a cold river," the Judge said as he clattered down the wooden steps of the porch. "I nearly succumbed to the stench emanating from his person."

"Better you than me," Elm said. He was leaning against the porch. His pose suggested he wasn't paying attention to anything in particular, but the constant motion of his eyes belied his laconic stance.

"However, I persevered," the Judge continued, "and while doing so, I managed to procure much needed supplies."

"Whiskey?"

"And bacon," the Judge said. He pursed his lips as if offended by Elm's summary catalog of their needs. "And *other* staples."

"Well, hopefully the sort that will be useful tomorrow."

"Useful for what?"

"Breakfast," Elm said.

The Judge cocked his head and regarded Elm. "What's on your mind?" he asked. He had noticed Elm's posture.

Elm gave a slight shrug. "How long will it take for this man to assemble this luxurious bounty?" he asked.

"Not very long," the Judge said.

Elm glanced at the book in the Judge's hand. "What is that?" he asked.

The Judge showed Elm the cover. *Ferret Finnegan and the Black Bear of Mishkewanke*. "A bestseller by Mr. Vance."

"Did he include the book with your purchase?"

The Judge shook his head. "I am going to avail myself of that privy yonder," he said. "And I may be a moment."

"You don't want to be seen reading a Meriweather Vance novel?"

The Judge snorted. "Hardly. I need something to wipe my ass with when I am done."

Elm looked past the Judge. "We may not be alone," he said.

The Judge glanced around and saw nothing but scrub and sky. "That's what the door on the privy is for," he said. "A man's got to have a little privacy when he is doing important business."

"You want to get shot while squatting?"

"Am I going to get shot while squatting?"

Elm raised his shoulders slightly. "Hard to say."

The Judge chewed on the inside of his cheek for a moment. "Are we going to be raided by bloodthirsty natives in the next fifteen minutes?"

"They may not be bloodthirsty. Or that punctual."

The Judge smiled. "Well, hardly worth worrying about then."

He nodded toward the privy. "Try to hold them off until I finish, would you?"

Elm shook his head at the inanity of the question. Satisfied that the situation—or lack thereof—was under control, the Judge wandered across the yard, whistling to himself. Laelaps trotted after him, as if summoned by the Judge's tune. Elm watched him go, thinking it was better if the dog was out of the way. Just in case things got out of hand.

3

Not long after the Judge disappeared into the privy, a trio of riders melted through the stand of trees along the trail. They wore brown buckskins and their hair was long and black. Two of the three had white and red markings on their faces, and all of the horses were inscribed with similar paint. The Indians approached carefully, keeping abreast with one another, but not riding in a clump.

Elm stayed near his horse and his rifle, but made no sudden moves that might spook the riders. As far as he knew, there wasn't a state of open conflict between the native tribes and the government of the United States, but relations were constantly changing. It was best to not appear threatening.

As the trio came closer, the swaybacked donkey snorted. He was familiar with these riders, or their horses, at least.

One of the Indians nudged his mount ahead of the others, and the chickens scattered as it approached the house. The remaining Indians hung back, and Elm spotted a rifle and a bow between the pair. The man in front was lean and muscular. His face was proud and his eyes were quick and dark. Elm thought the man to be about his age, maybe a few years older. Not yet old enough to be a chief, but well past needing to prove himself. Dangling from a rawhide thong about his neck was a shard of dark glass and a brass rifle cartridge.

The Indian dismounted, and his horse, without prompting, ambled toward the trough. Elm swore quietly. The damn beast was going to complicate lines of fire. If shooting started and the animals spooked, he was going to get caught between them.

He lifted his hands as he stepped out of the way of the Indian's horse. The Indian gave him a broad smile, and Elm acknowledged the man's cleverness with a small nod.

Keeping his eyes on Elm, the Indian called out a phrase in his native tongue. When a second try elicited no response, he switched to English. "Fat Bear," he shouted. "Are you in your cave, Fat Bear?"

The house shivered, as if it was waking from a long slumber, and the front door swung open. The trader emerged, blinking and squinting in the light. He spotted the Indians in the yard and his response was much more genial than his greeting had been for Elm and the Judge. "Red Eagle," the trader said. "May the wind carry you across the grass, and may your horses always find their way home."

Red Eagle touched a hand to his chest and then his forehead. "May your hands never be empty," he said. "And your purses always full."

"I do what I can," the trader said. He noticed Elm, and his beard wiggled for a second, as if his mouth was gnawing on some unspoken words. "What brings you to my trading post today?" he asked, returning his attention to the Indian.

"To trade, Fat Bear. Why else would we come?"

The trader's eyes danced like mayflies on a slow-moving river. "No reason at all," he said quickly.

Red Eagle's gaze fell on the three horses at the trough: his pony, Elm's horse, and the horse belonging to the Judge. It wasn't hard to spot the discrepancy between men and horses. The Indian said something to his companions, and the one on Elm's right —the one with the rifle and the black feathers tied in his hair—replied. Black Feather dropped his reins so he could hold his rifle with both hands. His knees tightened about his horse.

"Hey. Hey," the trader called out, making soothing gestures with his hands. "I'm almost done packing up some supplies for this gentleman here. Then he'll be on his way. Isn't that right?

He didn't wait for Elm to reply. "There's no fuss here. Nothing at all. You know me. All are welcome at Forestal's Trading Post. I don't treat people like him any different. I don't treat you any different."

Red Eagle stared at the trader, and his expression gave no indication of his thoughts.

"This land belongs to both red man and white man," Forestal said. "Remember? Red and white. We are family here. We don't spill blood on family ground, right?"

Red Eagle's features tightened. Behind him, Elm thought the Black Feather was going to raise his rifle. Forestal's attempt at diplomacy was almost disastrous.

"Do you have what we want?" Red Eagle asked.

Forestal nodded quickly, eager to conduct business. "Yes. I have what you want."

Red Eagle dismissed Forestal with a flick of his hand. "Fetch," he said.

Out of the corner of his eye, Elm saw movement in the grass near the privy. Laelaps had heard the Indian's word. As it was a familiar word, he was curious as to the game being played. *Stupid dog*, Elm thought. *This isn't a game.* He held himself rigid, refusing to turn his head. He didn't want to draw any attention to the dog. Or the privy. *What was the Judge doing in there?*

On the porch, the trader growled and swung his arms back and forth. He didn't like being ordered around, but after a moment of bluster, his ire failed and he stomped back to the house. Elm didn't let out the breath he was holding until the trader disappeared into the house.

The mood in the yard remained tense. A chicken clucked, and then fell silent, as if embarrassed by the noise it had made. The three Indians eyed Elm, and Elm eyed them back. He wondered if the old man had fallen asleep in the privy.

Laelaps yawned, showing his teeth, and then put his head back down on his paws.

Eventually, Red Eagle stirred from his stoicism. "Soldier?" he asked.

Elm shook his head. "Not anymore," he said.

"Did you kill Indians?"

"No," Elm said. "Other white men. Some black men, too. But mostly white men."

Red Eagle nodded. "You were a good soldier," he said.

Elm sucked at his back teeth. "I was good at following orders."

"And now?"

Elm met the Indian's piercing gaze and shrugged. "You?"

Red Eagle shrugged in return.

"Fair enough," Elm said.

"How about buffalo?" Red Eagle pointed at long shape wrapped in oilskin on Elm's horse. "Are you here to kill buffalo?"

Elm shook his head.

Red Eagle grunted. "What about your friend?" he asked.

Elm didn't see any point in protesting otherwise. Two horses. Two saddles. There was another person on the property. "He'd shoot his foot off trying to load the rifle," he said.

"Is that why he is hiding? Because he is frightened?"

"I doubt it. There is very little that frightens that man."

Red Eagle nodded. "I am like that."

The Indian with the bow snapped off a short phrase in their tongue, and Red Eagle's head whipped around toward the trail. Black Feather nudged his horse and raised his rifle.

There were more riders on the trail. Elm counted five, and four of them wore Union uniforms. The man not in uniform wore a weather-beaten duster and a wide-brimmed hat. He was a tracker of some kind, and he carried a Springfield rifle. The soldiers had carbines and the one wearing chevrons on his jacket had a pistol too. The men spread out as they approached the yard, and everyone stared at one another for a long moment. Elm's hands started to itch, and he suspected he wasn't the only one.

"You should be on your reservation," the man with the chevrons said to Red Eagle. "You shouldn't be here."

The soldiers sat stiffly in their saddles. They were trying to intimidate the Indians, but it was clear all the practice they had had was staring down sheep and pheasants.

The Indians were not impressed. They, on the other hand, were well-practiced.

The bearded tracker grew bored with all the staring. He had a flat nose and a wide mouth. He might have been handsome once, but the rough country had beaten the softness out of his face. "Who're you?" he said.

"Stonebrook," Elm said. He decided to provide a little more for the benefit of the men with the tracker. "I was with Company C with the 1st US Sharpshooters, during the War."

"War's been over for a while," the bearded man said.

"Aye," Elm said. "For most." He was watching the officer. The chevrons on the man's coat indicated he was a sergeant, which meant he probably had some experience. There was something about the way the man's mouth was fixed, like he sensed something wasn't right, but he couldn't quite place it . . .

"What are you doing here?" the bearded man snapped.

"Watering my horses," Elm said. "Getting some supplies."

"What kind of supplies?"

"Bacon," Elm said. "Whiskey. The important things."

The bearded man nodded. "The important things," he echoed. His gaze unfocused, and Elm wondered what he was thinking about.

The sergeant nudged his horse forward. "This isn't—" His eyes strayed toward Red Eagle. "Where's Forestal?" he asked.

Red Eagle, who was standing in the yard, stared contemptuously at the sergeant. He had no weapon, but he wasn't about to show any fear. Not to these men.

"The trader?" Elm spoke up as if the sergeant had been talking to him. "He's inside."

The sergeant narrowed his eyes. "Why hasn't he come out?"

Elm shrugged. "I bought a lot of supplies," he said.

"Hey, Forestal," the bearded man shouted. "There's a crowd on your lawn." He showed his teeth for a second. "We're getting thirsty and ornery."

There was no answer. The donkey made a nervous sound, and one of the horses snorted deep in its chest.

"I don't like this, Creel," the sergeant said to the bearded man.

Creel made a dismissive gesture with his hand, and Elm realized what had been bothering him about the party of uniformed men. The chain of command was askew. The sergeant and the other soldiers were too differential to the tracker.

"This is exactly what I was warning Captain Randall about," Creel said. "You never leave that fort. You don't know what is going on out here. Right under your noses." He shifted on his saddle, and the muzzle of his gun swung toward Red Eagle. "What are you doing here?" Creel asked.

Red Eagle didn't answer. Creel's hands tightened on his rifle. "I know you understand me, Indian," he said.

Black Feather twitched in his saddle, but Red Eagle stopped him with a word. "Trading," he said to Creel.

"Trading what?" Creel asked. He made a show of looking at the other two Indians. "You aren't carrying any goods. Nor do I see a wagon for transporting hides. Or, are you trading something else . . . ?"

The sergeant made a hissing noise with his teeth.

Creel cocked his head. "You trading information, red man?" he asked. "Is that what is going on?"

Before Red Eagle could reply, a thump came from inside the house. The front door swung open, and Forestal came staggering out. He had a rifle in his hands, and his face glowed with a fervent light.

Whiskey light, Elm thought. *He thinks he's found some strength in the bottle.*

Forestal planted himself at the edge of the porch. "Get off my land, Creel," he said. "You and your monkeys."

"They're not my monkeys," Creel said. His face had lit up when Forestal had come out with the rifle, as if the threat of violence was what he had been waiting for. "They belong to Captain Randall at Fort Hollis. They're charged with protection United States citizens in these here parts. Folk like me and you." He nodded at Elm. "Folks like him."

"I don't need any protection," Elm said, trying to stay out of the conversation.

Forestal nodded toward the Indians. "I'm not in any danger. Not from them."

Which Elm realized, in a flash of insight, was exactly the wrong thing to say.

"Don't need you or your fucking meddling," Forestal snarled.

Creel's tongue touched the edge of his lip. "Now, that's some uncalled for language right there," he said quietly. The tone of his voice was enough though to cause the soldiers to reach for their guns.

Forestal was rigid, and the glow in his eyes was already starting to fade. His hands were tight on his rifle. "I'll say what I want on my land," he wheezed.

"How long do you think they'll let you keep it?" Creel asked.

"Don't start nothing, Creel," Forestal warned. The soldiers traded glances, as if they were also uncomfortable with where this conversation was headed.

Creel looked at Red Eagle. "Man wants me gone from his land, but he doesn't have any issue with you being on it. Why is that, I wonder?"

Red Eagle didn't answer.

Creel lifted his rifle. "You're going to answer me—"

The privy door banged open, and the Judge stepped out. He had his gun in one hand and a sheaf of paper in the other. He looked like he was either an angel of death or a tax collector. Neither, of course, improved the tension in the yard.

"Clearly, we've all gotten off to a bad start," he said. He spoke in that tone of voice which he used to work an unruly crowd.

Please, God, no pontificating, Elm silently pleaded, but neither God nor the Judge were answering prayers.

"Before we start shooting, why don't we consider the lesson offered by Jesus when—"

Everyone stopped listening as soon as the Judge said 'start shooting,' which was the signal they had all be waiting for.

4

Creel raised his rifle, and the Judge got one shot off before Creel's rifle barked. The Judge ducked around the side of the privy, and the bullet from Creel's rifle tore through the thin planking where the Judge had been standing.

On the porch, Forestal raised his rifle and fired. One of the soldiers tumbled off his horse.

Red Eagle charged the soldiers. Elm was dumbfounded by the Indian's brazen assault. What in the world was the Indian doing? The soldiers were equally surprised, but the sergeant— perhaps demonstrating why he had the chevrons—managed to get his sidearm clear of its holster and fire two shots.

Red Eagle didn't deviate from his courageous charge. Elm couldn't imagine the fortitude required for such focus. No one charged a shooter like that without expecting to get hit, though perhaps that was the secret to such lunacy: how could you stand your ground when a howling warrior was coming at you like that, with a knife in his hand and murder in his eyes?

The sergeant panicked. Somewhere in his brain, he thought he'd have better luck using the revolver as a rock, and he threw it at Red Eagle. The Indian ducked, avoiding the revolver, and then leaped. He struck the sergeant full in the chest, knocking him out of the saddle.

The horse, no longer encumbered, whinnied loudly, as if it didn't know what to do with itself.

Red Eagle and the sergeant tussled briefly, and then Red Eagle was on his feet again. The sergeant stayed down and did not move.

The soldiers fired their carbines, and all the shooting spooked the sergeant's horse. Red Eagle lunged for the horse and got a hand on the stirrups. He was dragged along, neatly shielded by the horse's body, and when the horse was out of carbine range, he pulled himself up into the saddle. He let out a whooping war cry, his arms raised in victorious celebration of his daring assassination.

Elm, staring agog at what he had just seen, realized how much of a target he was. He scrambled backward, trying to get behind the horses and the trough. As more gunshots sounded, Elm grabbed for his rifle, but his horse pulled free of the hitch before he could get a grip on the oilskin wrap. The Judge's horse was already free, and both horses charged away from the shooting.

Screaming incoherently and firing his rifle as quickly as he could lever its action, Forestal kept to the high ground of the porch. In the yard, the remaining soldiers milled about, trying to control their horses and fire their carbines at the same time. Creel's horse was missing its rider, and Elm tried to find the tracker. Where had the man gone? No, wait, the horse had too many legs. Creel was hiding behind his mount!

Forestal was suddenly swatted aside as if he had been struck by a giant hand. A second later, the booming noise of a heavy rifle rolled down from the ridge.

Elm flinched as soon as Forestal was knocked down. He knew what had happened. He didn't need to wait to hear the report of the long gun. It was a sound he knew as readily as the sound of his own voice. During the War, the heavy thunder of the Sharps rifle had been how he had communicated with the Confederate armies. He knew that by the time the sound arrived, a good sharpshooter could have reloaded, adjusted his aim, and fired again.

He pressed himself against the house, trying to make himself as flat as possible. He couldn't see much of the ridge, which meant the sharpshooter probably couldn't see him either.

The cleft, he thought, remembering the leaning rocks he had spotted earlier. *That is where he is.*

He chided himself for not paying closer attention to his unease earlier. He had seen something on the ridge, and now he—and everyone else in the yard—were easy targets for the shooter on the ridge. Elm couldn't move from his location without exposing himself. Even if he had his rifle, the man on the ridge had the advantage of elevation. He had to stay out of sight.

Elm drew his sidearm and edged toward the scattered buffalo hides that had spilled off the porch. He grabbed the edge of a stinking hide and tugged it over his legs. A second one hid his thighs and abdomen. He wasn't completely hidden, but it was enough. He raised his revolver and sighted along the edge of the porch. If anyone came around the corner, they would walk right into a bullet. He exhaled slowly, holding his hand steady. He could be patient . . .

A soldier shouted out in the yard. He had spotted something and was calling to his companions. His voice was cut off by the report of a revolver. *The Judge*, Elm thought. *The old fool was still alive.*

More shooting followed, and amid the confusion, Laelaps began barking. Elm tensed, wondering why the dog was barking. Had the Judge been hit?

And then the shooting stopped.

Elm peered over at the privy. The door hung crookedly, as if it had been shot several times. There was no blood on the warped timbers, and he couldn't see either the Judge or the dog.

"Forestal! You still alive up there?" That was Creel. The tracker was somewhere to Elm's right. Near the donkey, he thought.

Forestal made noises, a mangled mix of invective and opprobrium, indicating that he was, in fact, still alive.

"Still got some fight in you?" Creel laughed. "Get up, you fat pig. Take another shot at me."

Forestal groaned and swore, and Elm imagined the trader struggling to get to his feet. But the fat trader's efforts turned into fit of coughing and gasping.

"Got ourselves a mess here, Forestal," Creel said. "Couple of bluecoats are dead. One of them Indians too. On your land. What's the Army going to think about that?"

Forestal's response was more guttural noises.

"They're going to think you've changed sides, aren't they? That you're working with them. Plotting against—"

"Go fuck your . . ." Forestal's words dissolved into a low moan.

"Speaking of fucking," Creel's voice got louder as he approached the porch. "That's what you've been doing, isn't it? A man can get lonely out here in this God-forsaken land. Gonna be cold this winter. Would be handy to have one of them around, wouldn't it?"

"Damn you, Creel." The porch shook as Forestal got to his feet. "Get—"

The rest of his sentence was cut short by a report from Creel's Springfield rifle.

Elm listened to the sound of Creel's boots as the tracker walked across the yard and climbed the steps of the porch. When he spoke again, he didn't have to shout. "You're going to bleed out, Indian fucker," the tracker said to trader. "And I'm going to watch."

Forestal growled like the bear he wished he was. Elm's grip tightened on his revolver. Could he stand and get a shot off before Creel noticed him?

"Is she in the house?" Creel asked. "You think she'll spread her legs for me? Maybe I'll give her to Vash. He'll know what to do." Creel laughed.

Forestal gasped, as if he was sucking in great gulps of air. Working up the strength to shout or scream or maybe even try, one last time, to get to his feet. But before he could manage, a wooden door banged in the yard. Someone came running across the yard, and Elm had an impression of a ghost in a white shift, her black hair streaming behind her. She had good lungs and a wild spirit. There was a large hunting knife in her hands.

She almost made it to the porch before the sharpshooter on the ridge took her down.

In the wake of the report from the Sharps rifle, the only sound in the yard was an agonized keening noise coming from Forestal.

One of the surviving soldiers approached the sprawled figure on the ground. Elm tightened his grip on his weapon. If the soldier looked up, he would spot Elm half-hidden beneath the buffalo hides.

"Uh, Mr. Creel," the soldier spoke up.

"What?" Creel snapped. Elm's attention wavered. His gaze darted to the edge of the porch. Creel was close.

"She's—she's dead."

"I know she's dead. I've got eyes, you damn fool."

"What, what are we going to do?"

"We're going to burn it. Burn the whole place down."

"Yes, but . . ."

"What?"

"What about Billy and . . . and Sergeant Chilton?"

"Put them on the horses."

Another soldier spoke up. "We don't have no horses," he said. "They ran off."

Forestal moaned, and Creel stomped on the porch. "Shut the fuck up," he snapped at the dying trader. "God damn it. Go fetch the fucking horses," he snapped at the soldiers. "They're dumb animals. They're aren't going to go far."

"What about . . . ?"

Creel marched down to the yard. "Don't matter about them. Just get the damn horses."

The soldier next to the dead woman turned, and in the split second when he might have looked at Elm, Elm's finger nearly pulled the trigger. But he held himself in check, and the soldier, his back now to Elm, marched off.

Creel said something Elm didn't catch as he walked over to the body in the yard. He stared at the body for a moment, his rifle held loosely in his hands, and then his shoulders stiffened. He raised his head and looked right at Elm.

Elm centered his sights on the center of Creel's forehead.

Creel stuck his tongue in his cheek. "Well, shit. In all this excitement, I plum forgot about you," he said.

"You did," Elm said quietly.

"You going to shoot me?"

"I haven't decided yet."

Creel didn't move much—his back stiffened and his hands tightened on his weapon—but Elm wasn't having any of that. He dropped the barrel of his revolver to point it at Creel's chest.

The two men stared at each other. "You aren't going to shoot me," Creel said after a moment. "You would have, if you were going to."

"I might still."

Creel's tongue touched the edge of his lip. Moving his head slowly, he directed his gaze toward the privy and then to the ridge beyond the house. "What about the fellow who was hiding in the privy?"

"What about him?"

"Rifle bullet will make a mess of his head."

"Your friend doesn't have the shot," Elm said.

Creel cocked his head slightly, squinting at Elm. "You sure about that?" His trigger finger moved a fraction.

Elm nodded. "He would have taken the shot already," he said. "If he had it."

"Is that so?"

"I'm okay," the Judge shouted from somewhere.

Elm's gaze flickered at the sound of the old man's voice, and that was the opening Creel had been waiting for. He jerked his rifle up, but Elm wasn't as distracted as Creel thought he was.

Elm fired. Creel's eyes widened in surprise and then rolled up, as if he was trying to see the new hole that had appeared in the middle of his head. He collapsed in two stages: first, to his knees, and then onto his face.

"I guess I decided," Elm said.

5

Elm found a shovel in the shed and dug a grave near the cotton-woods. The Judge ventured into the dark embrace of the trader's house and returned with a robe which he used to wrap the dead woman. It was nightfall by the time they finished burying Forestal and the Indian woman. The Judge said some words while bats flew by, squeaking their sorrow into the darkening sky. Laelaps howled at the moon as it crept over the ridge.

They stacked the dead soldiers and Creel in the privy, and used the shovel to brace the door shut. Elm hadn't been in the mood to dig another hole, but he didn't want to leave the bodies out in the open to attract predators. They didn't know what to do with the dead Indian—the one Elm had thought of as Black Feather—and in the end, they covered him with a wool blanket. *He'll be there in the morning*, the Judge said.

Neither man felt like staying in the house, though the Judge ventured inside long enough to fetch a bottle of whiskey. While he was gone, Elm scrounged some loose wood and kicked a few stones into a makeshift ring near the paddock. He and the Judge sat and stared at the dancing fire as the night deepened. They passed the bottle back and forth, though the Judge had a tendency to sip two or three times before he passed it back. Elm didn't quibble. The spirits were settling the Judge's ire, and Elm didn't want to drink himself senseless.

He wondered what had happened to the pair of soldiers who had gone off after their horses, as well as the sharpshooter on the ridge. Had they run into Red Eagle and the other Indian?

He and the Judge hadn't heard any gunfire, but that didn't mean there hadn't been any interaction between the soldiers and the Indians. It was likely there were other bodies lying out in the open, blood soaking into the ground, eyes gone flat and dark.

After awhile, the Judge's head drooped and he didn't react when Elm offered him the bottle. Elm pursed his lips and held kept the bottle—not that there was much whiskey left. He was about to finish it off when he heard the soft noise of a horse blowing air. Laelaps, who was lying next to the Judge, raised his head and let out a soft growl.

Two horses were standing nonchalantly at the edge of the firelight, as if they had been patiently waiting for Elm to notice them. Elm frowned. His senses were more dulled than he thought. Had the light of the fire lured them back? Why hadn't he heard them coming?

A shadow moved behind his horse, and it resolved into a man-sized shape that he recognized.

Red Eagle put his hand over his heart and inclined his head. "May your horses always find their way home," he said. "And may the wind always be at your back."

Elm nodded. He put the bottle down and raised his hand to touch his chest. "May, uh—" He struggled to think of some sort of appropriate greeting. What had Forestal and the Indian said to each other? He couldn't remember—more sign that he had drunk more than he had thought—and so he went with the first thing that came to mind. "May the horses of your enemies always step in gopher holes."

Red Eagle offered him a slight smile. "Why do you wish ill of the horses?" he asked. "They are not your enemy."

"I'm not the poetic one," Elm explained. Eschewing further explanation, he offered the whiskey bottle to Red Eagle, who declined.

"Your horses needed some guidance," the Indian said. "They are not very good at finding their way."

"Well, they're a long way from home," Elm said.

"As are you and your friend."

"Aye," Elm said. "That we are."

The Indian touched his chest again. He spoke a word in his native tongue. "That is the name my father gave me, but Fat Bear calls me 'Red Eagle,' and that is the name I wear when I speak with those who are not my kin. I am of the Kiowa. We have lived on these plains for six generations."

"My name is Elmore Stonebrook," Elm said. He indicated the snoring form on the other side of the fire. "That is Judge Willard Vernon Wallace, and that mutt beside is called Laelaps."

Laelaps let out a short bark.

"He says you are part of his tribe," Red Eagle said, a hint of a smile on his face.

Elm glanced at the dog, who thumped his tail against the ground. "He says that a lot," he said.

"And the one who breathes loudly and talks even louder? Is he part of small dog's tribe too?"

"Yes, he is," Elm said. "God help us."

Red Eagle cocked his head. "You buried Fat Bear."

"I did."

"And Pale Deer."

Elm raised the bottle in his hand and took a small sip of what remained in it. "Was that her name?"

"It was his name for her." Red Eagle dipped his head. "She was of my clan." He spoke the dead woman's name in his tongue.

"I am sorry for your loss." Elm glanced over at Black Feather's body. "I'm sorry about the death of your friend, too."

"He was a brave soldier. He died fighting the white man. It is a common fate these days, among my people."

Elm chewed on his lower lip, struggling to form a response to that statement. Eventually, he gave up. He wasn't a diplomat or an orator. He spoke his mind too bluntly too often—a trait of his which caused no amount of consternation for the Judge.

There were habits of the Judge's that annoyed him as well, so it all evened out in the end.

"The man with the long gun is still out there," Red Eagle said. "His hunger is not diminished."

Elm stirred from his thoughts. "What hunger?"

"He likes to cause pain. He likes to kill."

"And the soldiers?"

"They are all dead."

"No, not the ones here. The ones who ran away."

"They are all dead," Red Eagle said again.

Elm shivered in spite of the whiskey he had been drinking. "Did you—" he stopped. He realized he didn't want to know if Red Eagle and his companion had chased down the remaining soldiers. What was he going to do? It wasn't his job to uphold the laws of the territory or to defend the honor of the Army. Of course, the Judge would have an opinion on the matter, but the Judge was busy snoring. Elm wasn't about to wake him and engage in a long and drawn out discussion about who shot first, who oppressed whom, and who had more claim to this land.

"Awful lot of killing today," he said quietly.

"This land is bad, Elmore Stonebrook," Red Eagle said ominously. "It has been bad for many years, and the coming of your people has made it worse. You do not know the land like the Kiowa or the Cherokee. You does not listen to what the wind tells you. You do not see the weeping sickness for what it is. The white man digs holes in the ground—holes where he should not dig."

"Are you talking about graves?" Elm asked. "Are burial sites being disturbed?"

Red Eagle shook his head. "It waits for a spark," he said. "That is all it will take."

The Judge snorted in his sleep, and the sound penetrated his slumber. He shot upright, his hand clawing for his revolver—or for the whiskey bottle, one could never be quite sure with the Judge. Laelaps let out a bark of alarm, and Elm was startled by the old man's sudden movement. The Judge swung his head back and forth, the whites of his eyes glowing in the night. "What—what are you staring at?" he rasped.

The Judge's horse nickered, and the Judge peered blearily at both horses. "Where did they come from?" he gasped.

Elm started to explain, but then he realized Red Eagle was gone. He looked at the empty whiskey bottle in his hand and wondered if the Indian had been there at all.

Morning came, and the house retained to its shabby appearance as the weak morning light failed to dust off the shadows that had collected overnight. Clouds had moved in when the sun wasn't watching, and the sky was a featureless blanket of gray overhead. It hadn't rained, but Elm thought it would before the day was over. They decided to load extra supplies on the donkey and take it with them. As they set out, Elm said he wanted to see the top of the ridge.

The elevation change was even more gradual than he expected, and up close, what he had thought were rocks weren't much more than humps of dirt. Eventually, Elm stopped at a spot he thought was where the sharpshooter had been. The distance was well within the range of the Sharps rifle. With a practiced eye, he gauged how little he would have to compensate for the downward flight of a bullet.

He cast about for any sign—impressions in the dirt, discarded cartridges—but he didn't see anything. Elm wasn't surprised. If the shooter had been part of a regiment during the war, he would have been trained to not leave any trace. In that sense, not finding anything was confirmation of what he suspected about the sharpshooter.

"Is he good?" the Judge asked.

"He shot Pale Deer as she was running," Elm said. His gaze drifted toward the darker spot behind the house where they had buried Forestal and Pale Deer.

"Pale Deer?"

"That was the name Forestal gave her."

"How do you know?"

"Red Eagle told me."

"That's the Indian who brought back our horses."

"Yes," Elm said. "We talked for awhile."

"Right." The Judge nodded. "Part of your dream."

"I wasn't dreaming."

"Weren't you dreaming about Indians the other night too? That night when you saw something sitting at our fire."

"That was different."

"Of course it was," the Judge said, his tone of voice suggesting that he thought otherwise.

"Her name was Pale Deer," Elm said, ignoring the Judge's dismissal. "She was Kiowa."

"Kiowa," the Judge said. He squinted toward the morning sun.

"What?" Elm asked.

"Nothing," the Judge said. "I was just thinking."

"Thinking about what?"

"The Indians that were there," the Judge said. "What was the name of the one you . . . ?"

"Red Eagle."

The Judge nodded. "Red Eagle. Was he the one who charged the soldier? You remember that?"

"I was right there."

The Judge nodded again. "Yes. Yes, you were." He pursed his lips. "Never saw anything like that before. Have you?" Before Elm could answer, the Judge continued. "That soldier shot at him. I don't know how much training they get these days, or the quality of the firearms they are sending them out to protect the frontier with, but you would have thought that at least one of those shots would have hit the Indian."

"At least one," Elm said.

"And then he threw his gun at the Indian." The Judge chuckled. "Who does that?"

"Someone who is frightened," Elm said.

"Isn't that what the gun is for?"

"Only if it works, and if it doesn't . . . "

"I suppose you might as well throw it," the Judge finished for him. He chewed on the edge of his mustache as he stared down at the forlorn trading post. "This strike you as strange?" he asked eventually.

"Which part?" Elm asked in return.

"Exactly," the Judge said.

Laelaps barked in agreement.

Elm sighed and got back on his horse. He hadn't mentioned to the Judge what Red Eagle had said about the land. The Judge already had that hollow-eyed look he got. Elm knew better than to add to whatever fire was smoldering in the Judge's mind.

When they found the missing soldiers an hour later, Elm couldn't help but wonder about what Red Eagle had said. *It waits for a spark.*

6

Late in the afternoon, they reached the fort. Familiar with the Army's sense of decorum and design, Elm knew the squared off section of land would contain a barracks, an officer's quarters, a stable, and a storehouse or two. All composed of rough timber that had undoubtedly been transported by train and carted up the hill by wagon. There were two watchtowers—spindly platforms barely large enough for one man—at the northwest and southwest corners. The gate was located on the west-facing wall, which told Elm and the Judge all they needed to know about who the Army thought the enemy was.

If the donkey, who was trailing behind Elm's horse, hadn't been burdened with a pair of blue-coated corpses, they would have bypassed the fort entirely. The Judge was eager for a bath and a bed, but he acquiesced to Elm's desire to return the dead.

Three men in blue coats lounged near the fort's wooden gate. Only one of them was carrying his rife; the other two had propped their against a rough-hewn bench near the gate.

The Judge took off his hat and wiped his forehead with a handkerchief as he waited for the three guards to rouse themselves from their indifferent duty. "Good afternoon," he said affably. "Might it be possible to speak with your commanding officer?"

The soldier with the rifle squinted up at the Judge. "What for?" he demanded.

The Judge offered the young man a patient smile. The soldier's shaggy hair poked out from under his cap. His lopsided mustache appeared stuck to his face, like he had recently appeared in a stage play and had forgotten to take off his costume.

"Well, we wish to be relieved of a particular burden," the Judge said. "One that he might be inclined to take off our hands."

One of the other guards noticed the donkey's grisly burden. "Aye, Timms. What have they got there?"

Timms—the one with the lopsided mustache—peered around the Judge's horse. His eyes widened when he saw the two bodies strapped across the donkey's back. "Hey, what's going on?" he demanded. He brought up his rifle and pointed it at the Judge.

The Judge put his hat back on his head, and he was careful to rest both hands on the pommel of his saddle. "Your commanding officer," he said patiently. "We need to speak to him."

"Where'd you get those bodies?" the third soldier demanded. He retrieved his rifle and pointed it at Elm.

Elm tugged the donkey's lead, and the long-suffering beast picked its way forward. Elm's horse shifted as the pack animal and its cargo passed. Elm couldn't blame it. The work done by scavengers notwithstanding, the corpses were not a pretty sight. They had been viciously assaulted by a bladed weapon. The Judge thought the wounds had been caused by a hatchet, but Elm had argued with him. *He wants you to think this was the work of Indians,* he had said.

They had found the first body an hour or so after leaving the trading post. It leaned against the trunk of a lone dogwood. The second had been dragged a short distance by coyotes. Both men were still wearing their long coats and hats—dressed like Elm had seen them the day before—but their bodies had been stabbed and slashed multiple times.

They had been shot too: one in the face, and one in the back of the head. A small caliber weapon, mostly likely a revolver. Of the horses which the two men had been sent to fetch, there had been no sign.

The donkey stopped in front of Timms, whose eyes flicked back and forth between the Judge and the dead men. The Judge shrugged like he didn't think the problem facing the young man was all that complicated, and Timms's face reddened for a second before he lowered his rifle. "Sallie," he snapped, and the soldier who hadn't fetched his rifle stiffened. "Get this donkey."

"Why me?" Sallie complained.

"You're the one who ain't carrying nothing," Timms said.

Sallie looked at his hands and then looked over at his rifle.

"I'm watching these fellers. Get the donkey, Sallie," Timms ordered.

Sallie—red-faced and glowering—grabbed the donkey's lead. The pack animal resisted momentarily when Sallie tugged, and Elm thought the situation was going to become even more farcical than it already was, but the donkey, eager to be done with its burden, plodded forward.

Timms gestured at the bench where Sallie's rifle still leaned. "Leave your horses out here," Timms said.

Elm and the Judge dismounted from their horses. The third soldier retrieved Sallie's rifle, and Elm used a bit of rope from his saddlebags to configure a simple loop hitch for the horse. He motioned for Laelaps to remain with the mounts and hurried after the Judge and the soldiers.

He caught up with Sallie and the slow-moving donkey. The young soldier gave him a startled look, and Elm offered him a non-threatening smile. He nodded toward the flag hanging limply from a pole near the corner watchtower. "Which regiment?" he asked.

"Uh, Kansas Twentieth," Sallie said.

"Kansas?" Elm eyed the soldier. Too young to have fought in the war, which made him a volunteer. "How long you been with the regiment?" Elm asked.

"A couple—almost a year," Sallie responded.

They passed through the gate. Elm was familiar with the manner in which temporary camps became permanent outposts. The barracks were a rough lodge with gaps in the walls that were plugged with debris and scraps of leather. The stables were nothing more than a leaning roof raised over a crowded paddock. The officer's hut had a porch and chimney, but the porch lacked a railing and the chimney was crooked. There was a ramp along the inner side of the northern wall, and it slowly became a battlement as it reached the western wall.

Men scattered throughout the camp paid little attention to Elm, the Judge, or the donkey. Elm counted twenty-six, and after counting the men, his gaze landed on a wagon loaded with an object covered with a weather-resistant tarp. He idly wondered what was important enough in an Army fort to cover up against the weather. Something that didn't like getting wet, he thought, and his gaze lingered on the thick wheels of the wagon. Whatever the object was, it was heavy.

Elm stopped next to the Judge, letting Sallie and the donkey get ahead of him. Timms yelled for someone to fetch the captain, and Elm and the Judge watched the camp stir itself into a rudimentary action. Blue coats gathered. Guns were pointed at them. Soldiers jabbered at one another about the dead men on the donkey.

A man wearing a long officer's coat and a tall hat came out of the leaning building, and the confusion ceased. Sallie, who had been untying the dead men from the donkey, snapped to attention. The dead men, however, were not in the mood to salute, and one of them flopped off the donkey. The animal spooked, stuttering a few steps, and the other corpse slid off its back. Relieved of its burden, the donkey decided it had been dismissed and it kept moving. Sallie nervously darted after it.

"It's practically a carnival show," the Judge said out of the side of his mouth.

The officer was a gaunt man, hollowed out before his time, with thick eyebrows and a dense beard. While his coat was faded, his boots were clean and shiny. "What's going on here?" he demanded. His voice was a logger's saw rasping across stone.

"Captain Randall, sir," Timms shouted. "It's Bailey and Smith, sir. They're—they're dead."

"I can see that, private," Randall rasped. "And these two"—he indicated Elm and the Judge—"who are they?"

"They brought the bodies, sir," Timms replied. "And the—and the donkey."

Randall watched Sallie try to corral the donkey. "That your donkey?" he asked Elm and the Judge.

"No, sir," Elm replied. "It belongs—*belonged*—to man named Forestal."

The captain chewed on his lip for a moment. "Sergeant Marks," he called out. A short soldier with a wide head nodded and responded with a hearty "Yes, sir!"

"Who went out with Sergeant Chilton the other day?"

"Bailey, Smith, and Billy Douglas, sir."

Randall squinted at Elm and the Judge. "Where's my sergeant and the other man?" he asked. "You two know anything about where they might be?"

The Judge took off his hat. "We do," he said.

Randall's face darkened. "What happened?" he demanded.

"That conversation might be best had inside," the Judge said.

One of the soldiers said something about Indians, and if Randall heard the man, he gave no sign. "Who are you?" he asked the Judge.

"I am Judge Willard Vernon Wallace," the Judge said. "And this is Elmore Stonebrook. We were—"

"Judge? You riding circuit?" Randall asked, interrupting him.

The Judge spread his hands and smiled. "Are you in need of a jurist?" he asked.

The captain frowned, not liking how the Judge had avoided his question. "Inside," he said, waving a hand toward the building behind him. "You can tell me everything."

Elm and the Judge followed the captain into the officer's quarters, which akin to a homesteader's cabin: one room, a hearth, and a nook in the back that could be made private with a curtain. Opposite the hearth was a heavy desk and several chairs. The desk was handcrafted by hands that knew what they were doing, in contrast to the carpentry—or, rather, the lack thereof—on the exposed beams of the roof. A single window provided enough illumination to keep from bumping into the spartan furnishings.

The captain sat down and opened a side drawer in the desk. He took out a pipe, a tin of matches, and a tobacco pouch. "Report," he said as he started to stuff the pipe.

The Judge cocked his head, and Elm decided to lead the conversation rather than let the Judge get wound up about how they were not beholden to the captain in that way. "We're out of Independence," Elm started. "A week or so. We heard that we could resupply at a trading post run by a man named Forestal. We didn't know exactly where it was, but early yesterday morning, we heard shots and—"

"Shots," the Judge said. Captain Randall looked at him, his thumb working tobacco into the bowl of the pipe. "Gunfire," the Judge said. "The noise made by rifles and—"

"I know what he's talking about," Randall rasped. He fumbled for a match, struck it, and held it over the bowl of his pipe. The flame wiggled and stretched as Randall sucked air through the packed tobacco.

Elm, experienced with the dynamics of officers needing to remind their men who was in control, waited patiently for Randall to finish his pipe lighting ritual. Beside him, the Judge fidgeted and toyed with the brim of his hat. Elm gave him a glance that told him to curb his tongue.

"And then what?" Randall demanded when he was finished lighting his pipe.

"We rode to investigate the gunfire, sir," Elm continued. "When we reached the trading post, we found a number of bodies. Evidence of a fight between several parties. Being concerned citizens, we investigated the premises, but found no one living. After doing what we could for the dead, we rode on, intending to report this incident at the first opportunity. Earlier today, we discovered additional bodies—those two men out there—and we thought it best to bring them with us."

"What about the others? The ones at the trading post?"

"We had no way to transport them, sir."

Randall tipped his head back and exhaled a plume of smoke. "You have horses," he said. Smoke swirled above his head as he waited for Elm to answer.

Elm shrugged. "Aye, that we do."

"You couldn't have loaded the other bodies on your horses?"

"And who was going to compensate us?" the Judge asked, no longer able to keep his tongue still.

Randall tilted his head. "For what?"

"For freight haulage," the Judge replied.

"For what?"

"Do we look like we're in the business of hauling corpses across Kansas?" the Judge shot back.

"You brought two men on that donkey," Randall pointed out.

"And that donkey is never going to forgive me for that," the Judge said. "Which is why you can keep him."

"Keep him? Why would I want to keep a donkey?"

"Well, I didn't see an *empty* wagon, so unless you're going to overload some of those fine horses you have in that—"

Randall shot to his feet. "What are you talking about?" He had heard the Judge's emphasis and had taken the bait.

"I'm talking about—"

Elm put his hand on the Judge's arm. "The other men—Chilton and Douglas—they're at Forestal's trading post," he said. "They're safe from scavengers for a day or two, but not much longer than that. Regardless of what the Judge thinks about the donkey's disposition, I'm sure it will serve you well to transport the other dead men."

The Judge started to draw breath, and Elm squeezed his forearm, a silent admonishment to keep his mouth shut.

"That's our report. Sir." The last came after a brief pause, a gentle reminder that Elm was being deferential to the captain's rank.

Randall sucked on his pipe, mulling over what he had heard. "You served in the war, didn't you?" he asked after exhaling another cloud of smoke.

"Yes, sir, I did," Elm replied. "I served with Company C, 1st US Sharpshooters."

Randall nodded. "I came up with Colonel Stevens. The 79th, before we were brought under General Pope in '62. In time for Bull Run. You there for that fiasco?"

"I was," Elm said. "Part of the line at Henry House Hill."

Randall looked at the wall, seemingly lost in a fog of memory about the calamitous Union loss at what came be called the Second Battle of Bull Run. Late in the summer of 1862, Lee's Confederate Army had pushed into Virginia, and the Army of the Potomac had been charged with preventing him from reaching New York or Washington. However, much like the first battle at Bull Run, the Union commanders failed to coordinate well, and Lee nearly broke through the Union lines. Rebuffed, he had turned his attention to Maryland, hoping to resupply outside of Virginia. There was an election coming up, and Lee was hoping to frighten the Northern states and reduce morale.

Unfortunately for the Confederate war effort, he only got as far as Antietam.

Private Sallie provided them with directions to Citrine Springs: *down that road for a spell, and then a little farther south; you'll see the church soon enough.* If it weren't for the lure of a hot meal, a bath, and some female companionship, Elm suspected the Judge might have kept riding west. The old man had a tendency to get ornery when told what to do, and Captain Randall's not-so-veiled suggestion to stay in the area was precisely the sort of direction the Judge was likely to ignore.

"You didn't mention the other man," the Judge noted after they had ridden out of sight of Fort Hollis.

"Which one?" Elm asked.

The Judge flashed him a savage grin. "I emptied my gun during that fracas at Forestal's, and I doubt I hit anything," he said. "You fired one shot. You expect me to believe you don't remember who you killed?"

"His name was Creel," Elm said. "He wasn't a soldier."

"No, he certainly wasn't."

"Nor was the man on the ridge."

"The captain certainly perked up when you mentioned your unit, those sharpshooters."

Elm nodded. "That he did."

"Almost like he knows another sharpshooter."

"Almost like."

"You going to tell him what happened out there?"

Elm nudged his horse to catch up to the Judge's. "I'm not sure what happened out there," he said.

The Judge waved a hand at the uneven road slithering back and forth ahead of them. In the distance, the white spire of a church tower gleamed in the afternoon sun. "Perhaps you could tell me the story while our intrepid steeds piddle along like geriatric mules. Yonder cradle of civilization might crumble to dust by the time we arrive."

"He shot one soldier in the back of the head. The other turned around and got shot in the face."

The Judge leaned forward, expecting more, and when Elm shrugged, the Judge snorted. "The end," he said dramatically. He shook his head. "Your stories are passionless dribble. They lack the dramatic sweep of classic narrative arc."

"Oh, where is Mr. Vance when we need him?" Elm wondered.

The Judge made a face. "That outrageous violator of vocabulary? He would populate the tale with six more characters, an exotic location change, and insert an entirely superfluous love interest."

"So, you did read it."

"Read what?"

"The book you took to the privy. I thought maybe you had fallen asleep in there."

"I was not asleep. Nor was I reading."

Elm spread his hands. "It is none of my business what you were doing."

The Judge fumbled with his coat, managing to retrieve a disheveled book from his pocket. "I still have it," he said, shaking the book at Elm. "It might"—he turned the book over—"it might be missing the last few pages."

"You didn't start at the front?" Elm asked.

"I was—"

Elm hid a smile. "You were reading it," he said.

"I was not," the Judge protested.

Elm turned his gaze toward the town. "I want to find him," he said.

"Who?" the Judge asked.

"The man on the ridge."

"He might see you coming," the Judge pointed out.

"I hope so," Elm said. He gave the Judge a look devoid of any humor.

The Judge gave Elm a tight nod. "While you do that, I am going to have a hot bath," he said. "And find some company other than you for the night, if you don't mind."

"I don't mind at all," Elm said. "I am a little weary of your company as well."

The Judge offered the book to Elm. "In case you get lonely," he said.

Elm shook his head. "Why would I want that? It's missing the ending."

7

Citrine Springs was like many frontier towns—a cluster of houses and businesses that blossomed along the track laid by the railroad. For awhile, the town enjoyed its status as a terminus of the rail line, but the desire for westward progress was a never-ending hunger, and eventually, the railroad would start building again. Many followed, but those who had rooted themselves in the valley stayed, clinging to a fervent hope that their would survive being abandoned by the railroad.

Decision makers in Washington, gathered around a freshly drawn map of the border between Kansas and Oklahoma, chucked their chins and muttered to another. Representatives from the railroad companies whispered in their ears, tapping their fingers on the map *here, here,* and *here.* A secretary from the Department of Indian Affairs made noises about costs, allocations, and troop availability. In the end, Citrine Springs— by virtue of being forty-six miles from Wichita—got Fort Hollis, and the town's future was assured.

Each day, the sun passed over the main street of Citrine Springs, passing first over the clapboard church at the eastern end of town. The spire of the church was canted slightly out of true—the men who built the church were not the same men who had laid the track—and there was a large wooden cross nailed to the front of the spire. There was no bell in the steeple, for that would have been an unconscionable waste of steel in a land where progress was measured by miles of rail.

To the right of the church was a flat-roofed building with an elevated porch. It had been the train station, but once the rail reached Abilene and its sprawling cattle yards, management at the railroad decided to cut the stop in Citrine Springs. The station became a saloon, one of several in town, but in this establishment, everyone knew to hold on to their glasses when the train shrieked its approach.

As the sun rolled down the street, it peeked in narrow alleys filled with small shacks and cheap cabins. Beyond these tiny houses, the land transformed into a mixture of fields, orchards, and pastures, all of which were overseen by a scattering of ranch houses.

A little over halfway between the church and the hotel at the western end of town, there was a brick building with fancy curtains in the windows. A lurid banner hanging from the roofline promised all sorts of lurid entertainment, but the sun rarely saw any evidence of such. Most of the activity at Harck's Emporium happened after the sun was gone, and the moon— well, the moon would never tell what it saw through the upper-floor windows at Harck's.

Finally, the sun would pass over the Bateman Hotel, a square building made from orange and brown brick. The wooden trim along the roof and window frames had been red once, but the sun's relentless and persistent passage overhead had faded the trim to a dull pink. A broad porch with tall posts wrapped around the base of the hotel and every year or so its white paint was touched up. There were white curtains in the windows of the upper floors, and a broad sign attached to the southeast corner of the building proclaimed the hotel's name.

The hotel's namesake—Horatio Bateman—had been one of the founders of the town twenty years ago. The hotel, along with the store next door and the livery down the street, were still owned and run by Bateman's family. Horatio, alas, had passed several years ago. God rest his soul.

It was, as the sun could attest from its daily passage, a small town that had no reason to flourish and no particular reason to perish, but which persisted. Those who lived in Citrine

Springs—as well as those who made regular excursions to visit the store or the hotel—drank and gambled and waited for a reason to stop drinking and gambling. Was that persistence? Ah, well, raise a glass to that, then.

And speaking of which, here is Evangeline Harlstone—Miss Lily to some, Mrs. Harlstone to most—sitting by herself in the public room at the Bateman Hotel. Unaccompanied women were an infrequent sight in the public room, and Lily knew there would be talk. However, her tiny room at the back of the doctor's office was currently in use as a second infirmary bed, and she had been so furious at Doctor Ambrose that she couldn't stay in the office. She had stomped into the public room, demanded a glass of sherry from Thomas, and flung herself into a chair by the window, where she had brooded and sipped. Now, though, the glass was nearly empty. Was she going to ask Thomas for another?

That's how the trouble started in Boston, wasn't it?

The voice in her head was the voice of her older sister—a nagging reminder of Lily's failure to live up to certain expectations. It had been many years since she had seen Virginia, but that hadn't diminished the priggish and self-righteous tone that persisted in Lily's head. As far as she knew, Virginia was still in Boston, along with their perpetually-ailing mother. She hadn't written since she had left; she doubted her family knew where she had gone.

At moments like this—halfway through a glass of sherry and considering a second—Lily might acknowledge she had severed ties with her past, but all manner of folk went West to re-invent themselves. Why couldn't she do the same?

Although, Citrine Springs was a town no one cared about and which no one would miss when it was eventually swallowed by the grass. Her presence here—assisting the doctor when he needed help, and doing transcription work for Mr. Llewelyn and the Longspur Mining Company—was hardly a classic reinvention. The doctor was competent, even if his hands developed an awkward tremble by the end of the day, and Mr. Llewelyn only needed her once or twice a week. She would have thought there would be more correspondence at the mining company, but Mr. Llewelyn's reports always very brief: how many men were working, how much dirt had been moved, how much closer the operation was to completion.

It was this final part of the mining company reports which inflamed her curiosity. Mr. Llewelyn always referred to the goal of the company as "the Grand Design," and the few times she had discretely inquired, he had ignored her questions.

As she contemplated her nearly empty glass and reflected on the persistent mystery of the mining operation, the outer door swung open and Doctor Ambrose came into the room. Initially, she had been captivated by the rakish way he wore his long black coat, along with his shock of dark hair and his strong beard, but over time, she had seen it as the disguise it was. The coat, hair, and beard were meant to make the young doctor appear more worldly—more experienced. If his presence was daunting enough, no one would notice how nervous his eyes were or how much his hands trembled. When he discovered Lily's skill with a needle and the way she brooked no grief from the miners or other men in the town, he quickly realized she would be an effective shield.

Ambrose stopped at the bar and got a glass of whiskey. He brought it over to her table and collapsed in the chair opposite her. She fixed him with a fierce gaze as he gulped at his whiskey.

"Oh," he said, noticing her expression. "Did you—?"

"I'm fine," she said icily.

"Right," he said. He quickly finished his glass. "I'll get myself another one then," he said. "Are you sure you don't . . ."

"No," she said, even though she wanted to shout 'yes' at him. Yes, she wanted a glass of whiskey. Yes, she wanted him to not be such a spineless sniveler. Yes, she wanted—

As if he could sense her mounting fury, Ambrose—showing sudden and surprising alacrity—leapt out of his chair and darted back to the bar. He returned with two glasses, and sheepishly pushed one toward her.

She raised the glass to her lips and took a sip. The whiskey was fiercer stuff than the sherry. It burned her nose, her tongue, and the back of her throat. It felt like a hot coal as it slid down into her belly. She gasped, half-expecting a little puff of smoke to escape from her mouth.

Ambrose gave her a weak smile, as if he hoped the whiskey would quench the ire in her eyes, but his smile quickly faltered.

"You are going to talk to the sheriff," she said.

"Yes," Ambrose said. "Of course. Of course."

"Tonight."

"He might be—I wouldn't . . . I wouldn't want to disturb him tonight. I'll see him first thing in the morning."

She stomped her foot. "No," she snapped. "Talk to him tonight. And if you won't, I will."

"No, no," Ambrose said, waving his hands. "That's not necessary. I'll—I'll take care of it."

"That—that *animal*—almost killed one of those girls," Lily said. "Next time . . ."

Ambrose winced as if her words had physically hurt him. His eyes darted around the room, checking to see if anyone had heard her outburst.

"This is all very unfortunate," he said. "But let's not"—he held up his hands as she started to speak—"let's not make it more complicated than it is already. Please?"

Lily reached for her glass and took another sip. She let the whiskey burn all the words in her throat. Let it burn away the rage building inside her. *Remember what happened last time,* the voice in her head said.

Oh, I remember, Lily thought.

The whiskey couldn't burn hot enough.

8

After finishing his second glass of whiskey, Doctor Ambrose had mumbled something about checking on their patients. She knew he was fleeing her company; the doctor could read her moods plainly enough. She watched him scurry off, thought about calling out and reminding him of his promise to talk to the sheriff, but held her tongue as he slipped through the door.

Lily drank the remainder of her glass, grimaced, and thought instead of going to the bar and ordering another. But that would mean subjecting herself to the accusatory stare of the bartender—a fellow named Thomas, who, frankly, had no grounds to look askance at her. He cut his own hair, and was as unskilled at holding the scissors as he was at holding a bottle steady as he poured. And yet that man felt as if he could judge her with impunity.

As Lily was not going to the bar and not fuming in her seat—no, she most certainly wasn't—two men came into the public house. The older one—a man with a fierce gaze and a bushy beard—loudly announced his desire for a glass of whiskey, and it was the commanding tone of his voice that drew Lily out of her cycle of self-recrimination. She was reminded of Pastor Gleason's enthusiasm and verve when he got fervent about a passage from John or Luke during Sunday service.

The old man revealed a shock of white hair when he took off his black hat. Beneath his long coat, he wore a weathered vest and a collarless shirt that was not nearly as white as his hair. When Thomas ambled over with a bottle and two glasses, the old produced a gold coin from a pocket in his vest. Like many in the public room, Lily's attention was captivated by the theatrical flair with which he spun the coin across his knuckles.

Thomas went to grab the coin, but the old man kept the gold eagle out of the bartender's reach. He pointed at the bottle on the bar. "There is an order to this basic economic contract that we must enter into," the old man said. "Whiskey, first; payment, second."

Thomas frowned as if the man had spit and missed one of the chewing tobacco receptacles scattered throughout the room.

The old man rapped the gold eagle on the bar. "Pour a libation, my doubting man. Pour, before all the air leaves my lungs and my legs seize with cramps from standing here so long."

The other newcomer was so different from the old man that if she had not seen them enter together, she would not have marked them as traveling companions. His long coat and boots were stained the color of the wind and the rain, and his hat sat low on his forehead. His face was darkened with a beard that, while untended, was not as wild as the old man's. There was something about him that both drew the eye and made him forgettable. He stood near the bar and he ignored the old man's discourse. His attention was on the room, and his green-eyed gaze carefully measured each and every occupant of the room.

When his gaze fell on her, she sat up a little straighter. She did it unconsciously, like a flower turning toward the sun. He stared at her for a moment, as if he was memorizing her face and shape. She looked back, marking him as well, and he did not seem offended by her (slightly) whiskey-fueled brazenness.

"Might there be the possibility of a room and a bath in this fine establishment?" the old man said after Thomas finally poured a measure into each glass.

Thomas snatched up the gold eagle from the bar. "We have rooms," he said. He fumbled with the coin as if he was afraid it would burn his fingers.

"Ah, civilization." The old man drank the contents of his glass down in a single gulp. He clenched his teeth as the liquor bit the back of his throat. He put the first glass down and picked up the other one.

Thomas looked back and forth between the two men, slightly confused by the old man's behavior with the glasses. "One room?" he asked, scratching the side of his head.

"Two," the younger man said. "And I'll need a clean glass."

The old man finished the second glass, belched, and then picked up the bottle to refill both. "Yes," he said to Thomas. "Two rooms. I may have some company this evening."

The younger man plucked the bottle from the old man's hands. "Another glass, if you don't mind," he said to Thomas.

Thomas fetched another glass and put it on the bar. "I'll—I'll see about your rooms," he said.

The younger man poured a measure of whiskey. The old man, aware that he was the object of much attention in the room, waggled his empty glass like a man dying of thirst. "I have been too many days without proper medication," he said. His whiskers curled with abject sorrow.

"As have I," his companion said.

His attention was drawn toward the other side of the room. Two men were sitting at the table in the corner, their heads leaning toward one another. Realizing they were being watched, they broke off their secretive talk. One of the two got up, shoved his hat on his head, and left the room through the archway in the back of the public room.

Lily recognized them: Rufus and Pete—two local men who had been deputized by Sheriff Dixon. She had heard bits of stories from the girls at Harck's, as well as gossip from Mrs. Lasky and Mrs. Nelson. Dixon had only been sheriff a few years, and he had come into town in the company of other men, all of whom—it was whispered—had darker histories than the sheriff. One of them became the sheriff's chief deputy, and the rest had been hired by the Longspur Mining Company, first as shooters to clear the buffalo from the tracks, and then as security for the mine itself.

As the cattle trade surged in Abilene, Citrine Springs should have vanished from the map, but the Longspur Mining Company had prevented that. First there had been surveyors, who had crawled over the surrounding landscape like a swarm of ants; then, a wave of Chinese and Mexican laborers who lived in tents and squalor near the mine. They came into town once or twice a month, and it hadn't been difficult for the sheriff before Dixon—Lily couldn't remember the man's name now—to keep the peace. But as the mining operation grew, the town started to expand again, and when Mr. Llewellyn arrived, armed with a mandate to dig deeper and faster, the trickle of new arrivals became a flood. A pair of steam engines arrived from Chicago soon after, along with a half-dozen rail cars used to haul away the dirt and rock that came out of the mine. A mile of track was laid down too, connecting the mine and a hole where the rail cars dumped the dirt the miners had dug.

It has to go somewhere, Doctor Ambrose had explained to her one day. *You can't dig a mine without a lot of dirt. Where else is it supposed to go?*

But why haul it so far away from the mine? she had asked.

Ambrose had clucked his tongue—one of his infuriating habits—as if her query was so foolish it didn't even warrant a polite response. When annoyed, he would remind her how he had saved her in Chicago, how she would not have the luxury of living as she did—not to mention the marked pleasure of working under his august supervision—if he had not taken her under his wing and rescued her. What would your life be like if it weren't for me? he would ask. She knew better than to respond; he didn't want to hear her answer. He simply wanted to remind her of her place, of the debt he thought she owed.

Lily dipped her head and looked out the window. The man who had left the public room was in the street. It was Rufus, the shorter of the pair, and he had left the building through another door. He was hurrying as if he had some important destination in mind. *He's going to the sheriff's office,* she decided. She frowned, wondering why was he running to inform the sheriff.

She was still frowning, thinking about Doctor Ambrose and his empty promise to talk to the lawman, when she felt someone approach her table. She glanced up, and saw a pair of inscrutable green eyes looking down at her.

Elm had noticed the blonde woman's attention. She was not as distracted by the Judge's theatrics as many in the room. When the man at the back of the room scampered off, a tiny frown creased her forehead. He let his curiosity lead him to her table.

"Hello," he said. He lifted the bottle in his hand and nodded toward her empty glass. "May I join you?"

The blonde woman offered Elm an enigmatic smile. "Of course," she said, and she rose from her chair as he set down the bottle and his glass. Elm offered his hand, which she took. Her fingers were long and light in his grip. Her blonde hair was held in check by a comb of hand-carved walnut. Her cheeks were bright and her eyes were gray. She wore no rings, and a silver locket hung on a silver chain around her neck. Her dress was dark blue with long sleeves and a tiny collar. She was out of place in this public room—in all of Citrine Springs, likely—and yet, at the same time, something in her eyes said this was exactly where she was supposed to be.

"Elmore Stonebrook," he said. "But, please, call me 'Elm.'"

"Evangeline Harlstone," she replied.

Elm pointed at her empty glass. "May I offer you a libation?"

"That's a fancy word. I heard your friend use it."

Elm poured a measure of whiskey into her glass. "The Judge? Yes, he has a habit of dressing things up more than necessary."

"And you? You are not a fan of fanciful *dress*?" she asked.

He mulled her question over as he examined his glass. "Well, I suppose it depends on the audience," he said.

"I suppose it does" she replied.

"This whiskey, for instance," Elm started. He frowned at the unmarked bottle.

Lily leaned forward. "I don't think it has a name," she whispered conspiratorially.

Elm cleared his throat. "Well, if I were the sort of rogue who would approach a woman sitting by herself and offer her a pour from an unmarked bottle, I might be inclined to say it should be named after her, as a reflection of her beauty and taste."

"Would you now?"

Elm made a show of taking a sip from his glass. The raw spirit burned his throat. "But, having sampled . . . whatever this is, I believe such fanciful *dress* would be . . . ah . . . akin to putting a skirt on a cat, and you strike me as a discerning woman who would not be charmed by such shenanigans."

Lily took a sip. Elm watched her swallow. "My God. It really is awful," she said. "I think it may have better application as a varnish remover."

Elm's stomach twisted in agreement. A man could not survive on whiskey alone—the Judge's proclamations to the contrary—and he worried that this . . . *varnish remover* . . . would light a fire in his belly that would rage for many hours if he didn't get some food.

"What brings you to Citrine Springs?" Lily asked.

For an instant, Elm was back at Forestal's trading post. His hands on the shovel, dark patches of loose dirt strewn across the blankets wrapped around the bodies of Forestal and Pale Deer. His throat tightened, and he attempted to loosen it with the liquid fire in his glass. "I'm looking for someone." His words were made harsh by the whiskey.

"This person isn't a friend," Lily said, and Elm wasn't sure if she was responding to the roughness of his tone or some other sign he had given.

"No," he said truthfully. "Not a friend."

"Does he owe you money?"

"No," he said.

"Does he owe someone else money?"

"I do not know," Elm said.

"Is he a fugitive?"

"No," Elm said. "At least, not that I know of."

Lily pursed her lips. Her expression suggested she was tiring of this conversation.

At the bar, a woman in a crimson dress that squeezed her hips and left little to the imagination in regards to her breasts was listening intently to the Judge spin some outrageous yarn. Elm marveled at how her hair was nearly the same color as her dress. It was precisely the sort of unnatural plumage that would attract the Judge's attention.

"The man you arrived with," Lily said, changing the topic of conversation. "You said he is a judge."

"He was," Elm said. "Or still is, for that matter. I am not entirely clear on the particulars."

"Oh, one of those circuit judges? The ones who travel from town to town."

"Like that," Elm said.

"Do you work for him?"

Elm watched Lily's fingers tap against the side of her glass. "Why do you think that?" he asked.

"You seem reticent to name people 'friend,' but your familiarity with this man suggests you have been traveling together awhile."

"Therefore you deduce that he is my employer." Elm offered her a slight smile. "The simplest answer."

"You like simple answers."

"They're not . . ."

"Cats wearing skirts?"

Elm raised his glass. "Indeed," he said.

Elm watched her as she thought about taking another sip. The whiskey had brought a light flush to her cheeks. He realized he was staring and he directed his attention over at the Judge.

The woman in the crimson dress laughed at something the

old man had said. Her hand was on his arm. The Judge leaned over and whispered something in her ear, and she slapped his chest playfully.

"He is a friend, though, isn't he?"

"What?"

Lily pointed at the pair. "You are smiling, which suggests you are pleased that he has found company. You aren't just traveling companies. He means something to you."

"I suppose he does," Elm said. "But that is not why I am smiling."

Lily leaned forward. "Is it a secret?" Her eyes gleamed.

Elm laughed. "No, not really. The Judge likes to read."

Lily tilted her head. "And you? Do you dislike reading?"

"No, no," Elm said. "I enjoy reading as much as he does, I think. But the Judge? The Judge likes an audience."

"He wants someone to watch him read?"

"No, he likes to read out loud. 'Education comes from exposure,' he likes to say. 'A man knows the unknown when he acknowledges what he doesn't know and seeks to know more.'"

"Gracious. He sounds like Pastor Gleason." She saw his confusion and clarified. "He leads service on Sunday."

"Ah, yes. I can see how the Judge might come across like that." Elm smiled again. "He carries books with him, in his bags, and he will turn to them when he has an opportunity to do so. However, what made me smile in this instance is a book that recently came into his possession. What was it . . . ? Oh, yes, *Ferret Finnegan and the Black Bear of Mishkewanke*."

"I am not familiar with this book."

"It is—and I say this without intending to be dismissive—a forgettable story. The sort of book that is cheap and quick. Overly dramatic. Filled with too many adjectives. It might satisfy you momentarily, but it will not leave a lasting impression."

"Much like Glory herself," Lily said.

Elm examined the woman in the crimson dress. "Is that

really her name?"

Lily shrugged. "It suits her occupation," she said.

"I suppose it does."

"I still don't understand your amusement," Lily said. "It sounds like this book does not pretend to be something it is not. Nor does your friend appear to be someone who would be confused about this book's dress, if you will."

Elm nodded at her word choice. "Yes, well, this particular book was written by a gentleman named Meriweather Vance."

"And the Judge is not a fan of Mr. Vance's work?"

"No, he is not. He finds it beneath him."

Lily watched the Judge and Glory for a moment. "However, I suppose it is precisely the sort of cheap entertainment that Glory enjoys."

"Aye," Elm said. "I suppose it may be."

Glory tugged on the Judge's coat, pulling him away from the bar. The Judge allowed himself to be so moved, and Glory led him toward the staircase at the back of the room. Lily watched them ascend the stair. "You think she might convince him to read to her," Lily said. "Rather than coarser actions two people might undertake together."

"I suppose she might."

"Ah, the source of your amusement: you are imagining your friend's discomfort as he pretends to enjoy Mr. Vance's work."

"Indeed."

Lily blushed lightly under Elm's gaze. "What you do think of Mr. Vance's work?" she asked.

"I think the work is much like its author," Elm said.

"You've met him?"

"I have. We played cards one evening while riding on a Mississippi riverboat."

"That sounds like an interesting story."

Elm wrinkled his nose. "It's overly dramatic," he said, "and filled with too many adjectives."

"That is hardly fair, Mr. Stonebrook."

"How so?"

"If I continue my inquiry into your story, that makes me like Glory—eager to hear a story that you find to be ill-attired—and if I allow you to put me off, that makes me a prudish woman who has no time for cheap theatrics and bawdy entertainment."

"Such was not my intention, Miss Harlstone," Elm said. "You appear to be a confident and bold woman who is not overly concerned with such rash judgments that might be applied to your person."

"Boldly spoken, Mr. Stonebrook. I grant you clemency in regard to the earlier trap into which had you pushed me."

"Accepted with great relief, Miss Harlstone. And please call me 'Elm.'"

Lily picked up her whiskey glass. "You may call me 'Miss Lily,'" she said, and Elm enjoyed watching her smile after she took a sip.

9

The hotel room was at the end of the hall, and it was large enough to accommodate a bed and a washtub. The Judge plucked back the curtains on one of the two windows and looked out across the rooftops of the businesses and houses along the main road. Down below, a pair of men staggered off the hotel's porch and wavered up the road as if they were arguing over the route they should take. The sky had lost its vibrant color, and a few eager stars were already twinkling. Satisfied with the view, the Judge let the curtain drop and turned his attention to the room.

His companion—*Glory is my name and glory is my game,* as she had breathlessly informed him earlier—sprawled on the bed, which had a broad headboard and a solid frame with posts. The washtub he had requested was on a wooden platform. It was half full of steaming water. Money well spent, he thought as he unbuckled the tiresome weight of his gun belt.

Glory watched as he put the holster and belt on the table near the window, and she smiled suggestively as he took off his hat. With a practiced flip of his wrist, he tossed over the knobbed end of one of the bed frame posts. She giggled and arched her back, pushing up her already well-presented breasts. "Such aim," she sighed.

"Many years of practice, my dear," the Judge said. He shucked one arm from his jacket, grimacing at a twinge in his lower back as he did, and then he slipped the other arm free. Patting the pockets, he found the tattered remnants of the cheap book he had picked up at the trading post. The fur-bearing figure on the cover struck him as a more of a sad memorial to a fat trader than an inspiring image of a heroic mountain man.

"What's wrong, sugar?" Glory asked from the bed.

"Merely a passing phantom of a prolix memory," he said. He set the book down and proceeded to fold and lay his jacket out on the table.

"You sure know a lot of words," Glory said. "I would have just said 'it was nothing,' because I think that's what you meant."

"Do multi-syllabic utterances bore you?" the Judge asked.

"Nah," Glory said. She plucked at the front of her dress. "It's just that if we're talking, we ain't fucking, you know?"

"I do," the Judge said. He started unbutton his waistcoat. "However, as plentiful as your pastures are, my darling dove, I am going to lower my tired body into yonder tub before I lower it across your bountiful bosom."

"I don't mind a little dirt," Glory said. "You're cleaner than some of those fellers who come straight from the mine."

"I *do* mind the dirt," the Judge said.

Glory rolled onto her side, and her dress made a slithering noise as she squirmed. She propped herself up with one arm, and topped off her presentation with a well-formed pout.

As the Judge folded his waistcoat, he slipped a gold eagle into his palm. He revealed it with a flourish after setting his waistcoat on top of his jacket.

Glory's face lit up. "Where did you get that?" she said.

"Where it came from isn't as interesting as where it is going to go," the Judge said.

He flipped the coin toward the bed, and she followed its lazy arc. It landed next to Glory, and she grabbed it quickly.

"It's got a fancy lady on it," she said. Her eyes widened. "Is this gold?"

"It is," the Judge said.

"It's twenty dollars," she exclaimed.

The Judge sat down to take off his boots. "It is," he said.

Glory's eyes were bright. She gnawed her bottom lip. "I'll do whatever you want, mister, for this coin," she said.

The Judge dropped a boot on the floor. "I would like you to sit with me as I take a bath." He nudged the tattered book with a knuckle. "If you are so inclined—and if I can stomach the torturous prose—you may read aloud from this lurid narrative."

A wicked light bloomed in Glory's eyes. "Can I get in the tub with you?"

The Judge laughed. "Of course you can. Whether there will be enough room for all that water is another question entirely."

Lily declined to dine with Elm, but she didn't mind watching him eat. Thomas brought out a bowl of stew and several chunks of bread that Elm used to soak up the watery broth. He ate quickly, but he didn't gulp and choke down his food like the miners did. Under his scruffy beard, his face was lean, and there were dark shadows around his eyes and on one side of his face that could not be entirely blamed on the hotel's lighting. *He's been in a savage fight*, she realized, thinking of the faces of the women from Harck's who were at the doctor's office.

"What is it?" Elm asked, seeing the change in her expression.

"It's nothing," she said tightly. "You served in the war," she said, changing the subject.

"I did," he said. He dipped the last piece of bread into the broth. "Army of the Potomac."

"You were young."

"Not for long." He scraped his spoon along the rim of the bowl. "You had family who fought," he said. It wasn't a question.

She nodded. "My brother, Gilbert." She swallowed. "He died at Gettysburg."

"I'm sorry," he said. "Do you know where?"

"Devil's Den," she said. "He was with the Constitution Guard."

Elm nodded. "The 40th New York," he said. "They had a difficult task that day, and they fought well. I'm sure your brother's sacrifice was . . ." He waved his spoon. "That's of little consolation, I know."

"Yes, the men from the Army called it a 'contribution' in the letter they sent, which was not a word my mother found terribly appropriate. Or helpful."

"So, you are from New York?"

"Buffalo. And Boston." She paused. "And Chicago."

"Ever westward, huh?"

"Something like that."

Elm stared at her for a moment, and she held his gaze. Mention of her brother failed to stir any emotion in her breast, nor had it for many years. While her mother never recovered from the death of Gil, she had refused to let it break her in the same way. She had turned that sorrow into armor, in fact, and it had given her the courage to leave.

"I went to Europe after the War," Elm said, shifting the conversation away from her family tragedy. "It took awhile for me to realize I was running away from what I had seen and done during the War."

"Why did you come back?"

"I was born here. I fought for this country, and I guess I still believe in it." He offered a wry grin that didn't extend to his eyes. "Parts of it anyway."

"Which parts?"

"The parts that allow me to have dinner with someone like you, for instance."

Her cheeks grew warm. She was enjoying this conversation. It kept her from thinking about the two women recuperating at the doctor's office. Willa was in the patient bed and Catie was in her room. Ambrose had expected her to stay with them and sleep in the uncomfortable chair in the front room. It was one of the hazards of her role at the doctor's office, and she had tolerated it in the past—that knife fight at the Whistle Stop a few weeks back, for instance. The girls would be staying at the doctor's for awhile, and she wasn't eager to spend all those nights in the chair. She should look into a room somewhere else. At the hotel, perhaps, but she could already imagine the doctor's dismay at the expense. Maybe she should talk to Mrs. Lasky about that caretaker cabin beyond the north pasture on the family farm. *Only for a few weeks*, she thought. *Until the girls got better.*

"I'm . . . you have a conversation like this in every town you stop in," she said, putting aside the thoughts about where she was going to sleep.

"Not every town," he replied. His expression was earnest, and she wrestled with how she was supposed to react to such a confession, but then he smiled. "You thought I was serious."

"I—I wasn't sure," she stammered. The whiskey was muddling her thoughts. "I—I thought . . . Perhaps . . . I was confused by your words, and you gave the appearance of tallying a list in your head. I feared I underestimated your lechery—"

"Lechery? Your language cuts to the quick, Miss Harlstone."

"Mr. Stonebrook, this may be the frontier, but it is not *that* wild. It is still considered polite to observe some decorum when speaking to a lady."

He tapped the spoon against the side of the bowl. "I did ask your permission to sit here, didn't I?"

She inclined her head. "You did," she admitted.

"And I did admit that rushing to acknowledge your beauty and obvious charm would have been rude and crass."

"You did, but I recall it was poorly disguised."

"Poorly disguised?"

"Well, that is unfair of me. You did make a minuscule effort."

"Minuscule?"

"Shakespeare wrote sonnets; you resorted to a witticism about booze."

"Well, thou art more lovely and more temperate, surely," Elm said.

Lily's breath caught in her throat at his words, and she closed her mouth, stopping her cutting remark before it could escape. She hid the curve of her lips with her hand. She couldn't do anything about the blush rising in her cheeks, and she hoped he hadn't noticed, but she thought it unlikely.

She watched him as he chased the remnants of the stew with his spoon, marveling that this rough-faced man of the road had actually quoted Shakespeare as causally as if he were remarking on the weather. *Rough winds do shake the darling buds of May*, she thought, recalling another line from the poem—her mother had loved the English bard's sonnets. Lily found herself wondering how rough this stranger's hands actually were . . .

10

Catie hurt. It hurt to lie on her back. It hurt to lie on her side. When she rolled over, hoping to find a better position on the lumpy mattress, she hurt. It even hurt when she breathed, God help her. Catie couldn't cry anymore. The hiccuping, heaving torture of her emotions had used up all her tears.

She had heard the doctor talking to Miss Lily as they tried to make her comfortable. Heard him say things about her arms, about her ribs, about something inside her that was leaking. He didn't say anything about her face, though, but he didn't have to. Even with only one eye (the other being so swollen that she doubted she would ever open it again), Catie could see the way Miss Lily wouldn't look at her face. That downturn of the eyes. That outward tilt of the chin.

Catie remembered the public room at Mr. Harck's. She and a few of the other girls—Willa and Ruby and Glory—had been bored. Mr. Harck wanted them on display, even though there were no clients coming in off the streets. Most of the men of Citrine Springs were farmers or laborers—they did not have the time to wander in for a dalliance during the day. The miners worked in long shifts, and they wouldn't come until after sundown. By ten, the public room would be full of men eager to drink and fuck. There would be a steady parade of men going up and going down the stairs. Boots pounding on boards. Hands fumbling with glasses and coins. The piano man working the keys on the aged upright with the stoic determination of a faithless preacher. Mr. Harck, preening proudly from behind the bar, would see that all was right in the world.

A fresh spasm of pain wracked Catie's body, as if her body didn't want to her to revisit what had come later. She pulled her elbows in and forced herself upright. His name was in her throat, a low growl that gave her strength. That got her upright, chest heaving and aching. Eyes, stinging. The echo of his name pounded in her head.

Everyone knew about Vash. He was part of the group who had come to town with the lawman. Some of those men had been in the war together, and afterward, they had gone west to Texas and Mexico. She had heard stories about what they had done there, but the Longspur man hadn't cared about these rumors. He only cared that they were hard men who would answer to money. Most of the crew took over management of the mine, while the one who led them put on the star and became sheriff in Citrine Springs.

At first, the Longspur man's solution had been welcomed. There was less trouble at the mine. Around town, Dixon let it be known that he didn't mind what went on behind closed doors. As long as he wasn't bothered, then there was no reason for him to be the law now, was there? The old men who met for lunch on Fridays at the Bateman liked that Dixon wasn't bothered. Mr. Harck liked that Dixon never bothered to come to the Emporium. And the Longspur man? He liked that dirt kept coming out of the hole in the ground.

But then there was Vash. He was Dixon's man, but saying that was like saying that a man who held a tiger by its tail was the tiger's master. For a while, Vash hunted the buffalo and that was enough to curb his appetites. But when Vash had to go farther to find good hunting, the men at the mine forgot themselves. The doctor got busy, and when Vash came back, well, the doctor saw more business then too.

And then there was an incident with the Indians, which got the Army involved, and for awhile, everyone was bothered all the time. But winter came and it was hard and cold. It kept everyone indoors for many weeks. When spring arrived, all bright and green, the townsfolk and the miners had learned something about themselves while waiting for the weather to turn. Business at Mr. Harck's had been brisk in the spring and early summer. There was talk among the miners that they were going to find a vein soon, that they were going to find whatever they were digging for. Everyone was going to be rich, and the trains would come to Citrine Springs again.

We won't have to fuck the same six fellas, Willa had said to her. *We'll have new faces. Their nails will be clean. They won't stink of sulfur and sweat. They'll treat us nice.*

But as the summer heat baked the roofs and streets of Citrine Springs, the rail didn't quiver. They heard no train whistle. They saw no puff of smoke from a hot-burning engine hauling a full length of railcars, carrying those fresh faces with neat hands and tidy clothes. The grass grew tall and pale under the oppressive eye of the sun. The miners kept bringing dirt out of the hole. The girls at Mr. Harck's kept smiling at the same six fellas who always visited them.

It was dry and hot, and everyone knew a single spark was all it would take to light the grasslands on fire.

Catie was in the doctor's office. She recognized the wide hearth near the elevated table where he examined patients. The dirty curtain he pulled to give the sick an illusion of privacy. At the back of the room, there was a bed, and on the bed, there was a body. It was impossible to see who it was in the dull glow coming off the slumbering hearth. There were too many shadows.

With an effort that left her panting and sweating, Catie staggered over to the bed. She tried to sit on the edge of the bed, but her knees didn't bend right and she fell down. Catie cried out, unable to understand how she could hurt more than she already did. She leaned against the edge of the bed, unable to do anything more for a minute than whimper. Eventually, the pain ebbed, and Catie could force her throat to make other noises. "Willa?" she croaked. "Is that you, Willa?"

The body on the bed didn't respond. A heavy blanket covered the figure from neck to foot, and the body's head was wrapped with bandages. It was impossible to tell in the dim light if the person was alive or not, but Catie found strength in a thought: *Why would they leave her here if she wasn't?*

Catie crawled along the edge of the bed, grunting through the pain in her chest and stomach, until she reached the other end. "I dunno if you can hear me, Willa," Catie whispered after she got her breath back. "I dunno if God's already got you or not. All I know is . . ." Out of breath, she let her head fall forward and rest on the mattress. "He hurt us both," Catie whispered when she could muster enough breath. "And I don't know if you—I don't know—" A cough broke free inside her chest, and it rattled her body as it came out. She pressed her elbows against the bed to stop the tremors from agitating her ribs.

Her insides were all messed up. That's what the pain was telling her. Things weren't where they were supposed to be, and she didn't know if they would ever be right again. "And what for?" she hissed, a sudden surge of anger blocking out the pain. "So we can go back there again?"

Willa didn't answer, and the room spun around Catie. She pressed herself against the bed, trying to hold on. She knew she should go back to the other bed. The doc or Miss Lilly would be back soon. They would fuss over her. The doc would try to fix her, but there was nothing he could do but wrap her in bandages and tell her not to move. *Lie still*, he'd say. *It'll get better.*

She flashed on a face she hadn't thought of in years. *Lie still.* He had said those words too. *It will feel better in a moment.* But he had been lying, and she hadn't been the same girl after that. She had been . . . damaged, according to her father. Her mother couldn't look at her. The pastor at the church had refused to hear her confession. And when she had taken the money from box in the cabinet and stolen away in the middle of the night, no one had stopped her. *Lie still,* she had imagined whispering to them as she had crept out of the house. *It'll all be better in a moment. Once I'm gone.*

Catie raised her head and peered at the bandage-wrapped face of her friend. "It's never going to get better," she said.

Willa didn't answer, but Catie nodded as she had heard a response. "I'm gonna take care of us," she whispered.

It took her a long time, but she managed to get to her feet. "I'm gonna take care of you," she whispered again as she shuffled toward the door. *I'm gonna take care of everything . . .*

She lost something along the way. A part of her that she wouldn't miss, but which she knew was gone. It was—

Her legs ached. Her head hurt. There was something wrong with her eyes. She stopped, and looked back. There was nothing behind her but grass. *How did I get here?* she wondered, but the thought—like that fading sense of something dropped, something forgotten, something she should have held more tightly—didn't last long. There was a hole now, a hole that needed to be filled. And she could fill it, couldn't she? She could fill it with this anger. Yes. That was the ache in her chest. It wasn't her ribs. They still hurt, but she could breathe, as long as she was careful. Slow and careful. That's all that mattered. Slow and careful. *Keep it in for awhile yet.* The thought wasn't hers, but she welcomed it. Tucked it into the hole.

She was on the prairie. She didn't know where. It was all the same once you got out of sight of Citrine Springs. Miles and miles of the long grass. But here, the ground was bare. There was lots of loose dirt, almost as if someone had been digging. She looked about. She knew she wasn't at the mine, but a voice inside her head kept reminding her: *At the mine. He's at the mine.*

She found the hole. It wasn't a large hole, not like the one the Longspur man kept pouring money and men into. This was—relatively speaking—a small hole. It was deep, though. So deep the sun couldn't find the bottom. Not that the sun was looking.

It had fled the sky. There were only stars above her now, tiny dots in an otherwise black sky. There was no moon, and Catie wondered what she had done to make the moon hide from her.

Where am I? Catie wondered, and for a moment, she wasn't there—out on the prairie, under the silent stars. She was in the doctor's office, lying on the bed. Next to Willa. She could hear the slow sound of the other woman's breath. *Yes*, she thought. *I can hear her, telling me what needs to be done.*

Catie had no shoes on her feet. She was wearing nothing more than a bloodstained shift.

Yes. All the blood. That's what—

She shook her head, trying to remember what had happened. She had made a promise. Yes, that was it. *It'll get better.*

The hole wasn't *that* deep. She leaned forward. There was something down there. Something waiting for her. Something that would give her everything she wanted.

I'm gonna take care of everything, she thought.

A sensation ran up her legs. A vibration. As if a thing in the hole had shifted and the earth had recoiled from it.

But there was nothing in the hole! A very small part of her mind cried out.

She flicked that tiny voice aside. *Yes,* she thought. "Yes," she sighed, the single word slipping out of her mouth. *I will. I will make it better.*

She didn't even realize what she was agreeing to. Not the details, of course. She was too broken, too damaged to know the difference between what was real and what wasn't. Too delusional to stop herself from falling. All she wanted was to make the pain go away.

All she wanted was to save her friend.

I'm gonna take care of everything . . .

And then she wasn't at the hole anymore. She wasn't at the doctor's office either. She was in that squat, squalid shack he had at the mine. The ceiling was smoke-stained. There were stains on the wall and she shied away from thinking about the source of those stains.

He was there, of course. He was always there. A shadow that filled the room.

And yet . . .

She could see his face. There were scratches across his cheek, and she knew she was the one who had made them. *Yes, that was why he beat you,* the voice in her head said. *He hadn't stopped. He hadn't made it better. And you fought back, didn't you?* He had gotten angry—oh, his rage was an awful beast when it was released.

But it was her turn now, wasn't it? It was her turn to be the monster. To bite when he reached for her. To sink her teeth into his stinking flesh. To feel the hot blood as it filled her mouth. *Can you taste his fear?*

His eyes widened, and he got taller, but she wasn't afraid. She was beyond that all now. *It will get better,* she whispered to herself. Lying on the bed next to Willa. *It will get better.*

This is where the shadow in the hole had told her to go. This is what it had told her to do. She could taste his flesh in her mouth. The hot, smoky taste . . .

There was an oil lamp on the desk. She reached for it while he shouted at her. She didn't listen. She was past listening. She only saw the light of the lamp, and thought of the fire. *Hot, smoky . . .*

Burn it all, she thought, and part of her flinched. That wasn't what she wanted. No, no. That wasn't—

I'm gonna take care of everything, the shadow whispered.

Catie picked up the lamp. She raised it over her head. She looked at the face of the man who had beat her, who had cracked her ribs and broken something inside her. Who had raped her. She looked in his eyes, and she saw a reflection of what she had seen in the hole, of what filled that void inside her.

The lamp shattered when she threw it. The flames, eager to burn, crawled all over him. He screamed and flailed his arms. She wrapped her arms around his waist. *I'm doing this for you,* she thought. She opened her mouth to scream, wanting to shout her devotion out loud, but the flames roared into her throat and devoured everything.

11

The Judge snorted and snapped upright in the tub. The water was cold, and he felt like he had missed an important development in the narrative. No, not Ferret Finnegan. *That damn book*, he thought. Vance's book was stuck in his head. No, there was something else. Something more . . . He shook his head and looked around. His vision wasn't what it used to be, and the single lamp made for a lot of shadows. Was that . . . ? He blinked and focused. There was a naked woman in the room with him. At least, half a woman, bare ass and legs that went down to the floor. The rest of her was leaning out one of the windows.

"What's going on?" he demanded. He struggled out of the washtub, splashing water on the floor. *Yes*, he thought, *the two of us.* He and—*what was her name? Glory, that's right*—had climbed into the tub, which had made for cramped quarters but neither of them had complained. In fact, he had been quite energetic in his enthusiasm.

"Something at the mine," Glory said, her voice muffled by the window.

"What mine?" the Judge asked. He thought about the window for a moment, but mostly he thought about the rosy color of Glory's behind, and he sat down on the bed. The room was drafty—not surprising, all things considered—and he grabbed the corner of the blanket on the bed and threw it across his lap. Not because he was cold, but more so because the view of Glory's glorious—well, it was distracting.

"The mine." He forced his mind to focus on her words. "The rail line," he added. *Dear God*, his brain chortled, *she's—*

Glory pulled herself into the room, and the Judge breathed a sign of relief. She put her hands on her hips, and now the Judge had a different view to content with. Still naked. Still flush with the crisp night air. Still—

"Something has happened," Glory said. *Short on details, broad on presentation,* the Judge thought.

"I understood that, child," the Judge said. "And I would enjoy hearing the particulars." He waved a hand in her direction. "Could you find some clothes in the meantime?"

"I thought you wanted to see my tits," she said.

"I did. I do. I have." The Judge was having difficulty getting his message across. "And now I would like to—" He waved his hand again.

She sighed theatrically, and when she stepped away from the window, he leaped off the bed. Hauling the blanket with him, he hurried to the window and stuck his head out.

Down below, a chaotic swirl of bodies surged in the street. Not quite a mob, but more than a rabble. He sucked in a deep lungful of the night air, which helped clear his head (as well as his thoughts). He listened intently, trying to piece together what the rabble-not-quite-a-mob was doing. Something at the mine. Something about a fire.

When he glanced over the rooftops opposite, he realized that what he had mistaken as the fading gleam of the setting sun was a different sort of glow altogether.

A wagon rattled up. It stopped at a building across the street, and the man driving it went inside. The Judge watched as a woman pushed through the rabble-not-quite-a-mob and crossed to the wagon. As she climbed onto the high seat, the man returned. He put some bags in the back of the wagon, and then he joined the woman on the board. He snapped the reins and the horse lurched into motion. As the wagon rumbled down the street, the crowd strained and broke. Some of the people followed the wagon, some milled about in the street— concerned citizens who liked to participate in rabbles, but who drew the line at mobs—and the rest lost interest and went back into the hotel.

The Judge frowned at the dismal remnants of the crowd. How in God's name was he going to learn anything about this town if people didn't make an effort to demonstrate noisily in the street? He leaned farther out the window and caught sight of a familiar four-legged shape. "Ho, dog," he shouted. "What are you doing?"

Laelaps, hearing the Judge's voice, looked up. He wagged his tail.

The Judge made a shooing motion and the dog barked, happy to be noticed.

"Stupid mutt," the Judge grumbled. He was about to return to the room when he caught sight of Elm. "Go on," he shouted.

Elm lifted his head toward the window and pushed back his hat so he could see who was yelling at him.

"How are we going to learn anything when you are standing around like that?" the Judge asked.

Elm raised his shoulders, much like a horse shrugs to rid itself of a bothersome fly. He said something to the dog, who wagged his tail, delighted to be included in the conversation.

Elm stepped off the boardwalk and ambled in the direction of the livery, and the Judge fought the urge to yell after him. *You can't insist on the manner in which a man does the right thing,* he thought, *you can only get him pointed in the right direction.* With a final shake of his head, the Judge ducked back into the room, where Glory was waiting for him on the bed.

And speaking of following directions, she had made an effort to put some clothes on, though what she was wearing was not the fancy party dress she had worn earlier that evening. She was wearing his shirt, and it didn't escape the Judge's attention that she had failed to do up any of the buttons.

"There's a mine . . ." he started.

She nodded and leaned back on the bed. The shirt slipped away from her front.

The Judge did his best to keep his eyes on her face. "Tell me about more about this mine," he said.

She pushed out her lip and dropped her chin. It was an expression which—time and again—got her what she wanted, but this time—oh no, he wasn't going to fall for it this time. Not when there was something exiting going on.

"Why is the mine on fire?" he asked.

The road to the mine was a pale ribbon in the moonlight, and it slithered across a dark landscape. The road was pocked and uneven, and his horse picked its way carefully. Elm had time to reflect on his conversation with Miss Lily as well as the brief glimpse he had gotten of the man driving the wagon. The man he assumed to be Doctor Ambrose. Elm wondered about the relationship between Lily and Ambrose. Clearly, the doctor treated the young woman as an assistant, but there was something about Lily that said she would not suffer such callous presumption without cause.

He should have been more annoyed with the Judge for yelling at him from the window—in such a state of undress, as well—but the old man's peculiarities of personality were no longer cause for distress. Yes, that is the way the Judge would have said it: peculiarities of personality. *You can learn much about a man in the way he treats the staff*, the Judge would say, *or how he eats his food. Before he even speaks, you know how short-tempered he is, or how much he thinks before he opens his mouth, or whether he is miserly with his coin.*

And what would the Judge have said about a man who hollered commands at a gentleman not in his employ while wearing nothing more than a threadbare blanket?

The road turned and dipped, and as he came around the bend, he caught sight of his destination.

The camp was scattered across the bed of an ancient river that had long since departed this region. A steep bluff lay past the camp, and in it, Elm spotted a dark hole. Near that shadow-spawning darkness were several rail cars used to haul away rock and ore. The landscape was lit by fire—several tents and a pair of wooden buildings were ablaze, and judging by the fanciful color and movement of the fire, it was delighted to be untamed and out of control. Men worked a bucket line from whatever meager source of water was still running in the river bed.

Elm nudged his horse toward the line of men. Fire in a camp was a dangerous thing. During the war, there had been an incident where a cook fire had been left untended, and during the night, the wind had huffed on the coals. Eager flames had sprung up, leaping over to the frayed fabric of the mess tent. By the time an alarm was raised, the fire had spread, prancing across the top of more than a half-dozen tents. In the ensuing chaos, nearly a quarter of the company was injured, and most of the tents and gear were lost.

He tied his horse to a tent stake near the verge of the camp, and doffed his hat and coat before working his way toward the line. He couldn't do much about the lack of dirt and sweat on his face, but he figured that would change soon enough. When he got to the line, he inserted himself into a gap and started passing buckets—empties coming back from the fire behind him, full ones sloshing water on the ground as they came in the other direction.

If any of the men found his arrival strange, they didn't comment. He was working with them, and for now, that was good enough.

"We're not allowed out at the mine. And why would we go there, anyway?" Glory swung her foot back and forth as she pouted. "It's just a hole in the ground. They take dirt out of it. They load it into rail cars, and it goes away." Her foot indicated the work flow of the operation.

"What else?" the Judge asked as he pulled on his pants.

"What else what?"

The Judge sat down on the chair. "Men do not dig in the ground for the simple pleasure of making a hole in the ground. Yes, there is dirt, but dirt is merely in the way. There is something else there, something worth all of the time and money spent moving that useless dirt."

"Oh, like silver or gems?"

"Or gold," the Judge said. "Like that coin I gave you."

"I like gold." Glory sat up straighter. Her breasts pushed against the fabric of his shirt.

The Judge regarded his shirt and the woman wearing it. "Are they mining gold?"

While Glory pondered his question, the Judge put on his socks. "I don't think so," she said. "I never hear talk about gold."

"What do they talk about?"

"Dirt," Glory said. "There's a lot of it."

The Judge sighed. He felt like he was tied to a stake, and all he could do was go round and round and round. "How long have they been mining?" he asked.

"A couple years."

"And how long have you lived in Citrine Springs? Were you here before the mine opened?"

"Nah, I was in Wichita."

"Doing what?"

"Same thing I'm doing now," she said. A salacious smile worked across her face as she toyed with the buttons on his shirt.

"Why did you leave Wichita?" the Judge asked. He put his head down and focused on getting his other sock on.

Glory didn't answer, and when he was done wrestling with his foot covering, he looked up. She was pouting again, letting him know this wasn't how she wanted to spend the evening.

"Okay," the Judge said. "Just a few more questions, and then I'll be done."

"Promise?"

"I promise."

She swept his shirt back, revealing her breasts. "And then will you touch these?"

He pretended to give the question serious thought. "That, my dear, is an excellent idea," he said eventually. "But you know what? That shirt—and I say this with the utmost respect for the garment—is not necessary. It is getting in the way, is it not?"

She giggled, delighted to have convinced him that she was more fun than whatever was going on out at the mine. She leaned forward, slipping her arms out of the sleeves. The Judge, surprising her with his agility, leaped off the chair and grabbed the shirt before she could react.

"Hey!" She pounded her fist against the bed.

"Ah, but you said I could ask a few more questions first."

"You aren't staying," she said.

The Judge slipped his shirt on and fumbled with the buttons.

"You're married, aren't you?" Glory pounded her fist against her thigh this time. "You married men are all the same."

"Dear child, I am not married," the Judge said. "I merely have something more pressing to attend to."

Glory fell back on the bed. "You could be pressing your—"

The Judge scooped up the blanket from the floor and threw it over her delightful nakedness. While she thrashed beneath the blanket, he grabbed his waistcoat and jacket. By the time she had extricated herself—in a truly magnificent thrashing of naked limbs that, in another time and place, he would have relished watching—he had finished dressing and was standing by the door.

"When I return," he said, holding up a finger to forestall any angry protest. "I will make amends."

She grabbed a pillow and hurled it, along with a shriek of unladylike language. The Judge ducked out of the room, dodging both pillow and invective. Adjusting his waistcoat, he strode off toward the stairs.

It wasn't the young woman's fault. All the commotion in the streets had stirred his blood. He was eager to learn why a mining company was digging a hole and not finding anything. The fever for gold had swept this nation once or twice before, and like many fevers, it never entirely left the body. Did the mining company know something about this land that no one else did? Were they trying to stake a claim before word got out?

The Judge knew that greed made men do stupid things. He knew the jealous glances, the furtive pinching of coin, the whispers among those who had little about those who had a lot. He knew how men laughed when they thought they were flush beyond their wildest dreams. And he also knew that whores were like lightning rods. They attracted wealth and power. They knew things they shouldn't, and they shared secrets amongst themselves. And yet, Glory had been bored of his questions about the mine. .

She doesn't know, the Judge thought as he clattered down the stairs and passed through the near-empty public room. *And if she doesn't know, then the miners don't know why they are digging.*

That meant there was a secret, a secret well-kept, and if there was something the Judge liked more than the company of a well-endowed lady, it was the promise of secret knowledge.

12

It was dull work, waiting for a bucket to come, but it was no more dull than any of the work the miners did underground. They knew what to do, and they had no illusions that the work was going to get better or worse. There was a rhythm to the work, and the work would be done when it would be done. Some, however, were more eager than others, and these men fidgeted while waiting for a bucket.

Elm lost count of the number of buckets he had passed. A grizzled fellow with soot-stained cheeks made his way down the line with a jug and a pair of tin cups. Each man was offered a mouthful of whatever white dog 'shine was in the jug.

"We're beating it, aren't we?" Elm asked as the jug-bearer poured a measure for him.

"Aye," the man said. A gap-toothed grin crossed his face as Elm grimaced at the taste of the clear liquor. "Better that heat being in your belly than on your face," he said.

"Did you make that this afternoon?" he asked. The back of his throat felt as if it had been flayed.

The jug-bearer cackled. "Just about," he said.

"Are you handing it out so as to keep it away from the fire?" Elm asked as he gave back the cup.

"Don't breathe too hard in that direction," the man said, nodding toward the diminished blaze in the center of the camp.

Elm made a point of looking toward the ruddy glow. "Someone knock over your still?"

The moonshiner snorted. "Not my still," he said. "That's management's place."

The next man in line waved at the man with the jug. "Hey, you gonna keep pouring or what?"

"I'll pour when I'm goddamned good and ready to pour," the moonshiner snapped.

The man was given a empty bucket. "Stop holding up the line," he complained as he shoved the bucket at Elm.

A skirted figure approached the line. It was Miss Lily, and she was carrying two empty pails. Taking advantage of the argument between the man with the jug and the miner still waiting for his tipple, Elm shoved the bucket in his hand to the man behind him and hurried after Lily. He caught up with her as she reached the creek. "Let me help you with that," he said, reaching for one of the pails she was carrying.

"Oh, thank—" She stopped when she saw who was offering assistance. A bemused expression crossed her face.

Elm shoved the empty pair toward the pair of men standing in the shallow creek. "Lady needs some water," he said. The guy in the creek stared at him like he was an apparition. "Maybe she's taking a bath," he added, which only increased the man's confusion.

"It's for the doctor," Lily said. "The lady is quite content to wait until the danger of being burned to death has passed before concerning herself with bathwater."

"For the doctor," Elm repeated. He frowned at the man, as if he had been the one to make such the outrageous assumption about the lady's priorities. As the man bent to fill the pail, Elm indicated that Lily should give him her other pail as well. When both were full, he shook off her outstretched hand and nodded toward the tents. "Let's not keep the doctor waiting," he said.

Lily swept up her skirts and Elm hustled after her, a full pail of water in each hand. She held her tongue until they were far enough away to not be overheard. "Bath water?"

"Not many other reasons for water around here," he said.

"And yes, what are you doing out here, Mr. Stonebrook?"

"Helping with the war effort," Elm said, falling back on the standard response every conscript learned as readily as their own name and regiment.

She offered him an enigmatic smile. "Are you behind enemy lines, soldier?"

He hefted the pails. "I'm just carrying water for the doctor."

She raised an eyebrow. "Someone was doing just fine with that task before you showed up."

"Yes, but now your hands are free."

She stopped and put her hands on her hips. "And what else should I be doing with my hands?" she asked.

Elm flushed. "That's not what I meant . . ." he started.

"Of course not," she said. The intensity of her gaze made his embarrassment more pronounced. She cocked her head. "You have odd timing, Mr. Stonebrook," she said.

"Please. Call me 'Elm.'"

"What are you doing here, Elm?"

He hefted the pails. "Helping with the—"

"—war effort. Yes, you said that." She shook her head and continued walking. "Come along then. Make yourself useful."

Elm's heart was hammering in his chest, and he knew he was sweating. Lily's comment about enemy territory was not far from the truth, and yet here he was, standing around like a lovestruck fool, when he should be focusing on more important things. Like figuring out answers to all the questions he knew the Judge was going to have. *Keep your head, man,* he thought as he hustled after Lily. *Now is not the time for such foolishness.*

The Judge nearly missed the mining company office. It was a narrow building, wedged between the general store and a shipping company. There wasn't any porch, and the single window was covered with a heavy curtain. A narrow piece of wood leaned against the inside of the glass, and on it, "LONGSPUR MINING COMPANY" had been burned into the wood in a blocky script. The Judge pretended he couldn't read and kept on, strolling past shipping company and around to the alley in back. He was disappointed there wasn't a back door, and he quickly returned to the front.

A couple were strolling in the street, and the Judge politely tipped his hat as they went by. He loitered awhile, pretending to peer through the window of the general store—a fool's effort as the inside of the store was darker than a gopher hole on a moonless night. It kept his face turned away from the street, in case anyone was watching.

"Keep watch," he said to Laelaps, who had been dutifully trotting behind him.

He had felt a momentary pang of guilt for leaving the dog outside when he and Elm had gone into the hotel, but as Elm had named the damn mutt, didn't that also indicate an assumption of responsibility for the beast? And just Elm had gone riding off to God knew where, that did not mean the dog was now in his care. The dog wasn't a wayward puppy. He could attend to his own needs. He didn't need a guardian.

However, since the dog had decided—of his own volition, mind you—to follow the Judge during this nocturnal reconnaissance, he might as well make himself useful. What else was a watchdog for, after all?

When the Judge leaned against the door of the mining company office, the panel creaked, but didn't give. He jostled the handle and found the door locked. *Solid frame,* he thought. *Stout latch. They're not all bumpkins out here in the wilderness.* He reached into his coat for the fork he had lifted from the bar as he had left. Using his fingers to find the keyhole, he wiggled the fork in the slot. *Lightly,* he thought, *a gentle touch.* An image of Glory, lying on the bed, swam into his brain.

Would she still be there when he got back? The Judge thought she might be. *She would be an excellent alibi,* he thought. The woman had generous . . . *enthusiasms.* She had tried to read Vance's book while they soaked in the tub, but oh, that man's writing was terrible. Though, if his feet were held over a fire, the Judge might be able to locate a few passages that could be mistaken for rough script written by a hack pretending to be James Fenimore Cooper. Obviously, Vance had based his mountain man—the alliteratively named Ferret Finnegan—on Natty Bumppo, but there was an air of condescension in Vance's work. James Fenimore Cooper—for all his obvious narrative faults—earnestly believed in his writing. No, Vance knew he was writing garbage and—

The fork caught. When the Judge moved the latch, it lifted.

The hands always know what to do, he thought. He threw a mental salute to the image of Glory lounging in bed. *Thank you, my dear, for occupying my mind while my hands did their work.*

He surveyed the street. There were no errant strollers or pesky watchers. He was safe.

"Stay here," he said to the dog.

The dog whined and wagged its tail in a manner meant to tug at his heart.

"It's dark inside," he said. "There's nothing to eat."

Laelaps whuffed quietly.

"Look, I need someone who can read. Can you read? The Judge shook his head, answering his own question. "You're just going to be underfoot. Stay here. Be my lookout."

Laelaps whuffed again.

"I won't be long," the Judge promised.

The dog lay down and put his head on his paws. The Judge refused to feel sorry for the mutt as he opened the door and slipped inside. A momentary panic assailed him—*what was he going to do if the dog actually barked?*—but he dismissed that thought. No one was going to wander by and find him.

Lily led Elm to a tent on the far side of the camp, and as he followed her inside, he was assaulted by the stench of burned meat. The tent was narrow and dark. The sole source of illumination was a single lantern hung on a hook near the low ceiling, and Elm could make out a number of cots. The source of the smell was in the back of the tent.

Doctor Ambrose, his white shirt smudged with blood and soot, stood behind a makeshift table. Spotting Lily, he gestured at a nearby bed where there was a basin and a mound of dirty linen. "I need more bandages," he snapped.

Elm, realizing where the water was supposed to go, brought the pails over to the basin and poured the water. Lily started soaking strips of linen, which she handed to Ambrose as soon as they were wet through and through.

The patient on the table had to be a man, judging from his size. What few portions of his body weren't covered with bandages were dark from burns and bruises. The man's hair and beard were like layer of hard nettles stuck in the man's flesh. The figure grunted and muttered as the doctor wrapped his arm, though his words were an unintelligible babble of angry noises.

"Do you need more water?" Lily asked quietly after she had wet the pile of bandages waiting for her.

Ambrose's face was pale, and there were deep shadows under his eyes. He glanced at the basin and shook his head. "It doesn't matter," he muttered, almost to himself. "I'm not doing anything,"

"You are," Lily said. She reached out, but hesitated before she made contact with the doctor's arm.

"He's insensate from the pain," Ambrose grumbled. "He feels nothing. There's no point in trying to ease his discomfort."

"But later . . ." Lily trailed off.

Ambrose shook his head, indicating that he didn't think the man was going to live to see much of later.

"What about . . . ?" Lily turned toward the beds behind the doctor. On one of them, a dirty sheet covered a small body. A foot stuck out, and it was dark and strangely malformed.

Ambrose's lips thinned to a hard line. "There's nothing to be done for her," he said.

Elm pulled the sheet back, revealing the twisted and charred body of a woman. Her hair was gone and the skin of her skull was charred black.

"Who did this?" he asked.

Ambrose's gaze was haggard and hollow, as if he wasn't sure if Elm was real or if he was a phantom come to haunt him. His gaze slid to Lily, and then to the man on the table. "He did," Ambrose said. "Vash killed her."

It was dark inside the mining company office. After shutting the door, the Judge inched along the wall until his fingers touched the heavy curtain over the window. He shoved the curtain slightly—enough for a little moonlight to slip into the room, but not enough to provide a view for curious outsiders.

There was a desk off to his left and another one to his right. With a hand stretched out before him, he navigated to the corner of the righthand desk. There was a heavy wooden chair behind the desk, and beyond, an interior wall. A large painting hung on the wall. *A landscape*, he thought. His vision was adjusting to the gloom, but there wasn't enough moonlight to reveal fine details.

He let his fingers trail across the back of the wooden chair as he crossed the back of the room where he found a narrow table pushed up against the wall. His fingers encounter a tray and some kind of decanter. *Crystal*, he thought, feeling the smooth outline of the container.

He lifted the stopper off the decanter and sniffed the contents. He liked what he smelled, and he fumbled around for a moment, trying to find a glass. *Ah, yes, there.* Another tray, but this one had glassware.

He put the lip of the decanter against the glass, salivating slightly at the ring of glass against glass, and poured. The liquor went into his mouth like warm honey. He sighed, and the back of his tongue tingled. "Ah, the good stuff," he said.

He finished the meager amount he had started with and poured another measure. Filling half the glass this time. Or more. He could be excused such excess. It was dark, after all.

He rapped his knuckles on the sidebar. The sound was dull and heavy, but there was enough of an echo to suggest a hollow space. He bent over to investigate and found a movable panel. Inside, there were shelves, and on those shelves were boxes. He lifted one out and put it on the nearest desk. It was filled with sheets of paper, and he carried one over to the window, where the curious moon would provide better illumination.

"Formed in 1913 by Calhoun and Timacheus Longspur, the Longspur Mining Company has quarried stone, dug coal, constructed tunnels, and facilitated the growth of American enterprise et cetera et cetera . . ." The Judge skimmed the glowing list of accomplishments: regrading a portion of Missouri he had never heard of; negotiating exclusive mining rights with a handful of native tribes; a long list of inventions and patents.

The Judge squinted at the tiny print at the bottom. "The Longspur Mining Company has offices in St. Louis, Chicago, and Denver, from which it manages the excavation of more than thirty mining operations in six states and three territories." He clicked his tongue. "Busy, busy, busy," he said. "So many holes to dig."

Something nagged at him, like a bit of meat stuck between his teeth. His tongue would push at it, over and over. Eventually, he would think it had gone away, but an hour later, it would be there again. *Longspur*, he thought, sounding out the word in his head. He tucked the piece of paper in the pocket of his coat and returned the box to the shelf. *Long spur*. He stretched the name out, but that didn't help. He nosed through other boxes in the sidebar, but they were filled with mining minutia. Having exhausted his survey, he stood at the sidebar and sipped from the glass of expensive scotch. "Longspur," he said out loud, in case vocalizing made a difference.

And, yes! There it was. A case during his tenure on the bench in Baton Rogue. That's where he had heard the name. What had it been about? Water rights? No, that hadn't been it. Right of way? He drank more whiskey, and the liquor released more details from the dank recesses of his mind.

A pair of plantation owners had sued the Longspur Mining Company for dumping materials on their fields. Longspur hadn't disagreed with charges. In fact, they had offered to buy all the land of the aggrieved parties. However, these were family estates—one of them dated back to early French settlers who were in Louisiana before the land was acquired in Jefferson's nation-building purchase—and Longspur's offer was seen as an unconscionable affront. The family lawyers didn't want compensation. They wanted Longspur to desist all operations in the area.

The Judge couldn't recall the details of what the company had been digging for, but he recalled a rather impassioned argument about the impact such closure would have on the local community. In the end, while he found the plantation lawyers insufferable and the men from Longspur arrogant, he cited Longspur for negligence and ordered them to make reparations for the damages they had caused to the fields.

That had been in . . . when was that? Late '59? Early '60? It didn't matter. The Civil War started the following year, and both plantations were burned during the Union efforts to secure routes to the Mississippi River. After the war, Reconstruction made it difficult for the families to rebuild.

As far as he knew, Longspur never paid the fines levied against them.

Outside, Laelaps barked, and the Judge's head snapped up. He cast about, trying to decide which desk to hide behind. He noticed how much liquor was still in his glass, and while he dawdled, the latch lifted and the front door swung open.

The yellow glow of a storm lantern filled the room, and the Judge blinked against the sudden change in light. A man stood in the door frame. Light glinted off the badge on his chest and off the barrel of the gun in his hand.

"Am I interrupting?" the newcomer asked.

"I was just finishing up," the Judge said. He started to raise the glass to his lips, but the sound of a hammer being drawn back on a revolver made him pause.

13

The sheriff wore a fringed buckskin jacket, dark pants, and black boots. The brim of his hat was wide and flat, and his brown sideburns curled along the shape of his jaw. The ends of his mustache were waxed and curled. The silver star on his jacket made it clear he was the law in this town, even if his posture and the rounded curve of his belly suggested otherwise.

As the Judge stepped around the desk, the sheriff moved to the side of the door so that the Judge could neither rush him in the doorway nor duck out of his line of sight. The Judge, understanding the man was no fool, left the office without a fuss.

At the sight of the Judge, Laelaps wagged his tail vigorously.

"You needed to bark sooner," the Judge said to the dog, who barked enthusiastically in reply.

"That's the problem with hired help," the sheriff said as he shut the office door. "I have a couple of deputies who are similarly inclined."

"I am mollified to hear that," the Judge replied. He looked at the sheriff's classic Remington revolver with its high spur hammer. "It gives me hope about the state of law enforcement in Citrine Springs."

"Don't get too excited," the sheriff said. He tried the door after the latch fell, and satisfied that it was closed, he motioned with his gun.

The Judge looked in the opposite direction. "I was under the impression the jail was that way," he said.

"It is," the sheriff said. "But that's not where we are going."

"Where are we going?"

"To visit the man whose office you were just in."

"Ah, excellent. I would like to make his acquaintance."

The sheriff raised his eyebrows. "Breaking into his office and drinking his liquor is hardly a way to make a good impression."

"Well, I was attempting to learn something about this fellow's character," the Judge said.

"Do tell. I suppose I know something about your character too, don't I?"

"And what is that?" the Judge asked.

"You are inclined to take a tipple before you loot the cash box."

"What gentleman of leisure doesn't?"

"Speaking of leisure, start walking." The barrel of the sheriff's weapon drifted back to the Judge's chest. The Judge took the hint and headed east, away from the hotel.

Laelaps, without being told, came along as well.

"It's a tidy town you have here, Sheriff," the Judge said as he strolled along. "Streets are clean. Responsible law enforcement. Is there a satisfactory market for fresh produce?"

"It sufficiently meets the needs of the citizens," the sheriff said as he fell in a half-step behind the Judge.

"Oh, that is a very proper answer," the Judge said. "And coal? Does it 'sufficiently meet the needs' as well?"

"You can't eat coal," the sheriff said.

"Ah, but coal provides jobs, and jobs require infrastructure, which leads to commerce and financial opportunities." The Judge glanced back at the sheriff. "A man looking to improve his lot in life could stand to do well in such a town."

"Is that why you were poking around Mr. Llewelyn's office? Looking for some sort of business opportunity?"

"I was merely after some whiskey," the Judge said.

"You could have accomplished that at the hotel."

The Judge snorted. "Clearly, you haven't sampled what they have on hand there, sir."

"What are you doing in this town?" the sheriff asked. "There aren't any business opportunities—not like the ones you're hinting at—and you don't strike me as the wandering preacher type."

"Me? A man of God? Hardly. I prefer more mundane matters of law and order."

"Law and order, huh? You a lawyer?"

"Most definitely not. My name is Wallace. Judge Willard Vernon Wallace."

"Judge, huh?" The sheriff tucked in his upper lip as if he wanted to suck on his mustache. "Are you riding circuit?"

"Should I be?"

The sheriff gave him a cold grin. "Maybe I should telegraph someone in St. Louis. See what I can find out about who is assigned to this territory."

"You know, I made a contribution to a local parks commission the last time I was there," the Judge said. "They mentioned something about a statue. Perhaps you could inquire if they have erected that monument."

"I've never met anyone important enough to have a statue raised for them. Don't you have to be dead before they do that?"

"That all depends on the valuation of your contribution," the Judge said.

The sheriff stopped before a modest two-story house with unadorned gables and lace curtains in the windows. The sheriff banged on the door, and the door was opened in short order by a man wearing a dark jacket and white gloves. "What do you want, sheriff?" he asked brusquely.

"I discovered this fellow poking around the Longspur office," the sheriff said. "I thought Mr. Llewelyn would want to know before I tossed him into a cell at the jail."

"At this hour?"

The sheriff nodded toward one of the windows. A steady light from within made the curtains glow. "The man of the house is still up, Victor, so why don't you go ahead and announce us."

"Mr. Llewelyn is not the sort of man who entertains at all hours." The manservant peered at the Judge for a moment, and having satisfied himself about what he saw, he made to close the door.

The sheriff put his boot in the way. "Let us in, Victor," he said, and there was little humor in his tone. "Mr. Llewelyn will be very disappointed if you don't."

"I find that highly unlikely," Victor said, but he stepped back and opened the door for the Judge and the sheriff.

Elm wanted to ask the doctor more questions, but before he had a chance, more men came into the makeshift ward. All three were sweat-stained, and their clothes reeked of fire and smoke. One couldn't stand on his own, and the doctor indicated the others should help him lie down on an empty cot. Elm made eye contact with Lily, and indicated with his head that he was going to wait outside.

He paced back and forth for a few minutes, his brain churning with questions and darker thoughts. His gaze kept returning to the dark shape of the bluff beyond the camp, and he was about to succumb to the curiosity burning in his veins when the tent flaps lifted and Lily came out.

She fussed with her coat as if she couldn't get warm. "I think he's going to live," she said, her voice distant.

"Who?" Elm asked.

"Vash."

"Is that the name of the man on the bed?"

She shivered, and not entirely from the chill in the air. "His name is Vash," she said, her voice soft. "He works for Longspur. As a . . ." She stopped and let out a bitter laugh. "He's a monster. He threatens people. He beats women. When he isn't doing those things, he is out shooting buffalo or . . . or worse."

Elm concentrated on breathing slowly. He knew he shouldn't leap to conclusions, but his thoughts were circling like hungry vultures. The man in the tent. Was he the one who had shot Pale Deer?

Lily, oblivious to his thoughts—or maybe because she knew exactly what his thoughts were—told him more. "There is a place in town. It is run by a man named Harck," she said. "The women who work for him—though I hesitate to speak of their relationship in such generous words—these women come to the doctor on a regular basis. They have . . . certain issues that require the doctor's assistance now and again. Issues that could prevent them from working."

Elm nodded curtly, letting her know he knew how such arrangements worked.

"Occasionally, a woman comes to visit who is in need of more care"—Lily swallowed noticeably—"bruises, mostly, but sometimes, there are broken bones. Bleeding that won't stop. Deep cuts."

"And the doctor fixes them up and sends them back to this guy, Harck?"

Lily nodded.

"Why haven't—why hasn't the doctor spoken to the sheriff about this?"

"The sheriff?" Lily let out a short laugh. She spread her hands to encompass the tents. "This all belongs to Longspur. Who do you think pays the sheriff?"

The study was lit by lanterns in wall sconces as well as by a roaring fire in a deep fireplace. Bookcases surrounded the fireplace, and the Judge let out an involuntary noise when he saw the full shelves. A leather couch took up the center of the room, and there were two accent chairs—equally ornate and leather-covered. A writing desk sat near the window, and there was a piano-forte against the wall closed to the door.

A man about the Judge's age stood near the fireplace. He was dressed in a brocade jacket, and his white hair was long in the back—very European in its style. On his right hand, he wore a thick ring with a dark stone. He was casually holding a brandy sniffer. He looked up from his contemplation of the fire as Victor ushered the Judge and the sheriff into the study. A broad smile worked its way across his face, but it moved slowly, as if he had been waiting awhile and had forgotten the part he was supposed to play. "Ah, Victor. Guests!"

"Unexpected guests, sir," Victor said, a note of sepulchral annoyance in his voice.

"Oh, Victor. All guests around here are unexpected." The man gestured at the Judge. "No need to play the wallflower. Welcome to my home. I am Cornelius Llewelyn."

The Judge took off his hat as he crossed the library. "A good evening to you, sir," he said, holding out his hand. "I am Judge Willard Vernon—"

Llewelyn made to shake the Judge's hand, but as his fingers neared the Judge's, there was a quick pop of noise—like a firecracker going off—and the Judge felt as if he had been stung by a bee. "I say, what the devil?"

Llewelyn dropped the brandy snifter he was holding in his other hand. It shattered noisily. The Judge noticed a funny smell in the room, almost as if it were about to rain . . .

Llewelyn stared—eyes wide and mouth hanging open as if he had lost control of his face. "You . . . you . . . you," he babbled. Ignoring the glass and brandy on the floor, he lunged for the Judge.

The Judge steeled himself as Llewelyn grabbed his hand, but there was no shock as their flesh met this time. Llewelyn's expression was somewhere between glorious astonishment and beatific grace, and his two-handed grip on the Judge was like a small child holding tight to a beloved doll. "Yes, yes," he said. "Marvelous. Oh, this is quite marvelous. I knew it would happen. Yes, I did. I knew it."

"Knew what?" the Judge asked as he extricated his hand.

"Your arrival," Llewelyn gushed. "At precisely the right time."

The Judge looked at Victor and the sheriff. Victor's expression matched his own distress and confusion; the sheriff, on the other hand, looked downright amused.

"Well, then," the sheriff said, tipping his hat, "It would appear my instinct was correct. I will consider myself discharged of responsibility in regards to Wallace here."

"Yes," Llewelyn said. "Thank you, Sheriff Dixon. Thank you, indeed."

The sheriff nodded at Victor. "I'll show myself out," he said.

Victor started to reply, but his employer's enthusiasm overrode his cynical response.

"Victor," Llewelyn said. "Fetch some food, would you?" Glass crunched underfoot as he stepped. "Oh, and clean this up as well. We'll need another glass for—I'm sorry, I didn't catch your name. Wallace, was it?"

The Judge tugged at his waistcoat. "Yes, Wallace," he said. "Judge Willard Vernon Wallace."

"And when were you born, Mr. Wallace?"

The question caught the Judge off guard. "Uh, September," he said.

"What year? No, let me guess." Llewelyn had regained his composure, and there was a light in his eyes that the Judge found disturbing. "1812. Am I right?"

The Judge ran a hand through his hair. "Preposterous, good sir. I don't look a day over forty-six," he said defensively.

"Oh, that has nothing to do with it," Llewelyn said. "But I am right, aren't I?"

"You are," the Judge admitted.

"And on what day did you enter this world? Close to the end of the year, I suspect. Sometime in September, perhaps?"

The Judge inclined his head. "The twenty-third, in fact," he said.

"Oh, marvelous. The equinox. Of course. Of course." Llewelyn clapped his hands. "How far from the Mississippi?" he asked.

"Pardon me?"

"How far away from the Mississippi Rive were you born?"

The Judge narrowed his eyes. "These are a mite curious series of questions you are putting forth to me, sir," he said.

Llewelyn nodded sagely. "Are you familiar with the study of astrology?" he asked.

"Isn't that some twaddle about the influence the stars have over our lives?"

Llewelyn frowned, but his displeasure couldn't hold up to his delight and the grimace quickly disappeared. "Your derision fails to wound me, sir." He wagged a finger at the Judge. "We are all subject to powers greater than ourselves, are we not? Powers we can never hope to comprehend or control. But astrology—the enumeration of the stars in Heaven at your moment of birth and the subsequent influence which those celestial lights have upon your destiny—astrology gives us hope, you see . . . "

"Hope?"

"Yes, by studying the stars, we can understand the Grand Design unfolding all around us. We can fathom the part each and every one of us plays in it."

"We can?"

Llewelyn tapped a finger against his chin. "Now, like you, I was born in 1812, but I was born in December. The fourteenth. At my father's home in Philadelphia. It had been cloudy all week, but the sky cleared that afternoon. The stars were able to look down on me when, at a quarter past seven in the evening, the midwife eased me out of my mother's body. The moon was a witness to my birth, as well, and that night, it was squarely in Taurus, which is why I was so devoted to my dear mother during the years she faltered. When you consider Venus's presence in Scorpio and Mercury's in Capricorn, it is easy to see why I excelled in school and why my father was inclined to turn over the stewardship of the family business to me at such an early age. And—"

The Judge interrupted him. "And what has any of that to do with anything?"

"You were born during the day," Llewelyn said. "I can tell by your forthright manner."

"Actually, I was—"

"You were born—what is that? The twenty-third is the third week in September, so that must mean, yes!—you are nearly three months older than I. How fascinating! You are, sir, the oldest child of the new aeon that I have had the pleasure of meeting."

"The oldest what?"

Llewelyn's eyes narrowed, and for a moment, his enthusiasm faltered. "Are you are toying with me, Mr. Wallace," he said. "Are you testing my faith?"

The Judge gave his host an affable smile, even as he eyed the windows. Were they locked? Would he be able to yank aside one of those heavy curtains and turn a latch, or would he have to throw a chair through the glass? Was the sheriff outside, waiting for him to do something foolish like that? "Perhaps," he said, as he considered his course of action. "Perhaps, you are testing mine," he offered.

Llewelyn's face brightened. "Ah, indeed. What a clever turn."

The Judge was saved from further considerations of flight by the return of the house steward with a small cart. Arranged on several trays were cheese, sliced apples, chunks of bread that looked and smelled like it had been baked within the hour, and a bottle of French wine. The steward rolled the cart between the two leather chairs, and he drew out the cork from the wine bottle with the practiced indifference of a man who had forgotten how many bottles he had uncorked over the years. He poured a measure into a glass, sniffed it delicately, and then offered the glass to the Judge.

Llewelyn indicated that it was the guest's prerogative to taste the wine, and the Judge took a small sip. It was duskier than he liked, but it was neither too sweet nor too bitter. He nodded and Victor poured a full measure into a second glass. The Judge drank the rest of his glass and held it out for Victor to refill it. The steward stared at him for a moment and then put the bottle down on the cart. He retrieved a small hand broom and tray from a lower shelf of the cart and set to the task of cleaning up the broken snifter.

The Judge saved Llewelyn the embarrassment of having to pour wine for a guest. Once he refilled his glass, he quickly set about answering the sudden demands of his stomach. He plucked a piece of cheese, several slices of apple, and a chunk of bread from the repast, and without waiting for Llewelyn, proceeded to eat them in reverse order.

"Did I hear you say you were a Judge?" Llewelyn asked.

"Aye," the Judge said around a mouthful of food.

"And where did you sit?"

The Judge washed down the food with a large gulp of wine. "Baton Rouge," he said. "For awhile."

"And then?"

The Judge waved the hand holding the wine glass, as if to beg off from answering such banalities while he crammed bread and cheese into his mouth. Or perhaps his gesture was meant to encompass all the land between Citrine Springs and Louisiana. Either way, Llewelyn smiled politely and waited.

"And evil, sir?" Llewelyn asked, pouncing when the Judge had swallowed. "I would assume a man of your stature and position has seen a great deal of evil."

"I have seen my share of laziness and selfishness," the Judge said. "Many men can't be bothered to act beyond their own desires. Not every action has its root in malicious intent."

"Ah, so you would make a distinction between those with weak morals and those who actively aspire to villainy?"

The Judge studied Llewelyn, noting the subtle vibration running through the man's body. "I have seen evil," he said, deciding to play along with his host for the time being. "I have looked on its face and spat in its eye."

"Have you now?" His answer excited Llewelyn. "And did you best it?"

The Judge recalled a trio of cattle rustlers he had passed judgment on a few months ago. He couldn't recall the name of the town off the top of his head, but he did recall the ancient oak where the local folk had strung some ropes, in eager anticipation of his decision. *Et eorum animos ad Deum*, he had said, attempting to offer some solace to any family the men had in the crowd.

It hadn't mattered. The dead hadn't stayed dead. The three rustlers had come back that night and they had claimed one more soul before Elm had put them down again. Had they bested evil that night? The Judge knew they had done the right thing, but he also remembered leaving unexpectedly, their horses picking their way along a moonlit road in an unceremonious departure. "Evil's a tricky thing," the Judge said. "It doesn't always stay bested."

Llewelyn's face took on a well-meaning and sympathetic expression. "Yes," he said. "The life of the righteous man is fraught with trickery and deception." His expression brightened. "But once you accept your destiny, you will find it easier to pass judgment on the Devil's malfeasance."

"My what?" The Judge's hand paused near his mouth.

"Your destiny," Llewelyn repeated. "You are one of the chosen, after all."

"I am?"

"Of course you are," Llewelyn said. "And I have been waiting for you, because there is an immense evil that we must crusade against. Right here, in this valley."

14

Elm had offered Lily his horse when they returned to Citrine Springs. She had demurred, and they spent a few minutes politely sparring about who should ride and who should walk. In the end, they both walked, which didn't bother the horse who was glad to be returning to the livery, regardless of who sat in the saddle. When they reached the stable, she had thanked him again for his company and walked the rest of the way to the doctor's office by herself.

She had contemplated waiting for him, but had realized that would lead to an awkward conversation on the porch, where he might take offense when she didn't invite him in. Or maybe he wouldn't. She had been chiding herself on making that assumption, and then catching herself for being disappointed that he might not linger. And then confusing herself further by not knowing which scenario would be preferable.

She slipped into the doctor's office before she changed her mind and shut the door firmly behind her. She sagged against the wooden panel. While the stranger had been a delightful distraction, she couldn't shake the awful realization of she had done. She had let the doctor talk her out of going to the sheriff after they had initially cared for Catie and Willa—*it's not our place, Lily,* he had told her sternly—and now, look what had happened: another woman was dead. She had seen the body in the tent. The woman hadn't died from the fire. Her neck had been broken. A scream was building in her belly. How long were they going to stand by while this beast kept killing? How long were they going to do nothing?

She shook her head, her jaw tight. She ran a hand across her clothing, using the motion as a means of calming her mind. She was going to keep her anger in check. She was going to not let it out. She pushed and breathed, setting everything right in her mind, and when she felt like she could move without losing control, she crossed the room to check on Willa. *Focus yourself on those you can help*, she thought.

Willa's condition had not changed, and Lily adjusted the injured woman's blankets. More as an excuse to do something with her hands than to correct any discomfort that Willa might be feeling. Satisfied with her efforts, she went to check on Catie, who had been sleeping in Lily's own bed.

When she first peered into the tiny room at the back of the house, she thought Catie had somehow fallen out of bed. The blankets were a mess, and the lump on the floor turned out to be the pillows she usually put between herself and the outer wall of the building. There was no sign of Catie. Unlike Willa, Catie had been ambulatory, but Doctor Ambrose had told her to stay in bed and rest. Where had she gone? Lily wondered as she fussed aimlessly with the bedding.

A voice in the back of Lily's head chided her for spending time with Mister "Please call me Elm" Stonebrook. She could have returned from the mine with the cart and horse. She could have taken Mister Stonebrook—Elm—up on his offer to ride. *You should have been here*, the voice whispered. *You should have been watching over your patients, over these women no one cared about.*

A thought struck her, and its impact was so forceful Lily sat down on the bed. "No," she whispered. "No, no, no no no . . . "

The body in the tent. The woman whose neck had been snapped before the fire burned her body. It couldn't be—but it was, wasn't it? It had to be.

Catie.

The dog was waiting on the hotel's porch, and Elm smiled as Laelaps thumped his tail in greeting. "Keeping watch, are you?" He bent over and scratched the dog behind the ears. "Quiet night?"

The dog huffed and snorted, and Elm scanned the empty street. He was tired, and the foremost thought in his head was going inside and finding his room, but the dog's response—such as it was—made him pause. The street was quiet and dark. A thin light glinted in the widow of the doctor's office across the street, and overhead, the moon lay on its side, a lazy smirk carved into its face.

"Did the Judge go to bed?" he asked the dog. Laelaps trotted around him, and Elm frowned at the dog's movement. "I'm not sure what you are telling me," he said apologetically. "Or if you are even telling me anything." He leaned over and scratched the dog's head again. "You might just be happy to see me."

Laelaps wagged his tail and barked once.

Elm sighed, deciding the dog wasn't trying to impart useful knowledge. "He's a grown man," he said. "And I am tired." He glanced over at the doctor's office. "We're all tired," he said.

The dog continued to wag his tail. The moon stared drunkenly. Elm smelled smoke and knew it was partially from his clothes and partially from the breeze blowing from the mine. "I'll see you in the morning," he said to the dog, and he went into the hotel.

The public room was empty, except for a trio of card players in the far corner who were intent on their game. Elm leaned against the bar, looking for the young man with the hatchet haircut. He spotted the youth sitting on the floor behind the bar, leaning against the wall. Elm went around the bar and prodded the young man with his boot.

The young man's eyelids fluttered.

"You have a room for me," Elm said patiently. "My friend—the old man with the beard—he asked you to arrange some rooms."

The young man's face relaxed. "Yeah, yeah," he mumbled. "You and the preacher fella—"

"He's a judge," Elm corrected.

The young man flopped his hand. "You wanted separate rooms," he sighed.

"Aye," Elm said. "Separate rooms."

"He's in the fourth room," the young man said. "You're in the one closer to the stairs."

"And my bags?"

"Upstairs," the youth mumbled, already slipping back into the slumber Elm had disturbed. "'S'all upstairs."

Elm found the shelf with the room keys, and he took the one marked with a '3.' He eyed the bottles of cheap whiskey stocked nearby, and after a moment's reflection, decided against taking one upstairs. He was more interested in getting his boots off and lying down than sipping whiskey. The Judge would have scoffed at such a notion, but he wasn't the one who was still up, was he?

The room was small, and he had some trouble getting the sash raised on the window. But once he got the window open and his boots off, he felt like he could finally set aside the day's events.

He stared at the ceiling for a long while, listening to his thoughts. They kept returning to the young woman he had met. When he finally drifted off, the sound of her voice was echoing in his ears.

Ambrose splashed water on his face. The air in the tent was thick and torpid with the smell of burned flesh. He knew he would never get the smell out of his clothes. He would have to burn them, but he didn't want to think about that. No, because that meant thinking about fire, which lead back to what had happened at the mine, as well as the shriveled and blackened body on the cot behind him. He didn't like having corpses lying about. The dead bothered the living. On more than one occasion, patients under his care had lost their faith in living because Death had visited the room already. *He knows how to find us*, they would whisper. *He knows, and he'll be back.*

He rubbed at his neck with a damp cloth, trying to scrub his skin clean. He itched. Not there, on his neck, but on his back, across his shoulders, on his thighs. Where his clothes touched his skin. He wanted to strip them off and scrub his entire body until it was raw. Until there was no more of the stink on him. Like before, in Chicago. The fire in the ward. All those children.

Ambrose trembled so hard he had to lean against the table to keep from falling to his knees.

He couldn't—he hadn't been able to save them. He had tried. God knew he had tried. Even here, in this forgotten town, he kept trying to set things right. He set bones. He stitched up cuts. He wiped away the blood. And what about tonight? One of the miners had swallowed a lot of smoke and another had bruises and lacerations from a bunkhouse that had collapsed. Ambrose had helped them. It was his duty. His penance. Even the man who had been burned. He had helped him, too.

But the girl? He had felt a momentary twinge when he had examined her. Had he treated her before? Had he stitched her up, telling her that things would get better? He couldn't tell. The body was badly burned, and her head . . . it moved too freely when he had examined her. She hadn't suffered in the fire. Her neck was broken.

He knew who was responsible. He had cleaned up after the man on more than one occasion. Each time, when he told the girls that things would get better, he was also trying to convince himself. *The sheriff will do something*, he would tell the girls. *It won't be like this forever.*

Except he'd never spoken to the sheriff. He never went to the man and told him about the monster. He never said anything about Vash.

Ambrose found himself thinking about Lily and the stranger she had brought into the tent. She had gone to fetch more water, but she had returned with him. A man with fierce eyes, eyes that saw things. When the man had looked at him, Ambrose felt as if he had been summarily judged and found wanting. As if the man had known about the things the doctor had done— or hadn't done. About the lives that had been ruined.

Was he responsible for the actions of others? Was he supposed to weigh the value of a life in his case. What made *this* man or *that* man worth saving? Was the balance of their lives measured by what they had done or by what they might do, should they be saved by his care. Ambrose knew that such considerations were beyond all thought and responsibility of his profession. He was supposed to *save* lives. That was all that mattered. It was not his place to decide their worth.

Ambrose stared at his hands. During the war, he had carried a rifle, like some many others. But when it had come time to fire his musket, he had been afraid. Not for his life, he had realized, but because of what his musket ball was going to do to another man. Who was he to kill someone's son? Someone's husband? A brother?

He had refused, and the Army had no place for weak men like him. If it hadn't been for the Army's overworked and desperate field surgeon, he would have been marked as a coward and traitor. But the doctor had needed volunteers, brave fools who would be willing to save lives. And that was how Ambrose had found himself.

He put down his weapon and took up a stretcher. He wanted to save the abandoned, the lost, those who were thought dead. He went out onto the bloody fields, after the battle was done, and brought back the wounded. That work had soothed his troubled mind, and after the war, he threw himself into furthering his education. *Save lives.* That was his mission. His reason for living. Save every one of them. Nothing else mattered.

Until he couldn't. Until they died anyway.

Was this all some kind of punishment? Because he hadn't fired that musket. Because he hadn't taken a life. Had his entire life since then been a long charade? A lie, perpetuated over and over again. As long as he tried to keep his hands clean—*scrub that skin, scrub it so very hard*—he would fail. Someone would die—someone *always* died—and it would be his fault.

A rough cough brought Ambrose back to the present, and he was stirred from his ugly reverie. He struggled to his feet and peered at the nearest bed. The man who had sucked in all the smoke hadn't stirred. His gaze moved to the other bed, and his shoulders tightened.

Ambrose's heart started racing. All the thoughts that had been tumbling in his head tumbled faster. He was a doctor. It was his job to save lives. He didn't pass judgment. All were equal in his care. He shook his head, trying to brush away the darker thoughts. The ones laced with guilt and remorse. And fear. He saved lives. He healed people.

And yet . . . ?

What good had come from his efforts? How many had died in the fire in Chicago because of him? The woman, here in the tent, burned black by fire—oh, was that the hand of God, reminding him of his own failures? *You could have saved her.* Yes, that was the thought he had been trying to shut out. If he had acted earlier, if he had done something, she would still be alive.

No, he rejected that line of thinking. *I'm a healer. I help the sick. I'm not a judge. I cannot make those choices.* The blood on his hands came from trying to save lives, not end them. He wasn't responsible for anything else.

Ambrose realized he was still holding the strip of cloth he had been using to clean his face and neck. It was pink with blood. Was he bleeding? No, he had used it to moisten Vash's face, and then he had—His knuckles ached. He was having trouble breathing. His thoughts were racing as fast as his heart. What had he been thinking? What was he doing with the cloth?

Vash's body shook as his lungs struggled to move air in and out of his burned body. His head moved, and one of his hands flopped limply on the bed.

Ambrose let out his breath in a long hiss. He forced his hands to uncurl from the cloth. *What am I supposed to do?* he wondered.

Save them, came the answer. *Save them all.*

That was his job. His duty. The frenzied thoughts in his head started to slow, and many of them fell away into shadow. *Save them,* something whispered in his head. *Save them from a life of pain . . .*

Ambrose approached Vash's bed, his fingers working in the cloth in his hands.

He was a doctor. It was his responsibility to save lives. As many as he could. Even if . . .

Ambrose laid a hand on Vash's forehead. The man's skin was hot and wet. He was burning up inside, as if the fire still raged within his body. Ambrose's hand trembled as he turned Vash's head to the side. *This is the right choice,* Ambrose thought. *This is what must be done.* He fumbled with the cloth, bunched it up in his hand. *This is what I should have done years ago. I have to save them all . . .*

A spasm ran through Vash's body, and the burned man's mouth opened suddenly. He coughed and retched, as if he was trying to loosen something lodged deep within his chest. Ambrose reacted, but instead of drawing back in fear, Ambrose slapped his hand against Vash's hot forehead and shoved. Dimly, on some animal level, Vash reacted to the pressure of the doctor's hand, and when his mouth strained, Ambrose thrust the wad of cloth into that gaping hole. *I am not a killer,* Ambrose thought. *I am saving lives.*

Vash jerked and thrashed, but Ambrose—suddenly strong in his resolve—kept shoving the cloth deeper and deeper into Vash's mouth. *Get it into his throat,* he thought. *Choke this fucking—*

Vash's eyes sprang open, and Ambrose gasped.

There was only the stark whiteness of his sclera. His pupils were rolled back in his head.

Vash's hand shot out, and his thick fingers found the doctor's wrist. Ambrose winced. The man's grip was incredibly strong. Ambrose struggled. He let go of Vash's head as he tried to pull his arm free. He felt the glimmer of something at the edge of his perception—was that fear? *The cloth!* he thought. *I have to keep shoving it in. I have to finish this. I have to save him—*

Vash shook his head roughly, and Ambrose's grip slipped. He tried again, digging his fingers into the cloth. Shoving it farther back, trying to force it down the man's throat.

Vash's lips were pulled back, and his teeth gleamed. His jaw tightened.

Ambrose fought a constricted sensation in his chest, as if bands of leather were being tightened around him. *Just a little more,* he thought. *I've almost—*

Vash's hand tightened painfully on Ambrose's arm, and the doctor's resolve fled. He was suddenly aware that two of his fingers were deep in the other man's mouth. The terrible fury which had eclipsed him was suddenly gone, and all that remained was a cold panic. He had to get free. He had to get his fingers out of Vash's mouth before . . .

15

"A dedication to fighting evil is a heavy burden," Llewelyn said as he offered to refill the Judge's glass. "It is more than merely abstaining from puerile vices."

"It is?" The Judge was curious in spite of himself. He held out his glass so Llewelyn could pour.

"You've seen how pernicious gambling infects a community," Llewelyn said. "Oh, man can legislate all he likes. He can let other men guard him and watch him. But he will find a way, won't he? He will find a way to make wagers, to dally with coin, to engage in all manner of wanton games."

"All manner . . ." The Judge echoed.

"Well, the riverboats, for instance. Local governments can make gambling illegal in their jurisdiction, but what of those floating sin palaces that ply the great waters of the Mississippi?"

"Oh, those sin palaces," the Judge said. "Yes, what of them?"

"They are not bound by the same laws and restrictions, and yet, they are allowed to dock at any port. Anyone can board them, and while they are in the wretched embrace of the river, their inhibitions are loosened. They eagerly cast off those rules which they themselves abide by when on land."

"Ah, so you would legislate the river as well as the land."

"No, sir. You miss my point. I am merely noting one of the difficulties that lie in policing the spirit of man. You can restrict a man with all manner of laws and regulations, but he wriggles free at the first opportunity. Why? Why does man rush to escape the very good and just realm which he has created for himself?"

"Because a glass of whiskey, a game of cards, and some companionship are—" Noting the tension in Llewelyn's expression, the Judge changed his mind. "Why, indeed," he finished instead, opting to agree—in principle—with the other man's rhetoric.

This is not a spirited debate, the Judge acknowledged. *He has a polemic he wishes to deliver, and since you are eating his food and drinking his wine—which is surprisingly good, considering where are—you might as well hear him out.* Sighing inwardly, the Judge resigned himself to suffering Llewelyn's rhetoric. He tried not to think about Glory—was she waiting for him back in his hotel room? As soon as that hope flared in his head, he realized he was being exactly the sort of man—a wanton reprobate of a man—that Llewelyn was railing about. *God help me be better,* he thought, and then he immediately wished he hadn't sent that mental prayer.

Llewelyn noticed something in the Judge's expression, and he stamped his foot. "Judge Wallace," he exclaimed. "Your attention is drifting. Do you find my fervor tiresome?"

The Judge shook his head. "No, sir. I—well, to be fair, I am not a fan of fervor of any kind. A man is not measured by his enthusiasm for a strict morality or a narrow band of political expediency."

"How else does one measure a man?" Llewelyn asked.

"Must we?" the Judge asked.

Llewelyn's brow furrowed. "Are you unconcerned with the grace of God? Do you not want to live in accordance with His design?"

The Judge started to answer, but thought better of it, and instead, he made a weak gesture and offered a sickly nod.

Llewelyn strode over to the fireplace, his hands locked behind his back. As he stared at the fire, the Judge availed himself of more bread and cheese from the table. His glass was dangerously close to empty too—how had that happened? "I have disappointed you," he admitted, attempting to be civil.

Llewelyn raised his head, but didn't reply, and the Judge felt a twinge of something—was that guilt?—in his belly.

"I have been a servant of the law for many years," the Judge continued, knowing he was falling into the trap of silent disdain that Llewelyn had set for him. "And during that time, I saw a veritable array of the qualities of humanity—both good and bad. More bad, alas, and it is difficult for a man of my profession to remain wide-eyed and innocent about the Ineffable. It is much easier to believe evil is the stain on our souls we cannot scrub off. I did see truly good-hearted people, but oh, there are so very few of them. They are like tiny flecks of gold afloat in a persistent sea of venom and bile. I do not know how these flecks persist, but they do. No matter how virulent the waves. No matter how tempestuous the winds. They persist." The Judge shook his head. "The most damning thought a man in my profession can have is: Why? Why do these tiny motes bother? Why do they insist on surviving?"

Llewelyn turned toward the Judge, his eyes shining. "Ah, but you have that thought. You can't escape it. It is what calls you to you, isn't it? It isn't damning. It's hope. That is what is it. That is what God grants us. He grants us hope."

"Hope gets a man killed more often than not," the Judge said.

"As does turning his back on it," Llewelyn countered.

The Judge hesitated, his glass halfway to his lips. Llewelyn cocked his head and raised an eyebrow. The Judge drank down the contents of his glass, and the wine burned in his throat, like it was raw spirit. He gasped, and felt a surge in his gut. There were waves inside him. Waves and a tempestuous wind. The Judge's hand tightened on the empty glass as he looked away from Llewelyn's feverish gaze. "Aye," he said with a sigh. "As does turning your back."

"Judge Wallace, I see reluctance and shame plainly written on your face. You want to shut me out. You would like nothing more than for me to let you drink and eat in peace. Oh, sir, I see the armor you have built for yourself, but I also see it for what it is: a barrier to block out the world. Why? Why do you hide yourself? Set this armor aside for a few minutes. Hear me out. That's all I ask of you. Will you hear me out?"

"Aye," the Judge acknowledged. "I'll hear you out."

"Excellent, sir." There was a light bounce in Llewelyn's step as he strode around the Judge. "Let me get to the meat of it then: monstrous creatures walk this earth. You are familiar with them, yes?"

The Judge was taken aback by the twist in the conversation. "I . . . I have heard stories . . ."

"Ah, stories." Llewelyn waved a hand. "The witch that steals years from a man with a kiss? The phantom who feasts on the innocence of children? Those sorts of stories?"

The Judge, having recovered from his surprise, kept his face impassive.

Llewelyn paused, an eyebrow raised. "How about a cow whose gaze can turn a man to stone. Have you heard that story?"

The Judge, sensing Llewelyn wasn't going to let up until he played along, nodded tightly. "I've heard a few of those tales."

"How about the one about the wolf who walks on two legs?" Llewelyn smiled at the tiny flicker in the Judge's eyes. "Ah, yes. You do know that story. I would even say you have played a role in this story."

The Judge frowned. "Perhaps," he said.

"Have you not wondered where such creatures come from? Or why you were allowed to see such a creature?"

The Judge sucked in air. "I am not the only one," he said.

"No, of course you aren't." Llewelyn offered him a patronizing smile. "You aren't *that* special, Judge Wallace."

I deserved that, the Judge thought. The tension in his belly eased, and he reached for another piece of bread. Why was he so worried about what Llewelyn was going to say? The man ramble was merely a preamble—the Judge knew a raconteur's tricks—and he wished the man would get to his point. But at the same time, he didn't want to hear whatever secret Llewelyn desperately wanted to share. *No good will come of this*, the Judge thought.

"Most do not realize what they have seen," Llewelyn continued. "Most do not have the moral fortitude to recognize true evil. They cannot see it as plainly as you and I. They do not know what walks among us."

"And what is it that walks among us?" the Judge asked. "These cows with a stone gaze? These witches? Is that who you fear?"

Llewelyn would not be distracted. "The minions of the Devil are upon the world, sir," he said. "The complete ruin of God's creation is what they crave, and every action they furthers this end. They hunger. They thirst. They *lust* for our souls. And the only ones who can stand against them—who can see their pernicious actions and who can thwart their diabolical plans— are those who have been touched by God."

"And how—merely for argument's sake, you understand— do these *touched* accomplish this goal?"

"With pure hearts, of course, made blessed by our proximity to God."

"Ah, of course," the Judge. "I see how—"

"No, sir, you do not!" Llewelyn was as surprised as the Judge by his outburst, and it took him a moment to recover from his exclamation. "The Devil's discord is insidious," Llewelyn said. "It is a malaise that infects both mind and spirit. If you are not properly trained, it will devour you. If you do not allow yourself to believe, this poison will run you. It will ruin all of us." He shook a finger at the Judge. "It is not enough to wear your armor, sir. You must know what it is that you are shielding yourself from."

The Judge leaned against the arm of the nearest chair. "Very well, sir. Let us—for charity's sake, as you are an excellent host, all other things considered—let us move past the purely philosophical aspect of this discussion. We can stand here all night and circle one another in regards to which of us is the greater fool—rattling about in rusty armor, tilting at windmills no one else can see—but eventually, you will run out of wine. Therefore, let us ask a more germane question: what does the Devil want?"

"What does the Devil want?" Llewelyn started to sputter. "The degradation of—"

The Judge cut him off with a wave of his hand. "Enough of the flowery talk," he said. "No man—no agency, if you insist on defining the Devil as something other than a man—acts without some purpose. So, what is it that the Devil seeks to accomplish?"

Llewelyn's face reddened as he struggled to keep his temper in check. "The Devil seeks the moral degradation and ruin of man," he said, his voice strained. "You have not been listening—"

"I have," the Judge said. "And I have heard a lot of blather and fancy words. Let us dispense with the bullshit. Tell me why."

Llewelyn blinked. "What—what do you mean?"

"What does the Devil get out of—what did you call it? All this moral degradation and ruin."

"Satisfaction, of course," Llewelyn said quickly. "The carnal pleasure of destroying God's most supreme creation."

"And then what? 'Once more with rallied Arms to try what may be yet regained in Heav'n,' or something like that?"

"What does it matter after our souls are forfeit?" Llewelyn asked.

"I have spent many years listening to men speak of the desires and intents of others. 'It is not what he did, your Honor, it is what he meant to do that is important.'"

"You were a jurist."

"I still am, sir. However, when I had a bench and listened to all manner of cases brought before me, what mattered was not the facts of any matter." The Judge snorted derisively. "Facts are merely strong opinions, repeated over and over until everyone agrees so as to get the blowhard to shut up." The Judge shook his head. "No, what I sought and what I will always seek is the 'Why.' Why did these events occur in this manner? Why did these people act the way they did? Were they attempting to obviate some deep-seated pain?"

"The Devil feels no pain, Mr. Wallace."

"Well, I will present no opinion in that regard, Mr. Llewelyn, because to do so would be to presuppose certain facts which I am unwilling to grant. However, I will grant you this much so as to move our conversation onward: if I ever have the opportunity to meet the Devil, I ask him whether he feels pain.

"Until then, discussion of him and his infernal plans—whatever they may be—is mere conjecture and fantastic speculation. Such ideation, frankly, cannot be addressed without considering the intent of those who are offering it, clamoring as they may be from their pulpits or soapboxes." "Which brings me circumnavigationallly back to a core principle, to wit: Why?" He pointed a finger at his host. "Why are you trying so hard to convince me?"

"You are an objectivist." Llewelyn made the word sound filthy.

The Judge raised his glass. "I prefer 'realist.' Fewer syllables."

Llewelyn's grip tightened around his glass. "You have seen things," he said. "Ah, don't deny it. You have seen things. Things you cannot explain. Things that defy reality as any group of clear-headed and clear-eyed men might define the word."

"Aye," the Judge said. "I have seen things. Things I do not understand. Things that I cannot explain. But that does not mean I am bereft of my other senses or my wits. If I subscribe to the notion of God—in any form—then I must also acknowledge that such a being does not exist with some purpose. Rather, his Creation is not without purpose, or design, and therefore . . ."

"Ah, so you would argue that the Devil is subservient to God. That his foul actions are within the boundaries of a role that has been crafted for him."

"It would follow thusly," the Judge said. "One cannot pull the wool over God's eyes."

"Oh, yes. I see it now." Llewelyn's head bobbed up and down. "You do not wish to bear any responsibility for the world, but you hold out for salvation, nonetheless. But such faithlessness—for it be nothing else, when Judgment comes—means you want to be rescued but that you don't want to rescue yourself."

"I—I don't follow your line of reasoning," the Judge said.

"Noah and the Ark," Llewelyn said. "You know the story, don't you? How mankind had grown wicked. How the fallen angels had lain with the daughters of man and born children. God told Noah to save the animals and his family. The rest of humanity—and those foul monsters—drowned when God flooded the world."

"Ah, yes. *That* flood. But what does that have to do with anything we have been talking about?"

"The Devil wants to bring about the end of the world, Judge Wallace. That is what I have been trying to tell you. The Devil seeks to poison our minds and our spirits. He wants to make us as unclean as he is. If we don't stand against him, God will wipe his Creation clean and start again. He has done it before. He will do it again."

The Judge passed a hand across his forehead. The conversation was running in circles. Men like Llewelyn liked to argue in this fashion: round and round and round until everyone was exhausted. They could not—would not—be dissuaded from their notions, and all efforts to engage them on a practical level ended with hurt feelings and the smashing crockery or glassware. *He cannot see anything but his belief,* the Judge thought, *and that belief is unshakable.* He eyed the bottle of wine on the table, wondering how many more he might convince Llewelyn to open. *Why?* he asked, applying his singular principle to his own thinking. *Why prolong this?*

The Judge set his glass down on the table. "Fine," he said. "Let us jump to the quick: how are you going to save everyone?

How am I involved in saving anyone? This is what you have beating around the bush about. You have some grand scheme that will force the Devil to submit, thereby saving all of us from . . . what? Being drowned again?"

Llewelyn's face lit up with a broad smile. "Oh, yes," he breathed. "A Grand Design. Indeed. We are going to deal the Devil a mighty blow. "

The Judge smiled in return, though his grin did not extend all the way to his eyes like Llewelyn's. "Fantastic," he gushed. "This sounds exiting," he said. "How can I help?"

Privately, he thought: *This fellow has lost his mind . . .*

16

Ambrose felt like throwing up. He tried to hold his body still, but it kept moving back and forth, as if he was on a tiny raft adrift on a stormy sea. Up, down, up, down. He couldn't see the sky. He couldn't see the water. He couldn't even—He pitched forward, desperately trying to grab hold of something, and that was when he felt the pain again. It started in his hand, and like a flood of black water, it roared up his arm. He opened his mouth, half-expecting a torrent of foul water to spray out, but all that escaped was a bleating cry. His other hand—the left, the one he hadn't—Oh, God, no! His right hand. There was something wrong with his right hand.

He hunched over, shivering and sweating. Dimly, he realized he was sitting in a saddle. What he had mistaken for waves beneath a raft was, in fact, the slow motion of an animal. He was sitting on a horse! He wasn't in the tent. He was—where was he?

He was damp with sweat, and his mind continued to scrabble about like a trapped rodent. Every time his thoughts veered toward what had happened in the tent, a ferocious shiver ran up his spine, and his brain raced away from those memories. A bloody bandage covered his right hand. He had forgotten about it, and when he had instinctively tried to support himself, he had bumped his ruined hand against the saddle.

The monster had bitten one of his fingers off. Ambrose—for all his experience as a doctor—could not fathom how a man could do such a thing to another man. He hadn't imagined it. The proof was right there, cradled against his belly. Vash had gnawed and chewed while Ambrose had tried to extricate his fingers. When he managed to tear himself free, his middle finger was gone and his index finger was still attached to his hand by a flap of skin. He had bled all over his shirt and trousers before he could wrap a cloth around his injuries, and by the time he managed to stumble out of the tent, the cloth was soaked through. He had discarded it somewhere in the camp, replacing it with a shirt he had stripped from a laundry line. By the time he found a horse and fled the camp, the shirt was soaked through as well.

He didn't care. He had to get away from that monster. He had to find sanctuary.

His head dipped, and he snapped upright in his saddle. He made to grab at the horn of his saddle, but caught himself in time. Still, the sudden movement of his ruined hand sent a fresh wave of pain rolling through his body. He gasped and shifted in his seat so that he wouldn't fall off. *Sanctuary*, he thought, clinging to the faint glimmer of hope. *I have to find help before I bleed to death.*

He thought of Lily, and his breath caught in his throat. He didn't know where she had come from, but she had magically appeared one day at his office, as if delivered by a grace of God.

Not that God would grace him with any such solace, of course. Just look at all the blood on his clothes. No matter what he did. He couldn't scrub it away.

Lily had some medical training, and her constitution was strong enough that she could stand the sight of blood. Many of those who tried to be a physician's assistant failed to consider how much blood they would see at a doctor's table, and most learned too late they were not strong enough to witness what a doctor had to do in order to save a patient. Lily, on the other hand, never fainted, never blinked, and never trembled when she handed him his instruments. She was solid and dependable, and yes, over the last year, he had come to depend on her to run his practice. In Chicago or St. Louis—or any city with a respectable cadre of honest professionals, really—she would not be allowed to hold a knife or a needle, but out here in the God-forsaken wilderness of the plains, who was going to fault her for saving lives? She was an angel of charity.

I have to find Lily, Ambrose thought. *I need*— But as soon as the thought formed in his head, he shied away from it. *Look at the blood*, the voice in his head whispered. *What will she think? What of the others? They will see you. They will know.*

Ambrose shook his head, swaying in the saddle. *No, no*, he thought. *I tried to save lives. I'm not responsible.*

The horse stumbled, and Ambrose lurched, his legs squeezing the horse's barrel. His injured hand bumped against his hip, and the pain made him whimper. *I tried*, he thought. *I tried to do the right thing.*

Did you? The voice was cold and accusatory. *And now what? Running to her? Is she going to fix you? Is she going to fix everything?*

Ambrose shivered. His lips trembled. He couldn't go to Lily. Not like this. Not with all this blood on his . . . on his hands. What if Vash came looking for him? He couldn't risk exposing any innocent to that man's wrath. In his mind, Ambrose was back in the tent again, looking down at Vash's face. Vash's eyes rolled back in his head, his teeth growing, grinding. A spray of blood across the man's deranged features.

We have to tell the sheriff. Yes, that was what Lily had said when the two girls from Hack's had been brought in. Girls that Vash had abused. *Why would we tell the sheriff?* He had snapped at her. *What is that buffoon going to do?* Now, maimed and delirious, Ambrose wanted to laugh at his naiveté, but he was afraid he wouldn't stop. No, the sheriff couldn't help—wouldn't help. The truth was that no one in Citrine Springs would help. The mining company owned everything, and who would bite the hand that—

Ambrose banged his hand against the saddle and cried out as a wave of pain shattered all the thoughts in his head. The horse slowed, uneasy with the noises he was making. Ambrose leaned forward, brushing his forehead against the animal's mane. "It's all right," he croaked. "Everything is going to . . ."

A hollow laugh bubbled up from his belly, and he let it out. The horse huffed through its nose at the sound he made, and he knew it didn't believe him either.

Who would believe you? the voice sneered. *Who would listen?*

Ambrose raised his head. *The fort,* he thought. Yes, he could go to Fort Hollis. He could tell Captain Randall what had happened. He had proof, didn't he? His missing fingers. All the blood. Yes, he had proof. Randall couldn't ignore all the blood.

He fumbled for the reins as he peered about in the dark. Where was he? Wasn't that—

There was a glow on his left. It wasn't firelight. It wasn't moonlight. It was too steady. Too pink. It was something else. What was it?

Ambrose wrapped the reins around the blood-soaked shirt plastered to his forearm. He felt nothing as he tugged the leather straps. The horse puts its head up as he pulled. It didn't want to go that way, but Ambrose, his attention focused on the light, kept pulling. Slowly, reluctantly, the horse turned and started plodding toward the glow.

I'm going to the fort, Ambrose thought.

Fire, came another thought, *that will keep me safe.*

Blood and fire.

His face felt strange. His lips moved, but he couldn't remember the words that were coming out of his mouth.

I can make the pain go away. I can save you . . .

He rode toward the pink light, his lips twisted in a ferocious grin that would have frightened him if he saw it.

Elm slept uneasily. His dream was filled with dark water, and he struggled to stay near the surface. Dark things moved beneath him, and he knew that if he went under the water, they would be waiting for him. He had to find his way to some other place, and so he kept swimming, even though his arms and legs were so heavy.

Eventually, he reached a pale beach, and beyond the beach, through a screen of trees, he found himself back at Silverglen, but it wasn't the way he remembered it from his childhood. It was the ruin he had returned to after the war. The fields were fallow and the gardens were overgrown with weeds. A portion of the main house had been burned, and a large animal had used the space under the grand staircase as a den. There were bones scattered throughout the main entry—some small, some large, and several pieces that were from at least one human skull. The tapestries were gone as were all the paintings. There were holes in the walls, and when he peered in one, he heard rustling noises deep within.

He wandered through the house, listening to the creak of old timber and the scuttling sounds of things within the walls. When he called out Miss Rebecca's name—which he hadn't done when he returned after the war, because it was obvious that no one lived at the estate—he heard mocking echoes. Why did he call out her name now? Was it because he was in that place where she had been an enormous part of his life? Or was it because of what she had meant to him?

Why do you not call out for me?

It sounded like Orchili's voice, and he realized he was more unsettled by that idea than of what he imagined was crawling in the walls.

He went up the grand stairs, looking for Miss Rebecca's room. He had never been in her bedchamber, but he knew which one it was. He saw her often enough at her window. The window was gone now; there was nothing but a ragged hole in the wall, a gaping emptiness that he felt in his gut. Black crows which had been stalking about the room took wing as he entered, taunting him with raucous cries. *Call our names!* they screamed. *Call out for us!*

A message rendered in soot and blood was scrawled across one wall. Tiny stick figures fled from a jagged shape wreathed in flames. Beneath the figure, there were rows and rows of other figures laid head to foot, like bodies stacked in a field. He knew these fields. Antietam. Gettysburg. Shilo. So many dead.

When he turned around, there was something crouched in the door of the room. A shadow with tooth and claw.

Elm was not afraid of the things he saw in his dreams. Unsettling dreams of blood and monsters had filled his sleep since the first night after he had killed a man with his rifle. *If you don't dream of blood and death, you aren't human*, one of the other sharpshooters had told him. *It's where all the terrible things you do get buried. Some nights, those dead will haunt you.* As the war dragged on, fewer and fewer men slept through the night. There was a lot of blood and death to be buried. After the war, he still had the dark dreams, but they diminished in their frequency. More so when he traveled across the ocean. But when he returned to America and started traveling with the Judge, the dreams had come back, darker then before.

He was marked by what he saw, and the more he saw, the more it marked him. The physical wounds he had sustained earlier that year were fading, but other injuries lingered. When he dreamed, he still felt the wolf's teeth on his forearm . . .

A torrent of wings filled the room—red and gold like a sudden burst of sunlight through a tear in dark clouds. Before he could react, Elm was snatched up and carried out the window. The beast crouching in the doorway howled, outraged to be denied, and the wreckage of Silverglen fell away beneath him. Buffeted like a leaf by a frenzy of birds, he was carried up into the clouds, where white and blue lightning flashed all around him. The birds which had rescued him fled, like sparks rising from a hot fire, and he no longer felt like he was flying. He was falling. Again.

The ground came up fast. He only had a moment to throw up his hands in a futile effort to protect himself before he struck the dirt. He couldn't breathe for a second, but that was all. The impact felt no worse than falling off a horse, and he lay still for a moment, gathering back the breath which had been knocked out of him.

The birds were gone. The storm clouds had broken, revealing a sky, bright and blue. He lay near the edge of a cliff, and he crawled to the rim and looked down. The land below was rugged and jagged; there were broad bands of orange and red and brown in the rock. There was a stream at the bottom of the wide ravine, and directly below him, the ground was littered with twisted and broken bodies—men, women, and children. They were all still alive, and they stared up at him, mute but not unfeeling.

Shocked, Elm scrambled back from the edge, and he bumped into something hard and unyielding. He fell over and stared up at the massive shape towering over him. It was a buffalo, with mismatched eyes—black and yellow. Patches of its skull were missing, like it had been partially devoured. When it turned its head, he saw the bones of its neck. There was no blood on its fur, but there were shadows, writhing and squirming in the beast's wounds.

Elm scooted back on his rump, but he couldn't go too far. The edge of the cliff was behind him.

The buffalo creature raised its head and let out an all-too human shriek.

He wanted to crawl farther away, but he didn't dare. His fingers dug into the dry ground of the cliff edge.

The buffalo swung its head from side to side, giving Elm a better look at its disturbed eyes. One was gone entirely, simply an empty eye socket filled with darkness. The other was like a boiled egg covered with yellow pus. Elm felt like that eye was the one that was blind. The buffalo saw him with the empty socket.

The monster groaned, and Elm flinched at the sound. He knew that sound. He heard it on the battlefield. It was the mournful sob of a man who knew he was going to die, but who couldn't get there fast enough.

He looked away, seeing once again the writhing bodies at the base of the cliff. Their outstretched arms looked like they were entreating him to join them. *Jump! We will catch you.*

The buffalo pawed the ground, its hoof scouring an ugly line in the dirt. Elm tensed, his mind like all those black crows, suddenly trying to flee Miss Rebecca's bedchamber. The buffalo charged, its head down, horns lowered. Elm threw himself flat against the ground. He closed his eyes, unable to watch the approach of the haunted monster. The ground shook.

Don't be afraid.

This time, he recognized Orchili's voice.

They only have what strength you give them.

He felt something brush his hair, like her hand, and he unconsciously turned his head, leaning into her touch.

He opened his eyes. The buffalo creature was gone. The only sign it had been there at all was the black furrow in the dirt.

He rolled onto his belly and looked over the cliff.

The beast was still falling. As it tumbled, its hide came off in long, smoky ropes. Soon, all that remained was a puzzle of pale bones. Something trapped inside its ribcage slipped free just before the carcass hit the ground. He heard a loud sigh, as if the mortally wounded at the base of the cliff exhaled their last breaths all at once. Then the jumbled skeleton of the buffalo struck the ground, and shards of bone sprayed across the empty landscape.

He caught a glimpse of a red bird before it vanished in a flash of sunlight.

Bones, scattered at the base of the cliff, reminded him of the like the spring sprouting of a thousand daisies. Life, rising out of death.

The Judge snorted himself awake. He flailed his arms, grabbing at empty air, and nearly fell out of the chair. Chest heaving, he blinked and gasped, trying to remember where he had been and how he had gotten from there to here. His tongue was dry, and his head pounded in time with his heart—a nagging reminder of why a man does not mix wine and whiskey. Though, that was all the fault of that ridiculous fellow who had prattled on and on about God and the Devil, at a time when all reasonable men were either at a table with coin and cards or in bed with a woman. And speaking of which . . .

He peered blearily around the room. Moonlight through the windows revealed a tangled lump of blankets on the bed. Protruding from the tangle was a naked foot—slender and attached to a well-formed calf. The chair creaked as he pushed himself upright. He tottered toward the bed, peering at the blankets, and he eventually spotted a mass of unruly red hair poking out from the top. *Ah*, he thought, *some things were still right in the world.* He put his hand on the bed, steadying himself, and he noticed his feet were bare. He was wearing both pants and undershirt, but the rest of his clothing had—where had it gone?

He had no memory of returning from Llewelyn's house. Had the sheriff escorted him back? Had he left his boots there? The palm of his left hand was tender, and when he sat down on the bed, he realized his shin ached. Had he fallen down? Why had he fallen down? Glory moved on the bed, and her foot slipped back under the blanket. The Judge eyed the spot where her naked flesh had tantalized him, and for a moment, all he could think about was whether she was naked under the blankets and whether he should investigate. Well, two thoughts, but one followed from the other, which was another indicator that the world was righting itself. The Judge appreciated such evidence. It created some perspective against which he could measure the rest of the evening.

Here is something your senses and wits can understand . . .

The Judge shook his head as he remembered Llewelyn's trick with the candle.

What is this? Llewelyn had gone to the mantel and retrieved an unlit candle in a metal stand.

It's a candle, the Judge said.

Is it lit?

And the Judge—not fully understand the game Llewelyn was playing, but full enough of wine and cheese to play along—had answered: *It is not.*

Llewelyn held the candlestick tightly. His forehead creased with concentration, and the Judge felt something twist in his gut. As if he knew what the man was attempting to do. And what it would mean if he did. The Judge smelled fresh rain, as if someone had just opened a window and let a spring squall into the room. Llewelyn's face glistened with sweat. Was that a curl of smoke rising from the candle's wick?

And then, with a noise like a pig farting, a tiny flame started.

Fiat lux, Llewelyn whispered. *And with this light, we can see.* He thrust the now-lit candle at the Judge.

The Judge quickly pinched out the flame. *There are easier ways to start a fire*, he said.

Can you do it? Llewelyn asked. *You are older than I, by nearly three months. Your gift must be demonstrably greater.*

What gift?

The gift of the angels, of course. We all have it. Those of us who were born in that year.

The Judge shook off the memory, like a dog shaking water off its fur. He couldn't dismiss it entirely, for one very simple reason. He closed his hand and rapped his knuckles against the wooden frame of the bed. When he opened his hand, a gold coin lay across his palm. He wrapped his fingers over the warm coin, squeezed it once, and when he spread his fingers, the coin was gone. The coin's passage pressed against his throat, and he moved his jaw, swallowing away the tension in his ears.

You are the oldest, Llewelyn had said. *The oldest of those who were born the year the Devil came to America.*

Frowning, the Judge brought the gold eagle back again. He rolled the coin across his knuckles, and when it tipped past his pinkie finger, he turned his wrist as if to catch it, but it had vanished. With a sigh, he made it appear in his other hand, even though his hands were not near one another.

He didn't know how such magic was possible, but he knew he could do it. He could summon the coin with a thought, and he could make it disappear just as easily. It was not the same trick as lighting a candle, but it was . . . well, what had Llewelyn said? *We are knights, marked by God. Our crusade is to rid the world of the Devil and his minions. And to that end, we have been given special considerations . . .*

Quod erat demonstrandum, he thought. It was a Latin phrase Elm liked to spring on him when he tortured the poor load with some convoluted explanation that stifled further argument. *It must be true because he says it is,* Elm would translate to those unversed in the pithy nuances of dead languages.

The Judge made the coin vanish one last time. His stomach tightened from the passage of the coin. He had to be careful. Too much of that nonsense and the power of that other place would start pulling at him instead of the other way around. Tugging at his mind. Whispering to him. *Let us pass . . .*

He wondered if Llewelyn felt the tug too, or was he blind to the possibility that such gifts were not divine in origin but from a darker source. *Fiat lux,* Llewelyn had whispered. *And with this light, we can see . . .*

But what were we looking for? the Judge wondered. *And why?*

17

When the sun came, its light crossed the Mississippi River first, transforming the fog on the slow-moving water into a veil of silk. Birds, slumbering in the willows along the bank, stirred, shaking a nocturnal chill off their feathers. Fish slapped the river as they rose and fed, their scales glinting in the glowing benediction of the sun.

West, now, across fallow fields and empty pastures. Crops have been harvested and herds have been driven to rail yards, where they were packed in dark boxes and shipped north. The sun spooked a breath of wind, which hurried through the endless grass. There were still buffalo on the plains, and they raised their heads as the sun's light brushed across the land. They tested the wind for the chill they knew was coming. The nights were long and getting longer. Soon, they would see less of the sun because the sky would be filled with a heavy weight of snow-bearing clouds. But today, the wind of light and fresh. There was no scent of snow. The buffalo returned to their morning routine, gnawing at grasses which grew faster than they could eat all of it.

The sun patted the buffalo as it passed, warming their thick hides. It sailed over a pair of men and their horses, and it winked as they paused to raise their voices in honor of its passage. It spilled light over the edge of a bluff, like milk spilling off a worn table, and the light spread across the valley floor in a widening pool. In the distance, a tiny splinter of white marked the church of Citrine Springs, and the sun knew it would get there soon enough.

But first, it wanted to see if it could sneak up on the hole in the ground. It wanted to see if it could see the bottom of the well.

The puncture wound in the plain might have always been there, because there were many holes in this land, and the sun could not be bothered to remember all of them. Some of them had been there before men had come to this land; some of them had been dug by man, and the sun enjoyed peering into these holes because they were not natural—perhaps it would see something it was not supposed to see. But this hole wasn't that old—relatively speaking, of course, the sun had been circling this rock for a few long time—nor had it been dug by man. More so, the sun was never able to see the bottom of the hole. No matter how it angled itself for a better look. Once or twice a year, in fact, it was practically overhead, and it should have been able to see what lay at the bottom of the hole. But no matter how much light, the sun poured into this hole, it never saw any bottom.

And then men had discovered the hole. At first, they had covered it, infuriating the sun. Why were they hiding it? Why were they keeping it for themselves? It tried even harder to see what lay in the hole, but while the sun's light was persistent and bright, it was not clever enough to move stone and wood.

Every morning, the sun would hurry across the Great Plains, hoping that men might have moved the covering they had put over the hole. And one morning, the sun's fervent wish had been answered. The hole was open again! But—and the sun flared hot and furious when it saw what was happening—men were trying to fill the hole! They had brought long boxes of dirt, and men, working in long lines with shovels and buckets, were dumping the soil into the hole. The sun stayed overlong, showering the sweating men with its radiant fury, but they had not stopped. Every day brought another container of dirt. Every day, more dirt was shoveled into the hole. Every day, the sun was denied knowing what lay in the hole.

But this morning, as the sun hurled itself across the sky, hoping to reach the hole before the men and their dirt boxes arrived, it saw a light on the plain. It wasn't much—certainly not enough to be noticed under the blooming radiance of the sun—but it was there, nonetheless. The sun was perplexed by this glow, for wasn't all light nothing more than a reflection of its own luminous magnificence? The sun wondered if the moon was playing games, but the moon had already fled the scene. No, this gleaming, which stubbornly refused to be suborned by the omni-present brilliance of the sun's light, came from something else entirely.

But the sun could not step down from the sky and poke about in the hole. It could look, but it could not touch. It could tarry, but it could not stop. It was always looking ahead, past the next tree, past the next mountain—always straining to see beyond the curve of the earth. Its light lit up the walls and spire of the church in Citrine Springs. Shadows were flushed from the walls of Fort Hollis. The mighty steel ribbon that ran to the east, and the sun, always eager to follow a trail, hurried along the track. The rail would take it all the way across the plains, over heavily wooded mountains to the place where the surf gnawed on stones. There, the sun would leave the land behind and sail across an endless expanse of azure. It would leap into the surf, done with its daily task of running off the shadows on the land between sea and shining sea. It would frolic with schools of shimmering fish, it would chase pods of whales, and it would fall into a lazy backstroke—for the passage across the sea takes the rest of the day, after all—and it would forget about the puncture wound in the Midwest. The sun would not reflect or wonder about the light coming out of the hole in the ground. Not until tomorrow, when it would remember, when it would hurry again, hoping to see the bottom of the hole. But, by then, who knew if the light would still be there . . .

Edgar Dutton was numb. He wore no coat, and for the last hour, he had been shivering on the board at the front of the wagon. The horse picked its way along the rail line that had been laid by the mining company. His hands were stiff and he had difficulty gripping the reins. Even the sun, which had eagerly licked his face with its warm tongue when it had crested the horizon, had brought no respite from the cold burning in his bones.

Edgar Dutton was numb because he knew he was going to die.

In his experience—which wasn't much, but who wanted that sort of knowledge?—Death arrived with little to no warning, and those who felt its passage most were those who were spared. Like last month, when the mining cart had slipped its brake and come careening down the slope in the east tunnel. Dutton had been shoveling dirt with George Miller, and he and Miller had heard men shouting. Sound was funny in the mine tunnels. Some days, they could hear every word of a conversation being held at the top of the shaft; other days, like that one, all they could hear was a chattering noise, like skulls rattling their teeth.

Miller had wandered up the track, and all of a sudden, Dutton heard things clearly: the clatter of cart wheels against the metal rail, followed by a dull thud, like the sound dirt makes when it is shoveled into a cart. A breath of cold wind slipped inside his collar, tickling his spine, and Dutton knew something bad had happened. He expected to see a cart, but none came, and when he had gone after Miller, he had found out why.

The cart had derailed when it had struck Miller, and it lay on its side beside the track. Of Miller, Dutton only saw the lower half of his body. The rest was crushed beneath the cart.

Miller might have known he was going to die a brief instant before the cart had struck him. Death had put an arm around him and whispered in his ear. *Don't look.*

Dutton envied the other man. He knew he wasn't going to be so lucky. Death was coming. In fact, it was in the wagon behind him right now. Along with the body of that burned whore.

Dutton had inhaled a lot of smoke when he and Felks had gone into the burning building, where they had found Vash and the woman. When he tried to breathe, it felt like hundred of needles were pricking his insides. He had wanted whiskey, sure that the spirit would push the pain away, but the doctor had forbidden him to drink alcohol. *Water and clean air*, the doctor had said. *That's what you need now. And rest.* He hadn't wanted to stay in the tent—not with the burned woman and Vash—but every time he sat up, he felt lightheaded and the needles came back. *Stay and rest*, the doctor said. Surprisingly, Dutton had fallen asleep.

When the dark shadow woke him, he had, at first, thought he was still caught in his dream. *Get the whore*, the shadow had whispered, and when Dutton had resisted, the shadow grabbed him by the throat and hauled him off the cot. It bent him in a way that made him forget about the needles in his lungs, and moonlight finally revealed the face of the shadow. *Gather the meat*, Vash growled, *or it will be your face I eat instead.*

I'll do it, Dutton moaned, looking away from the burned flesh of Vash's face. *Don't hurt me.* Vash released him, and when Dutton caught his breath—shallow gasps that barely filled his throat—he found he was all alone in the tent. Just him and the dead body. The doctor was gone. Vash was gone. Had he fallen off the cot and woken up from a nightmare? Or had it been real? Dutton wasn't sure, but what he did know with a horrible certainly—like a black stain spreading in his brain—was that Vash's hunger was real.

He scrambled over to the corpse. She was lighter than he expected, but a corpse is never an easy thing to move, and he struggled to drag her to the door of the tent. When he got her outside, there was a horse and wagon waiting. Vash threw the corpse into the wagon as if it weighed next to nothing. *Take me to the hole*, Vash said.

When the sun's light colored the landscape around him, a brief flicker of hope flared in Dutton's chest. Perhaps, he was wrong. Perhaps this was all an extended nightmare. He could still wake up. The idea warmed him.

But when he saw the hole—and the light coming from it— his heart shriveled in his chest. Each breath brought stabbing pain.

He knew about this place. This was where the rail cars went. They were brought here and emptied, even though—according to the rail crew—the hole was bottomless. But now, there was something in it, something making a pinkish light.

Dutton fumbled with the reins, but his hands refused to tighten on the leather straps. He wrapped his arms around his belly and leaned back. Where was that light coming from? He tried to give voice to his question, but all that came out of his mouth was a dry rattle.

The wagon rocked as Vash moved behind him. A hand fell on his shoulder. "Closer," the burned man hissed in his ear.

The horse picked its way slowly toward the rosy glow surging out of the hole. It flowed and bubbled, almost like it was water.

When Vash's fingers ground into his flesh, Dutton jerked involuntarily. The horse, responding to Dutton's fear, stopped and tossed its head. The wagon rocked as Vash climbed out, and Dutton sagged on the board. For a moment, he welcomed the pain of breathing. It meant he was still alive.

Out of the corner of his eye, he watched Vash retrieve the sheet-wrapped body of the dead woman, but he wouldn't look at the hole as Vash carried the body toward the light. Dutton sucked in a lungful of air, gritting his teeth against the furious fire stabbing in his chest, and turned his head away.

A hissing and bubbling noise started in his head. It made him think of the noise the train made when the engineers filled the hot box, stoking the steam that powered its engine. Dutton put his hands over his ears and clenched his jaw. It made no difference. The noise was in him.

The horse fidgeted like it could hear the noise too. It wanted to run, but it was hindered by the wagon and Dutton's weight. Dutton wished he could cut the beast free, but he had no knife. He looked in the bed of the wagon, but there was nothing there but a shovel and a shotgun. He couldn't cut the horse free with the digging tool, but perhaps he could . . . He looked away, embarrassed, shocked, and horrified by the thought which had poked its way into his brain. *No, no*, he thought. *Not that.* His hands were too cold. He couldn't even hold the reins.

Something touched his shoulder and he flinched, sure it was Death, draping an arm around him. Like it had done with Miller. *Don't look,* Death whispered in his ear, and Dutton, whimpering with a mixture of joy and dread, covered his face with his hands. The reins slipped free of his grip.

The horse, sensing the slack, pulled at the wagon. Dutton fell off the board and landed hard on the cold group. His heart pounded in his chest. The dry voice whispered in his ears: *don't look, don't look.*

He did, and wished he hadn't. He wanted to undo that moment, reverse time and remove the image burned into his brain. Instead, he scrambled to his feet and ran. He tripped over the wooden ties of the rail line, nearly falling, and his boots crunched on the gravel between the rails. Ahead of him, there was nothing but open land and sky. Nothing but the grass, which parted before him as he ran.

The hiss came after him. It slithered into his ears, like bees working their way into his brain, and he beat at his head, as if he could shake them loose. The noise got louder, and Dutton ran faster. But the faster he ran, the more his lungs cried out for air. He had to breathe! His heart was beating so fast. Dutton had to get away from Vash and the hole, from that image of the burned man tearing something from the corpse and raising it to his mouth.

Something grabbed his ankle, and Dutton went sprawling. The grass lashed at his face, and he felt like it was trying to wrap itself around him. He flailed his arms and hollered. Wasn't that what you were supposed to do if you ran into a wild animal? Make yourself bigger and fiercer. Warn it that you weren't easy prey. Dutton rolled around in the grass, bellowing like a cow stuck in the mud. Because he was stuck, wasn't he? He couldn't get his foot free. He tried to find his legs in all the grass. Why was it so long? Why was it waving around like there was a big storm coming. His mouth was full of liquid—hot liquid that tasted like metal—and he spat it out.

The grass slithered and hissed, and whatever was holding his foot tightened its grip. Dutton couldn't see past his knee. There was too much grass. He couldn't understand how he was tangled, but it certainly felt—

He was jerked so hard that his head slammed against the ground. The grip on his ankle was painful now. Like he had stepped in an animal trap, but the devices used by fur trappers were staked to the ground. They didn't move. Not like this.

Dutton grabbed at the grass around him. He gasped in pain as the stalks slashed at his palm. He tried harder, but his fingers kept slipping. There was—there was blood on the grass. There was—

Dutton screamed as he was dragged through the grass. The stalks whipped at his face, cutting his cheeks. His ankle burned, and the ground dug and tore at his back. He tried to dig his fingers into the ground, tried to slow himself somehow, but he couldn't get a grip.

He heard the hissing again. It came from the grass. It came from the hole on the other side of the rails. The hole where Death waited for him . . .

18

With exaggerated care, the Judge put his lips on the rim of his cup and sucked air and coffee with equal measure. He swallowed, sighed contently, and resolutely placed the cup on the table—firm punctuation to his non-verbal exclamation. He looked about the public room, his gaze lingering on the pair of heavies by the door, and then launched into the whole routine once more. Lift, slurp, swallow, sigh, replace.

"You going to do that all morning?" Elm asked.

"Do what?" the Judge asked.

Elm was sitting across the Judge, trying to eat a plate of dingy hash. He, too, had a cup of coffee, and having sampled it, he knew it wasn't as euphoria-inducing as the Judge was pretending. He pointed at the Judge's cup with his fork. "That drama there."

"Oh, I am merely enjoying this bountiful—"

"Are you going to pitch a hissy when your cup is empty?" Elm asked.

"A what?"

"A hissy." Elm waved his fork. "Bang your fists on the table. Leap out of your chair. Tear your hair out. You know: pulpit play-acting."

"Ah, that sort of hissy." The Judge took another noisy slurp. "It depends," he said after he had returned the cup to the table.

"Can I finish eating before you flip the table?"

The Judge gave Elm's request some thought. "Perhaps," he offered.

Elm resumed shoveling food around his plate. He made no effort to eat faster. "Is this drama for that fellow behind the counter?" he asked.

"Is he watching?"

Elm raised his eyes briefly. The man standing behind the counter was not the young man from the night before. When Elm had wandered down and inquired about breakfast, the man had looked blankly at him. His clothes were roughly made, but functional, and Elm noted the sidearm hanging from his belt. His beard was untamed and his hair had been shaped by a hat a size too small. It bunched on his head like a plume of rough feathers.

Elm made a show of noticing the other men in the room, who were, generously speaking, cut from similar cloth. *I'll get it myself,* Elm said, and he turned toward the kitchen. The man decided he didn't like the idea of Elm being in the back room and grudgingly agreed to fetch some food. *And coffee*, Elm reminded him.

Elm suspected the man spat in one, if not both, cups before bringing them over to the table. He decided not to dwell on what the man might have put in the food. He simply added the affront to the list of injuries one sustained while traveling with the Judge.

It was a long list.

"The help in this establishment lacks polish," the Judge noted. "One would think their mothers might have beaten a rudimentary notion of decorum into them before throwing them out into the world."

"I'm not entirely sure they had mothers," Elm pointed out. He let his gaze roam around the public room. He and the Judge were the only real patrons. The dour man behind the bar and his friends weren't here for food or drink.

The pair were sitting at a table near a window, playing cards with all the enthusiasm of gravediggers waiting for a priest to finish reciting the virtues of the village's most respected citizen.

"He's the saddest looking frog I've ever seen." The Judge tried to curve his mouth into an imitation of the barkeep's dour expression. "That hurts my jaw," he exclaimed.

"I suppose we are meant to know we have minders," Elm said. "Though, they could be as inept as they appear . . ."

"One would hope it is the former and not the latter," the Judge said. "Otherwise, we could be in trouble."

"You don't say." Elm scraped the plate with his fork. "Who did you offend last night?"

"I was in my room the entire evening," the Judge protested. When Elm gave him a look, the Judge picked up his coffee and went through the whole noisy routine again. "I may have stepped out for a bit of air at some point," the Judge admitted.

"Of course you did," Elm said.

"That fire wasn't my fault."

"For once, I agree with you. I can't imagine how it could be," Elm said. "Which makes this cloistering all the more curious."

"Cloistering?" The Judge slurped coffee. "What are we? Fucking nuns?"

"Should we ask them?" Elm asked.

The Judge cocked his head. "Politely?"

"Well, I have noticed a difference in how people respond, given the tenor of how they are approached. I hesitate to suggest a direct correlation between cause and effect, but . . ."

The Judge looked down the length of his nose at Elm. "I am mildly offended by what you are implying," he said.

Elm raised an eyebrow. "Only mildly?"

The Judge shrugged. He cradled his cup in both hands. "It's not yet noon," he said. "I am attempting to ameliorate my outrage across the full span of the day so as to not injure myself."

"A wise decision, especially for a man of your advanced age."

The Judge bared his teeth at Elm in what some might consider a feral display of aggression, but which Elm knew was more of an instinctive reaction to a perceived assault on his vanity.

Elm pushed his plate away and sat back in his chair. "Well, I guess I should test my theory."

"Which theory is that?"

"That they are here for you."

The Judge gave Elm a wounded look, but he didn't argue.

Elm stood. At the bar, the bored man with the ill-tempered hair shifted slightly but gave no sign otherwise that he cared a whit. Elm wandered over to the table with the two men. "You should ask him to come join you," he told the pair. "It will improve his disposition."

The one on Elm's left slapped his cards down on the table. "Do I look like I care about your opinion?" He shoved his chair back from the table. His companion, a broad shouldered man with a gut threatening to overspill his belt, wasn't as ready to jump up and do battle.

"I'm just offering a polite observation," Elm said to the outraged man. "Something to make your task more—"

"Sounds like you're looking for trouble," the man said.

Elm took in the man's greasy hair and limp mustache. "That wasn't my—"

The man imagined something Elm's expression and he shot to his feet. He shoved his coat back and reached for his gun. "You—" He stopped, his hand on the butt of his weapon.

Elm's gun was already out, and its barrel was firmly pressed into the ear hole of the man's fat companion.

The room's silence was broken by the sound of the Judge slurping coffee.

"Now," Elm said. "Let's start again, shall we? You and your friend may continue this charade of playing cards, and my friend over there will keep making that damn noise with his cup. I, on the other hand, will no longer be witness to any of this." He pressed the tip of his gun harder against the man's skull. "I trust we all understand each other?"

The man with the droopy mustache fingered the butt of his gun. "Pete," his rotund friend whined. Pete made a show of thinking about Elm's statement for a second more, and then moved his hand away from his gun.

"I am going out for a bit," Elm said to the Judge.

"I shall be here," the Judge called back. "Waiting for these fine gentlemen to tell me why they've been sent to keep me sequestered in this dreary place."

"I could shoot this one," Elm said. "If that would help." The fat man didn't like that idea, but the only counter-argument he could offer was a low gurgling noise.

The Judge waved a hand. "I think their attitudes are improving, as we speak. Isn't that right, gentlemen?"

Fat man found his voice. "I . . . Pete, I don't wanna die . . ."

"Shut up, Rufus," Pete snapped. "You ain't going to die."

Elm frowned at Pete. "Not yet," he said, "but the day is long and my patience is mighty—"

"All right," Pete snapped, raising his hands away from his belt. "We got no issue with you, mister. None at all."

"I thought not," Elm said. He withdraw the tip of his gun from Rufus's ear. "Have a lovely day, gentlemen."

Without looking back at the Judge or at the man behind the bar, he left the Bateman Hotel. And only when the door had closed behind him did he holster his weapon. He had overreacted with the pair by the door, but the trio of watchers had soured him. He had been in a mood last night when he had returned from the mine, and the dream that had thrashed him hadn't helped either. He had wanted to talk to the Judge, but the watchers had curtailed any earnest conversation. And the Judge? He had been in a mood as well, and when that man was annoyed, the whole world suffered.

Laelaps, who had been patiently waiting for someone to come out and pet him, raised his head. His tail wagged, and as if buoyed upward by the motion, he got up and trotted over to Elm. "The man is infuriating," he said to the dog.

The dog huffed in response, as if he knew exactly who Elm was talking about.

Meanwhile, the man who had put Rufus, Pete, and the dour fellow behind the bar to their task of watching the Judge was suffering an annoyance of his own. Mr. Llewelyn had instructed Sheriff Dixon to keep an eye on the Judge, and typically Basil Dixon was a man who did his own work, but he had been put off this morning by a pounding in his skull.

Not literally, of course, though he would have preferred that, since he could have shot the son of a bitch doing the banging. He hadn't shot anyone in a while, and while he wasn't the sort of man who believed violence was a useful solution, he would occasionally lament that he wasn't that sort of man.

But shooting folks for no reason other than to assuage the pressure in his head led to other complications, and that was why Basil Dixon was in Citrine Springs, after all. It was a little shit-stain of a town in the middle of nowhere, and no one cared about it, its inhabitants, or what happened there.

No one had cared since the president of the Central Pacific Railroad had driven a golden spike into the line at Promontory Summit, connecting the CPRR line from California to the Union Pacific railroad line that extended all the way to Omaha. And when the meat packing companies in Chicago decided they were going to load cattle from Abilene, the stockade managers in Citrine Springs could only stare in despair as railcars jammed full of cattle whistled through town.

Then the blizzard of '69 fell upon the plains like the Last Judgment of God, scouring all the struggling seedlings from the dry ground and lashing all the meat from the bones of the straggling buffalo who had not yet been shot by buffalo hunters.

Most of the homesteaders who had come out after the war had long since lost their wide-eyed innocence about starting families and hacking a harvest from the unforgiving soil. Those who could went west to California and Oregon—panning for gold was an easier life than trying to raise a family in a land that hated them.

There were some who stayed, of course, stubborn loners and hard-scrabbling jackasses who didn't know when to quit. They were too busy trying to eke out a living to bother with one another. The only people they tolerated were those who kept to themselves and who had no interest in gossip and salacious stories about other places. The rest of the country might as well be a foreign nation to them.

Dixon wasn't going to stay in Citrine Springs forever. Just long enough for the Texan State Police to find new scoundrels to chase. In the meantime, all he had to do was make sure the rest of his gang stayed out of trouble. Some of them—that hairy lunatic Vash, for one—did not do well with sitting around, sipping whiskey and contemplating naps. They needed something to do—purpose, if you will, which was a little ironic, given how unsuited to purposeful lives they all claimed to be. They needed routine, some kind of structure to their days and nights.

And the solution to Dixon's problem was the Longspur Mining Company and the rabbit warren being dug in the bluff outside of town. No one knew what the mining company hoped to find, which made it hard to tell how long they would be digging. Dixon was more interested in the man who did the back-breaking work. Who watched over them when they were hauling dirt out of the ground? Who made sure they didn't wander too far when they weren't in the mine? Who made sure they came back to work the next day? The Longspur Mining Company needed local management, and it hadn't taken Dixon long to convince the company man that he and his associates would be well suited to running things.

In short order, Basil Dixon became sheriff of Citrine Springs. Half his team were deputized, and the other half were assigned to the expanding mining camp. Longspur was happy, Dixon was happy, and his men were—well, they stayed out of trouble, which was all that mattered, really. Dixon could stop worrying about visitors from Texas and spend his time fretting about these damn headaches.

He'd had them since the Battle of Five Forks, where Sheridan's Union Army had routed Pickett's Confederate forces. They had been preparing for a charge, men jostling one another in their nervous impatience. Waiting for the order. Suddenly, the head of the man standing in front of Dixon had burst, like a melon struck with a hammer, and Dixon had been punched in the head. Dimly, Dixon heard the order. Around him, men started hollering and moving. He wanted to go with them. He didn't want to be left behind. But his legs weren't working right. Nor where his arms. The sun was terribly bright, and there was a foul taste in his mouth. He tried to spit, fell down instead, and when he opened his eyes again, he was lying on a cot in a field hospital. His head was wrapped in a blood-soaked cloth and his uniform was caked with the dried brains of the other soldier.

The doctor told him that he had had a close call with a Minié ball from a Confederate sharpshooter. The ball had killed the man in front of him and ricocheted off his skull. *You were lucky*, the doctor told him. *God skipped over you the other day.* Over the next few weeks however, Dixon hadn't felt that lucky. The head wound left him with bouts of fever, nightmares, and near constant vomiting.

How long? he asked the doctor. *How long is this luck going to continue?*

Days, weeks, maybe longer. Probably until you die, the doctor said. *Which could be next week. It could be forty years from now. Who knows?*

His head healed, but inside his skull, things weren't right, and Dixon spent the rest of the war waiting for the seizure that would kill him. It never came, and when the war was over, Dixon drifted west and did more soldering in Texas. When that wasn't as lucrative as he would have liked, he turned to other opportunities. In short order, he had found himself a band of like-minded brothers, as well as the attention of the Texas State Police.

The Texas Rangers had been disbanded a decade earlier when Texas had left the Union, but after the War, the state needed some kind of law enforcement. The U. S. Government had a reconstruction plan, but there was no way in hell Texans were going to put up with justice being handed down from the North. No, they would take care of their own business, as they always had, and so the governor had created the Texas State Police. Eager to win the hearts and minds of Texans everywhere, the new law enforcement agency rounded up every able-bodied ruffian, scoundrel, bank robber, and wild gunslinger who dared to set foot in the state.

Vash had wanted to stand his ground and fight, which wasn't surprising because that was always Vash's response. Dixon had considered leaving him behind, but Creel wouldn't have any of that talk—they had served in the same unit during the war, and Dixon understood that level of dedication, even though such loyalty made matters more complicated.

It's always complicated, Dixon thought as he adjusted his hat over his face. The headache had been waiting for him when he had woken up that morning, and it had been tempting to stay in bed, but he knew from past experience that lying down didn't help. Sitting upright was better, and as long as he didn't tilt too far back in his chair . . .

He winced as a sharp pain made his left eye weep uncontrollably. It was like getting stabbed by a ice pick.

The pounding came again, and Dixon realized the sound wasn't coming from the inside of his skull. Grumbling, he lifted his hat from his face. Sunlight lanced his weeping eye and he shivered.

"What is it?" he called out. It had better not be one of those idiots he had sent to keep an eye on the Judge. He should have made better arrangements last night after escorting the old man back to the hotel after his chat with Llewelyn. But he had been tired, and his shoulders had ached—a sure sign, if he had been paying attention—that the headache was sneaking up on him.

Just another damn complication, he thought. *If the Judge has rabbited, I'll send Vash.*

The door opened, revealing a man wearing the blue and gray of an Army uniform. He led with his hat, which made it clear that he was the sort of soldier who other soldiers saluted when he entered a room. Dixon hadn't been a soldier in a long time, and so the urge to leap to his feet and snap off a salute was nothing more than a distant twitch, deep in his tailbone. The sight of the ranking officer from Fort Hollis, however, meant— in a word—*complications*.

Captain Randall had a narrow face and deep set eyes, which lent him a perpetual air of disappointment, as if he marched about the grounds at Fort Hollis expecting to hear bad news. His mustache was too long and it drooped over his lip, reminding Dixon of hairy caterpillars he often saw in the spring.

Randall was accompanied by a pair of clean-cut recruits, whose boots clattered noisily against the floor. Dixon closed his eyes, swallowing an urge to yell at them. The noise of their boots was like someone banging on pots with spoons. When they were done parading about, he swallowed the heaviness stuck in his throat. "Captain Randall," he said. "To what do I owe the pleasure of your visit today?"

"I am displeased," Randall snapped. "And to ensure there is no confusion about my displeasure, I am here to express it personally."

"Marvelous," Dixon murmured. *Today is the day*, he thought, *today is the day where my skull finally bursts*. He coughed, hiding an inadvertent smile. If his head popped, then he wouldn't have to suffer yet another tirade from this preposterous preener. *A welcome end*, he thought. *A truly welcome end*.

Captain Randall was oblivious to Dixon's thoughts. "When we last spoke," he said, "I mentioned some stories I had been hearing about men in your employ—"

"I don't have employees," Dixon pointed out. "I was appointed by the mayor."

"By Mr. Llewelyn and the Longspur Mining Company, you mean," Randall snapped.

Dixon spread his hands magnanimously.

"Regardless, these men are your responsibility, and whatever malfeasance they perform, it reflects on you."

"If they are engaged in impropriety, I will look into it as the duly designated officer of the law in this town, Captain, but let's not get too worked up about laying the blame for their actions at my feet."

Randall's lip curled back. "I knew you wouldn't take responsibility."

"You have yet to mention what I should be taking responsibility for," Dixon pointed out.

"I am . . . I am missing some men," Randall said.

"Ah." Dixon looked at the men crowded behind the captain. "The last time I checked, I wore this"—he fingered the silver star on the lapel of his jacket—"while you wear those." He pointed at the insignia on Randall's uniform. "More bluntly: I'm not responsible for any of your enlisted men."

"I believe *my* men were providing an escort for *your* men."

"I don't recall requesting such an escort."

"Regardless—" Randall stressed the word, reminding Dixon of his own use of it a few moments prior. "Your men are responsible."

Dixon breathed out slowly, refusing to get worked up by the Captain's tone. *I'm missing something*, he thought, trying to figure out what the captain wasn't telling him. *He's nervous enough to have brought men with him.* "Which?" he asked, drawing out the conversation in an effort to discern what was really on Randall's mind. "Which men are you talking about?"

"Vash and Creel." Randall's lip curled again when Dixon didn't reply. "You are considering some manner of excuse," the captain sneered. "Why don't you dispense with the lies, Sheriff? If you aren't going to bother with me, then I will take up my issues with Mr. Llewelyn directly. We'll see how he feels about displeasing the US Army."

Dixon finally removed his feet from his desk. He wasn't sure how much Randall could influence Llewelyn—or the mayor, if the captain so decided. Besides, those two idiots were, in fact, his responsibility. Not in the way Randall thought, but because of Hidalgo—because of what had happened before. Debts were owed, and debts were still to be paid. Out here, a man measured himself by his debts.

"Mr. Vash and Mr. Creel maintain order at the Longspur Mining Company's operation at the Pine Bluff Mine." Dixon stared at Randall as he explained the obvious to the army man. His voice was flat. His gaze was flat. One company man telling the other the way of the world. "Why would they require an escort of Army soldiers when they are perfectly capable of fulfilling their duties on their own?" He cocked his head to one side. "Unless your patrols have stirred up the Indians again. Isn't there a settlement of Kiowa still—"

"There are no settlements," Randall said quickly. *Too quickly,* Dixon thought. "They've all been . . . relocated."

"By the grace of the United States Army, of course."

Randall showed Dixon his teeth. "By the terms of the treaties between nations, Mr. Dixon. Terms which most of these tribes wisely abide. There are a few who refuse, of course, because they are ticks. And if it were up to me, they would be dealt with like all ticks should be."

"Well, it is probably best for all of us that it isn't up to you," Dixon interjected.

"The Kiowa can't be trusted," Randall said. "They ignore the treaty. They have no right to remain on the plains. And if it wasn't for Fort Hollis, they would have already slain all of you in your sleep. All of this land is under the protection of the United States Army, and when you misappropriate resources under my command, you—"

Dixon held up a hand, cutting Randall off. "I spoke with Vash yesterday," he said. "He said nothing about an Army escort. Are you certain these men didn't wander off on their own accord?"

"Men under my command do not wander off, Sheriff." The captain was affronted by the idea. "This was a polite warning, sheriff," he continued. "I intend to speak with these men of yours. And if they have put men of my command in danger, I will not hesitate to arrest them."

Dixon looked up at the captain. The man's image swam, and he wanted to swipe the tears building in his left eye, but he didn't want to draw attention to them. "Now?" he asked. The ache in his head was strong enough that a tiny quaver found its way into his voice, and he hated himself for letting his pain show.

"Now," Randall said. He showed his teeth again, and Dixon's heart beat loudly in his chest. An echo reverberated through his skull, and he fought an urge to weep.

His headache was going to get worse.

19

When Lily woke, her tiny bedroom was filled with light. She started upright, her heart hammering in her chest. How had she overslept? She thrust back the covers and quickly threw on her dressing gown. She found Willa in the patient bed—still tucked in, still breathing—but there was no one else, and all the thoughts she had tried to keep at bay last night came rushing back. She staggered over to the nearby chair and sagged into it, fighting to hold back more tears. Hadn't she cried enough last night? *It will never be enough*, she thought.

It had found her again, that dreadful futility which gnawed at her spirit. It had nearly devoured her in St. Louis, and she had thought she had lost it when she came to Kansas, but she knew now that she would never be truly rid of it. It didn't matter how far she ran, it would always find her. It would always slip back into her brain, reminding her that she couldn't save them all. Yes, one or two, here and there, but there would always be more, wouldn't there? There would always be imperiled women. Her sister, broken in spirit and cast aside by her husband. The young girl in St. Louis, who would never walk again because of how she had been beaten. In Philadelphia, in Boston: it didn't matter what she did, she couldn't save them. And so she had run away, hadn't she? She couldn't be responsible anymore; she couldn't let herself feel for others because all it meant was more pain for her.

Her gaze lingered on Willa as she remembered the dream she had been having. Like a vengeful ghost, Willa had come into her room. She sat on the edge of the bed and stared at Lily. The bruises on her face were dark blotches, and one eye was swollen shut. Her other eye was a baleful gleam in half-light, and her gaze had pinned Lily to the bed. She struggled to move, to breathe, and when she tried to speak, she couldn't make the words come out of her mouth. They were caught in her chest, like birds tangled in brush. Willa leaned forward, her bandaged hands fumbling at the blanket. She hadn't been trying to help Lily speak; she had been pulling the blanket tighter around Lily. Constricting her. Making it even harder for her to breathe . . .

A hand rapped on the door of the doctor's office, and the dream spooked in Lily's head. She gulped air, welcoming the interruption, and as she rose, shakily, from the chair, she glanced nervously at the bed. Half-expecting that Willa would be staring with her unbruised eye.

But Willa didn't stir when the knock was repeated. Lily brushed her hands along her dressing gown, pushing aside all the fragments of sleep and dread clinging to her mind. She fussed with her hair as she crossed to the door, and when she opened it, she managed to fix her lips in an almost cheerful smile.

The smile got easier to hold when she saw who was standing on the porch.

The man from last night—the one who had helped at the mine and who had walked her home—took off his hat when he saw her. His smile was earnest, and her heart quickened at the sight of it. "Ah, good morning, Miss Harlstone. I hope I am not disturbing you."

"Good morning, Mr. Stonebrook," she replied. "I am not disturbed by your appearance."

His hand strayed to his dark hair. "Am I sporting some kind of rooster tail?" he asked.

"You are a fine looking man," Lily said. She was startled by the words that had leapt out of her mouth, but she knew she couldn't take them back. A flush rose in her cheeks, and she became embarrassingly aware of her own state: her feet bare, wearing her old dressing gown, and God knew what her hair looked like. Her hand tightened on the door panel as she fought the urge to slam it shut. She could hide under the blanket in her bedroom until he left. She could start this day over.

"Well, thank you for that," Elm said. "A compliment from an attractive lady is always a good way to start the day." Her cheeks warmed even more, and instead of slamming the door, she leaned against it. For once, she didn't say anything. It was a lie—this moment of respite from her thoughts—but she wasn't going to rush through it.

Elm cleared his throat. "I was hoping to have a word with Doctor Ambrose," Elm said. "Is he in?"

Lily sighed. "He is not," she said. Her throat tightened, and the flush faded. She felt like she was going to float away, and her hand tightened on the door for support.

Elm tapped his hand against the brim of his hat. "I suppose I could come back later," he said. "Though I am not sure how to pass the time until then . . . " He glanced at the street. "Unless, of course, there is someone who could inform me about the history of this town. Is there a museum or historical register of some kind?"

"A museum?" Lily found the idea amusing. "Here, in Citrine Springs?"

Elm shrugged. "I have only seen the hotel over there and this place. It seems like there is probably more to this town than these two buildings."

"There might be," she said.

"Do you suppose I could trouble you too . . . ?"

The flush warmed her throat again. "I could be troubled," she said.

His gaze skipped across her. "Would you—" He fumbled with his hat. "Perhaps some other attire might be more appropriate."

She fought the urge to look down. She knew what she was wearing. "What is wrong with my attire?"

Elm's fingers tapped on his hat. "A sturdy pair of shoes, perhaps," he suggested.

And now, she did look down, but she brought her gaze back up to his blue eyes. "Yes," she said. "I suppose those might be a good idea. Anything else?"

It was Elm's turn to flush, and when she let the door close and returned to her room to dress, she found her mind clear and bright. The dream was gone, and the disturbing thoughts had fled to the dark corners of her brain.

Arriving at the mining camp, Dixon did his best to observe the disarray without drawing attention to his displeasure at the state of the camp. It was impossible to miss the burned frames of the two buildings—the storage barn and the camp house where his men slept. Nearby tents were streaked with ash, and several looked as if they had partially assembled, or disassembled, and then forgotten. There was no rail car in the loading bay, and it didn't look like anyone was actually working the mine. There were men wandering about; the camp wasn't abandoned. It was as if no one could be bothered to do any of the work they were here to do, and Dixon had an inkling as to why this was the case.

So did Captain Randall. "Where is the foreman?" Randall demanded of the young man standing near the paddock. The man—who looked more than a little dazed by the men in uniform—shrugged and shook his head in response to the captain's question.

"Run and fetch him, boy," Randall snapped. "We haven't all day." As the young man wandered off, looking to be in no hurry whatsoever, Randall dismounted from his horse. "What happened here?" he demanded.

"There was a fire," Dixon said, sticking with the obvious.

"And why is no one working?"

Dixon adjusted his belt. "You'll have to ask the foreman," he said.

Randall gave Dixon a scathing look, which Dixon did his best to ignore. The sheriff dismounted from his horse, and since the kid watching the animals had wandered off, he looped his reins around the paddock's rope. Randall stomped around, his boots raising dust, and after several circuits, the Army captain's patience ran out. He marched off in the same direction the young man had gone. Dixon glanced at the other soldiers, who were well-practiced at having no opinion, and leaned down off his horse and ambled after Randall.

He spotted Tyrone Jenks, lumbering toward the paddock like a man shriveled by sunlight. The man's coat was filthy and wrinkled, and his beard was more unkempt than usual. His hat was pulled low on his head, and he had the air of a man who was having difficulty remembering where he was going and where he had come from. Of course, that how Dixon always thought of the man, but this morning Jenks was even more distracted than usual.

"Ho, there," Captain Randall called. "Are you in charge around here?"

Jenks stopped, looked around, took a step in a direction away from the captain and Dixon, and then stopped again, realizing that both men could see him. "Aye," he said. The word was followed by a spasm of coughing that sounded like Jenks was trying to dislodge something deep in his chest. When the spasm passed, Jenks worked his mouth and then spat. It was an impressive display of an utter lack of civility, and on another day, Dixon might have been proud of the man for his causal indifference to authority. "I . . . I suppose I am," Jenks said. He caught sight of Dixon standing a few paces behind the captain, and a frown wriggled its way across his face.

"I'm looking for a couple of men. Vash and Creel. You know these men?"

"I . . . I know Vash and Creel." Finding an answer to each of the captain's questions seemed to require a great deal of effort for Jenks.

"Where can I find them?"

Jenks blinked, and his eyes darted toward Dixon again. The deference was not lost on Randall, who turned and glared at Dixon. "Where are these men?" Randall asked, returning his attention to Jenks.

"They're . . . I don't know . . . sir." Jenks waved at the burned building. "They ain't sleeping there no more."

"I didn't ask you where they bunked." Randall said icily. "Though, judging by the lack of activity in this camp as well as the disheveled state of its management, perhaps I have grossly overestimated the capacity of the Longspur Mining Company and its operation here."

Jenks scratched the dirt with the toe of his boot. "I'm not their boss," he said, a petulant sulk in his voice. "They don't have to tell me where they're going."

Randall let out a loud sigh. "When did you last see them?"

Jenks gave the question some thought. "Yesterday?"

"For the love of God, man. I'm asking *you* the question."

Jenks shot Dixon a pleading look. "I . . . I'm not—maybe it was a few days ago." He did a little dance, like he was having trouble holding his water. "I'm not in charge of them," he whined.

Randall turned to Dixon and shook a finger at him. "This is ridiculous," he snapped.

"You were the one who wanted to come out here," Dixon reminded him.

"You are hiding something from me," Randall said.

Dixon made a show of looking around the desultory camp. "I can't imagine where I might be hiding something," he said dryly.

Randall got in close, the brim of his hat nearly touching Dixon's. "Where are your men?" he said through gritted teeth.

Dixon held his ground. "Roust every lazy sluggard from their tents," he said. "Make them all stand at attention in their undergarments like one of your Army inspections. If that will make you happy, go ahead and do it. Just get the fuck out of my face." Dixon paused for breath. Randall's jaw was tight, and there was an unusual flush to the man's pale skin. "And when you are done poking these men in their privates, maybe you should consider what is right in front of you."

Without taking his eyes off Randall, Dixon pointed at the burned building. "As Mr. Jenks said: they aren't sleeping in the mess over there. So, maybe—God forbid—they're in more pleasant company. Maybe they're under a pile of whores at Harck's Emporium."

"And why would they be there?"

"Why would any man spend time at Harck's, Captain?"

Randall's face reddened. He swept his furious gaze over Jenks, the burned buildings, and the rest of the mining camp. "Your attention to discipline is atrocious," he fumed. "You have no control over these men." He pointed at the blackened walls of the camp house. "That is your fault," he said, a tinge of fury in his voice. "You let this happen, and—and—" He stopped, as if he had suddenly become aware of the sound of his voice. He made a show of adjusting his hat and uniform, as if to remind Dixon and Jenks who he was and who he represented. Satisfied that his show had properly punctuated the conversation, he stormed past Dixon, heading for his entourage and the horses.

Dixon watched as Randall retrieved his horse, and with the soldiers who had accompanied him, the captain left the camp in a cloud of dust. The ache in Dixon's head was still there, pulsating behind his left eye, and his tongue was dry in his mouth. He thought about the bottle of whiskey in the drawer of his desk and wondered when he might get a chance to pull the cork and pour a measure into a glass. *Not anytime soon*, he thought. With a sigh, he turned to Jenks. "Where are they?" he asked.

"I don't know," Jenks said.

"Randall there thinks they went somewhere with an escort. Why would they need an escort?"

Jenks wouldn't meet his gaze.

"Jesus Christ," Dixon said. "They were hunting something other than buffalo, weren't they?" He shook his head. He had always known Vash's feral lunacy would bring too much attention, and it was his own naiveté for not anticipating something like this. He eyed the charred frame of the camp house. "What happened?" he asked, changing the subject. Though, the tension in his head said he was still talking about the same thing: Vash.

"We took care of it," Jenks said, refusing to look at Dixon.

"How did it start? Was anyone hurt?" *Why didn't anyone tell him?* was the unasked question.

"A couple . . . Vash and . . ."

"Vash was here? I thought you said it was a couple of days ago?"

"He had a couple of . . . and—it's complicated," Jenks said.

Dixon wanted to shake the man. *Don't use that word!* He wanted to shout. *It's not complicated.* He pressed his thumb against his eyelid to keep it from fluttering.

"A couple of what?" His voice sounded like it was coming from someone else's throat. You had to talk to Jenks this way, like you were talking to a skittish dog. Jenks hadn't been the same since Hidalgo. Hell, none of them were, but of the group, Jenks was the one who seemed to carry all the weight of their actions. "He brought women out here, didn't he? He brought whores out here from Harck's. Is that what he did?"

Jenks ducked his head. "I know, I know. You don't like them bringing girls out here. But I didn't know they had done it. Not until . . . Not until we had to . . ."

"Had to what, Jenks?" Dixon knew the answer to the question, but he asked it anyway.

"I took 'em back to town," Jenks said. "Took 'em to the doctor's office. They were—" He shook his head. "It ain't . . ."

He didn't finish his sentence, but Dixon had an idea of what was on the man's mind. *God damn it,* he thought. *Why couldn't Vash stick to hunting buffalo?* His mind rebelled at what else Vash might be hunting on the plains, even though he knew.

Jenks found something else to talk about. "I don't know how the fire started," he mumbled. "All of a sudden, there was smoke and screaming and—Felks and Dutton—they went in. While it was burning. They got them out. Both of them."

"Vash and Creel?"

Jenks shook his head. "Vash and the girl." His hands clawed each other. "I didn't know about this girl. I took the others to town. I didn't know he had another one in there. I didn't know."

"What girl?" Dixon snapped.

Jenks lifted his hands and shoulders. "She was all burnt."

Dixon was having trouble hearing Jenks over the noise in his ears. "Tell me what happened. Where is Vash? And Creel. Where is Creel?"

Jenks sucked in air, stung by the sharpness of Dixon's tone, and when he exhaled, a shudder went through his frame. "He's not here," he said.

"Who? Vash? Creel? Which one?"

"I—I don't know about Creel," Jenks said. "But Vash . . . Sometime this morning—I dunno, an hour or so before dawn—I was having a dream about being drowned. I couldn't breathe. It was all around me. I was—I couldn't breathe, and I woke up, but it wasn't a dream."

"Make sense, man," Dixon snarled.

"He was sitting on me. I opened my eyes, and he was right there, sitting on me. Waiting for me to wake up. Said he was hungry. Wanted me to fetch him something to eat. Something wasn't right. The doc said he'd be out for a while. From all the pain of his burns." Jenks shook his head. "But last night? Something in his head was making him say crazy things."

"Vash has always said crazy things," Dixon said. "He's been like that since . . . "

"I know. I know. But this was different. This was—I don't know what it was, but it frightened me. It really did. It wasn't like . . . It wasn't like that day when—"

"I know that day," Dixon snapped, cutting Jenks off before he started sniveling about the shootout in the bank.

"I . . . I told him I couldn't fetch him anything with him sitting on me like that, and he got off me. He gave me a nasty grin—oh, it was such a nasty thing to see on his face—and . . . and I ran. He let me go, yelling after me that I needed to get him something to eat, otherwise he was going to . . . he was going to . . ." Jenks trailed off, and the look in his eyes sent an involuntary shiver up Dixon's spine. "I . . . I told him I was going to get him some food, but as soon as I was out of the tent, I just ran." Jenks voice became a plaintive whimper. "I ran and hid. I could—I couldn't face him."

Dixon absently tugged on the end of his mustache. The buzzing in his head was a constant hiss of noise. Something fluttered at the edge of his vision, and when turned his head, it hid from him. "Vash got burned in the fire?" he asked.

Jenks nodded. "Him and the woman. And . . ."

Dixon snapped his fingers. "Christ, man. What else is there?"

"It's Dutton. He went into the burning house. He and Felks—they fetched them out. The girl and Vash."

"Yes, you said that. What about Dutton?"

"He's gone. I don't know . . . Last I heard, his lungs got all filled up with smoke. He was having trouble breathing. The doc said he might get better in a few days, but until then, he . . . he was supposed to lie there and . . ."

"What about Felks? Has he wandered off too?"

Jenks flinched at Dixon's tone. "He's, ah, I think he's in one of . . ." His voice trailed off and he waved a hand toward the ragged rows of tents.

"That's it, then?" Dixon asked eventually. "Vash brings a bunch of girls to the camp, beats a couple of them up, and you take care of it for him. And later, there's a fire that nearly destroys the entire camp, and Vash and Dutton and some whore get burned. Have I got it all, or is there something else? Some other way you've screwed all of this up?"

Jenks waved his hands in a *What was I supposed to do?* gesture, and while Dixon understood the panic that drove Jenks to be spineless, he let his anger flare. Couldn't someone have done something? *Of course, someone could have*, a voice in his head replied. *And that person should have been you.*

There was a bad taste in Dixon's mouth, and he yearned for that whiskey bottle in his desk. "What about Creel?" he asked, swallowing the acrid taste on his tongue. "Where was Creel in all of this?"

"None of us have seen a lick of Creel. He left with Vash, a couple of days ago. As far as I know, he ain't come back. It was just Vash."

"And when Vash came back, he didn't say anything about Creel?"

Jenks's mouth firmed into a bloodless line. "Vash didn't say anything about nothing," he said.

"Of course he didn't." Dixon blew out his cheeks. "What a fuck-up, Jenks."

Jenks started to nod, but stopped himself when he realized he shouldn't be agreeing with Dixon. He couldn't keep still, however, and a tiny shiver rattled up his spine. "It wasn't my fault," he tried, and Dixon knew he was talking about more than the mine. There was a long history that Jenks wasn't responsible for. That he shouldn't have to carry guilt about. "Vash brought the girls to his place. That's where the fire started. I was just sleeping—"

"Shut up," Dixon barked. "Of course it is Vash's fault. It's always that bastard's fault. I could grow cobwebs sitting in that chair in the sheriff's office if it weren't for Vash."

He stared in the direction Randall and the soldiers had gone. *I should have done something a long time ago*, he thought. *I should have shot him when I had the chance.*

20

The card game reached an awkward impasse when the Judge took all of Rufus's and Pete's money. The end result had always been a forgone conclusion, even though the Judge had treated the game as if he was playing with sun-dazzled children. With a theatrical sigh, the Judge returned their losses and suggested they try again. The second time around, Rufus played even worse, due to his simmering rage at being treated like a fool by the Judge. *I do myself and him no favors by thinking otherwise,* the Judge thought as he lead Rufus into a trap where he could spring his four of a kind on him. *Coddling the man was only treating him like every other person had during his life, and look where it had gotten him? Better that he be given a true accord of his worth, regardless of the hurt feelings that might flow from such treatment.*

And Pete? Sums of any sort were beyond the man's capacity— as evidenced by phrases like "three of the little ones" and "two bills and some copper" that were offered as he made bets. All of which made the Judge want to shake the man soundly and deliver a strong lecture about the value of a basic education.

In an effort to maintain both his resolve and poise, the Judge amused himself by composing ribald limericks in his head, and when that paled, he turned to recalling favorite lines from Walt Whitman's self-named poem in *Leaves of Grass. I loaf and invite my Soul,* the Judge thought, *I lean and loaf at my ease, observing a spear of summer grass . . .*

Salvation finally arrived in the form of Mr. Llewelyn, wearing a heavy wool coat and a beaver fur hat. When the Judge caught sight of the other man, he nearly leapt out of his chair and embraced him. Llewelyn's cheeks were pink from the brisk outside air, and there was a merry light in his eyes. "Ah, Judge Wallace," he exclaimed. "How delightful to see you here."

"Where else would I be?" the Judge asked with an air of utter innocence. Internally, he seethed at the man's smug expression. He would have made himself available to see Llewelyn had the man asked, but this nonsense of being kept in the public room had been maddening.

As if he sensed some of the Judge's internalized anger, Llewelyn's beatific facade cracked for a moment. He forced his way past his momentary lapse by delivering a hearty laugh at the Judge's comment. "And now I am here as well!"

"Indeed," the Judge replied dryly.

"Splendid!" Llewelyn clapped his gloved hands together. "If these men do not mind, I would like to spirit you away for an adventure."

The Judge eyed the supple calf-skin leather of Llewelyn's gloves. *Big city extravagance*, he thought. *Reminding these folks that he doesn't belong here.* He put another mark in the mental ledger he was composing about the man. The marks in the negative column were starting to add up . . .

Llewelyn glanced at the scattered money on the table. "I say, is that a gold eagle?" He reached for one of the coins.

The Judge scooped the gold coin off the table before Llewelyn could touch it. "It is a mere novelty," he said.

Llewelyn made a noise with his lips. "That is hardly the case, my friend. You should be careful with a coin like that. This is not some fashionable house in a respectable neighborhood. There are people in this region who might attempt to lift it from your person."

"You don't say." The Judge gave Pete a scornful look, as if he was shocked by the idea that Pete might be inclined to do something unbecoming of a gentleman. Pete looked away, and on the Judge's left, Rufus glowered.

The Judge continued to ignore Rufus's provocative glare. "Since Mr. Llewelyn has come to rescue me from this internment of absolute despair, I should bow out of this game and leave the coin to you." He turned over his cards.

Pete stared at the table. "You had four sevens," he said in a quiet voice.

The Judge looked down at his cards. "So I did," he said. He made the gold eagle spin across his knuckles. "Well, I suppose I should keep this, in that case." He tucked the coin into the palm of his hand.

Pete looked at Rufus, a morose expression on his face. "I had a pair of jacks," he whined. "Best hand I've had all morning."

Rufus slapped his cards down on the table. "Three sixes," he snarled.

"How does he do it?" Pete wondered.

"Practice," the Judge said. He noisily slid his chair across the floor as he stood. As he did, he clenched his fist around the coin, tucking it away in its secret place. A crease appeared in Llewelyn's forehead as if he had felt something twinge his heart in a strange and yet vaguely familiar way. "Now, Mr. Llewelyn, I am eager to embark upon whatever conceit you have in mind, but I do hope it includes some manner of victuals because I am famished." The Judge clapped his hands together. "Are we going on a picnic, perhaps?"

"A picnic!" Llewelyn chortled. "Do you ever not think about eating?"

Llewelyn's tone made the Judge hesitate. "Ah, but a man cannot survive on a diet of ideas alone," he said.

"Oh, yes. I am in complete agreement with you, Judge Wallace. Ideas are what transforms us, but they do little to fill the belly. Never fear. We shall dine on the way." Llewelyn beckoned for the Judge to follow him.

Curious in spite of himself, the Judge adjusted his hat and followed Llewelyn out of the hotel. He blinked heavily against the light, even with the shade offered by the brim of his hat.

He thought he was seeing was a mirage. But when his eyes adjusted, he saw that, indeed, there was a fine black coach standing before the Bateman with a pair of equally admirable horses hitched to it. Standing beside the conveyance was Victor, Llewelyn's steward, dressed in a heavy coat and shapeless hat that made him look like a furious mushroom.

As Llewelyn stepped up to the coach, Victor opened the door. "Let us take a short ride together," Llewelyn said, indicated the leather-covered bench inside.

"Do I have a choice?" the Judge asked, squinting at the coach and the man. He was filled with a sudden unease about climbing into the conveyance. He felt a tightness around his chest, as if the coach was a cunningly disguised cage.

Llewelyn made a face. "I do wish you would try a little harder, Judge Wallace," he said with a pout. "This will not be any fun if you are going to be like that."

With a sigh, the Judge trotted down from the hotel porch. When he reached the coach, he furious mushroom man gestured at the Judge's waist, indicating the Judge's sidearm. The Judge considered refusing, but he relented. After unbuckling his gunbelt and giving it to Victor, he climbed into the coach. He sat on the back seat so he could see where they were going. The leather was soft and supple under his hand, and the interior woodwork of the coach was of fine workmanship. Velvet curtains could be untied and lowered to block the view, and nestled against the side opposite the door was a cloth-covered hamper.

Llewelyn climbed in and sat across from the Judge. Their knees brushed as Llewelyn leaned over and pulled the door shut. He thumped on the ceiling with his fist, and with a lurch, the coach started to move. Llewelyn beamed at the Judge's interest in the hamper.

"I told you we would not discuss great ideas on an empty stomach," he said. He waved a hand at the hamper. "There's at least one bottle in there. Glasses, too. Please pour us a tipple."

The Judge offered Llewelyn his first earnest smile of the day. "Well, sir, this is a perfectly reasonable start to an afternoon's excursion."

Llewelyn laughed as he worked at pulling off his gloves. "Oh, it gets better, Judge Wallace. It gets much, much better."

The Judge lifted the lid of the hamper and the aroma of freshly baked bread filled the coach. The Judge inhaled deeply, reveling in the smell. He investigated the contents of the hamper. In addition to several loaves of bread, there was fruit, cheese, and two bottles of spirits. The Judge plucked two glasses from velvet-lined holders attached to the inside of the hamper lid. He filled each glass halfway and offered one to Llewelyn. After taking a healthy sip and luxuriating in the warm glide of the whiskey down his throat, he leaned against the cushioned back of the coach bench and regarded Llewelyn with a hooded gaze. "Now," he said, all previous amusement gone from his voice. "Why don't you tell me what the fuck is going on?"

Ambrose came awake with a start. He thrashed madly, his motions raising dust. He stared dully around him, trying to remember how he came to be in what looked like a farmer's loft. Sunlight streamed through gaps in the walls of the barn, transforming the dusty chamber into a golden bower. His mouth was dry. There was hay in his hair. A darkened bandage was wrapped around his right hand, and there was . . .

He frowned at his clothing. It was stiff—stained with something—was it blood?

The last thing he remembered was riding a horse. He had left the camp, intending to ride back to Citrine Springs. There had been something he needed to do there, but he couldn't remember what it was. "An accident," he mumbled. The words felt strange in his throat, as if he hadn't used his voice in a very long time. Or if he had been shouting a great deal.

Unconsciously, he raised his hand to this throat, and his eyes focused on the bandage wrapped around several of his fingers. How had he injured himself? Why couldn't he remember anything?

He shied away from his bandaged hand, and he turned the motion into a clumsy roll onto his knees. Without using his bandaged hand, he struggled to stand. There was a railing nearby, and he staggered over it, hoping to see something familiar. The lower floor of the barn was a maze of shadows and sunlight, and the patchwork of light and dark made his head spin. He leaned against the railing, fighting an urge to vomit.

There were a handful of horse stalls below, and from his vantage in the loft, he saw that all but one were empty. The gate of that stall was half-open, and the dirt floor around the gate was dark.

Ambrose realized there was a heavy smell in the air. It was a familiar odor, though, in this environment, it was strangely out of place. *Blood,* he realized. *I smell blood.*

The dark spot on the floor was blood. A lot of it.

He turned and gave a longing look at the piles of hay in the loft. He could burrow into the hay, lose himself somewhere in the dustiness of that dry feed. No one would know where to find him. No one would come looking, at least not here, in the loft. He could rest. He curl up and hug himself until . . . Until . . . Until what? What was he hiding from? Why was he hiding?

A reflection of light caught his attention and he turned his head toward the gleam. It was a spot of sunlight caught and reflected off something down below, like an eye, winking at him. *I see you,* the light was saying. *You can't hide.*

Ambrose's knees trembled. He clutched the railing for support. *Just burrow into the hay,* a tiny voice whispered in his head. *Like a rodent. A pest. Vermin.* He shook his head, trying to dislodge the voice that wasn't really there. His gaze fell on the ladder that led down to the ground floor, and somewhat unsteadily, he moved toward it. He couldn't stay in the loft. He wasn't—he was the town doctor. People needed him. Someone was wondering where he was. He had . . . he had patients, didn't he?

Yes, he thought as he clumsily gripped the ladder with one hand. *I have patients to care for.* He started down, struggling to remember the faces of his patients. Why were they in his care? What ailments were they suffering from?

A flash of white teeth made him jerk. His foot slipped. All that kept him from falling was his left hand, locked around the wooden rung. He kicked his legs, getting his boots back on the rungs. He pressed his body against the ladder, hugging it to his chest. Squeezing his eyes shut, he tried to not think about falling. He tried to calm his breathing. He tried to not feel the sudden flare of pain in his hand, in his missing fingers.

Ambrose made it down the ladder. Reluctantly, he pried his left hand from its frantic grip. He was sweating, and his back itched beneath his stained shirt. Strands of hay had found their way into his shirt and they were sticking to his slick skin. Tickling him. Touching him. Irritating him. Absently, he plucked at the bandage around his right hand, fighting an urge to scratch at the skin beneath the cloth.

Timidly, he made his way toward the open stall. The stain on the floor was large. In his experience, that amount of blood meant someone—something—had bled out. He reached the gate and peered into the stall. The shape he had seen from the loft was a horse—his horse. Lying near the dead animal was a wood-handled saw. Its teeth were smeared with gore. Someone had carved the horse up.

Ambrose's knees weakened and he leaned heavily against the wooden door of the stall. He had no memory of doing this horrible thing, but the blood on his clothes suggested that he was responsible. *Why?* He thought. *Why would I do this?* An image of white teeth flashed in his mind. Biting. Gnawing. *Chewing.*

He stumbled away from the stall and the dead horse. His stomach rebelled, and he retched, spewing a flood of bile and dark fluid.

His right hand ached. *Vash*, he thought. His gaze slid toward the horse stall. *Vash did this,* the voice in his head whispered. *While you were asleep. That is what happened. That terrible man came into the barn and—*Ambrose's stomach threatened to turn itself inside out again. In his head, he could see Vash standing in the stall, the saw in his hand. He could hear the horrible rasp as the blade went back and forth, cutting meat. Grinding against bone.

He hunched over, vomiting again. His gaze fell on the bloodstained fabric of his pants, and distantly, a part of him knew the voice in his head was lying. *Vash*, he thought as he straightened. He kept his gaze up, refusing to look at his bloodstained clothes. *It has to be Vash.* He could bear the idea that it might have been someone else. *Vash.*

He had been silent for too long. *No more*, he thought. *I have to do something.*

His right hand ached.

"I have to do something." It didn't sound like his voice, but it had to be. There was no one else in the barn. He was all alone.

21

Lily turned, putting the church behind her, and she spread her arms to encompass the length of Citrine Springs. "I'm afraid that—as a tour guide—I do not have much to offer in the way of historical anecdotes."

Elm's gaze tracked from the distant exterior of the house owned by Mr. Llewelyn, the man in charge of the Longspur Mining Company, to the Bateman Hotel, to the sheriff's office and the doctor's office, and then to the livery, general store, and on down to the church at the western end of town. The edge of Mr. Hack's Emporium peeked out from behind the Bateman Hotel. "As a tour guide, you managed to not get us lost," he said. "Your skills are wasted at the doctor's office."

Lily swayed from side to side, a nervous flutter in her belly. "Take care, Mr. Stonebrook. Such words will make me wonder about your motives."

"You give me too much credit, I'm afraid," Elm said. "Such subterfuge is beyond me."

Lily's smile faded. "Now you are patronizing me, Mr. Stonebrook."

"My apologies, Miss Harlstone. Such was not my intention."

She made a noise acknowledging his apology as she bent over to scratch Laelaps's ears. The dog wagged his tail happily at her touch, and she continued, digging her fingers into the scruff of his neck. When the dog was good and wiggly from her attention, she straightened up and looked at him. "You've gone away from me," she said, noting his silence and his faraway gaze. "What are you thinking about?"

Elm had been watching a black coach stop in front of the hotel. He hadn't seen one like it since London, and it was a strange oddity in this weather-worn town. "I was recalling an adventure the Judge and I had," he said. Laelaps barked, and Elm shook his head. "Not that one, my friend," he said. "Before you started traveling with us."

"Do tell this tale, Mr. Stonebrook," Lily said.

"Once, the Judge and I were asked to locate a man's missing wife," Elm said. "We were somewhere along the Ohio River. A farming community which had only been there since—I don't know—a few generations. Long enough for there to be subtle discord between those who had first settled the land and those who had come when commerce and industry made the land more workable. Anyway, a young farmer hired us, and the Judge went into town to inquire about the missing woman." Elm shook his head. "The Judge tends too . . . well, he knew what he was doing, and his inquires were couched rudely enough that it was clear he suspected the farmer's wife had taken up with some other man. She had neglected to inform her husband of her decision, and the town was conspiring—not actively, mind you, merely out of embarrassment—to not see what was happening among them. 'When you know there is a hornet's nest in the brush,' the Judge said to me, 'you don't waste time pretending it isn't there.'"

"It is a sure-fire method of getting stung," Lily said.

"Aye. But who was going to get stung?" Elm raised an eyebrow. "Not the Judge, certainly."

"That poor man," Lily said. "Did you find his wife?"

A shadow passed over Elm's face. "We did."

"Was there heartbreak?"

"Worse," Elm said. "That hornet's nest? It was more like a slumbering bear."

Lily raised her hand to her lips. "Oh. Are you . . . are you speaking literally? Or is this still a metaphor?"

Laelaps's commentary was a short bark.

"It was—never mind," Elm said. "It was not a very pleasant experience. A number of folk were hurt." He knew he was being vague, but he had probably said too much already. In the short time he had spent with Lily, he had read a strong intelligence in her, as well as a streak of something stronger. She read people well, and she was going to know if he lied to her, and he didn't want to do that. *Best to say little*, he thought.

Too late, came a response in his head, a voice that sounded a lot like the Judge's. *And shouldn't you be doing more important things than natter on with this woman?*

Oh, like sip coffee loudly and sit on my ass? He snapped back. The voice in his head—the imagined caricature of the Judge— said nothing. It was easy to imagine the Judge doing exactly what he was being accused of: enigmatically coffee slurping. As if that was all the answer Elm needed, even though it was no answer at all.

Lily watched Elm argue with himself, when it was clear he was done telling her about his adventure with the farmer's wife, she looked away. "It is a pleasant enough town," she said, shifting their conversation without actually changing the subject. "But who knows what lurks beneath such a innocuous veneer."

"Yes," Elm admitted. "I suppose that was the point I was trying to make."

"And you fear *something* . . . something dark and ominous is lurking here in Citrine Springs?"

Elm hesitated. Last night, the Judge had seen something. He hadn't said as much over breakfast, and Elm had spent enough time with the old man to know how nigh impossible it was to get the Judge to talk when he was not in the mood. Typically, such reluctance was merely an indicator that a portion of the man's history was weighing on him, and Elm had his own share of demons that he carried with him. Neither felt the need to fill the empty hours when they were riding with idle talk about their pasts. He and the Judge hadn't actually ever discussed why they were riding together. Elm suspected the Judge would bluster and dissemble if asked. Nor had they talked about their recent experience on the Mississippi riverboat, though it had brought them closer together. Not in a familial way—though you could argue that what bound them was, in fact, blood.

Elm didn't know if the Judge's mood had anything to do with the men they had met at the trading post, or with the man who had shot at them from the ridge. But something had gotten under the Judge's skin, and there would be no deterring the man until he had vanquished that itch.

And speaking of itches . . .

Vash. Elm had heard Creel say the name when he had threatened Forestal, and he had heard the name again last night. That was the name the doctor had used when referring to the burned man in the tent. *Vash.* It was possible there was more than one man with that name in the area, but Elm thought it unlikely.

"Your thoughts have taken you from me again," Lily said.

"I was . . ." Elm waved a hand at the land beyond the buildings. "What is it that the mining company hopes to find out there?" he asked. "It's the reason everyone stays, isn't it? That hope for something . . ."

"What do you mean?"

Elm nodded toward the Bateman. "That building is, by my guess, the oldest here in town. The rest are much younger, but to look at them, you would think they are older than you and I. The winters around here are cold and cruel—which ages buildings quickly—but I suspect it is more likely that these structures were built quickly." He pointed at the flat-roofed building with the wraparound porch near the church. A sign with letters carved quickly in a slab of wood was nailed to the facade. *The Whistle Stop,* it read. "That was the rail depot."

"It was," Lily said.

"But the trains don't stop here anymore, do they? Ranchers drive their cattle somewhere . . . north of here, is it?"

"Yes," Lily said quietly. "To Abilene."

"I've heard of Abilene," Elm said. He turned to face the church, but his gaze went past the white-walled building. "The wickedest town on the frontier, is what I have heard." He shook his head. "But I haven't heard of Citrine Springs." His tongue touched the corner of his mouth. "Why is it still here?" he wondered, almost to himself. "It must be the mine, but why isn't that operation bigger? Why doesn't the rail go to the mine?"

Lily had been thinking that Elm was no more than an itinerant gunman, ruined in some fashion by the war. No longer fit for farm life or the dull work of an office, he hired on as the companion—and probable bodyguard—of the Judge, who was riding circuit of the lands west of St. Louis. It would be an easy job, for few bothered a judge on the road, save for the occasional brigand who had no interest in abiding by the law. But Elm had quick eyes and a quick mind. His laconic demeanor and casual interest in her idle chatter during their brief tour along the main road had been anything but.

"There's an army camp out there," he said, his eyes still looking west.

It wasn't a question.

"Yes," she said. "Fort Hollis."

He nodded. "Fort Hollis," he repeated. He turned around again, his gaze examining each building slowly and methodically, as if he might have missed something. But she knew he hadn't. "How can the Army protect you if they are so far away?" he asked.

"Protect us from what?"

"Indians," he said.

"What Indians?"

Elm looked at her. "There aren't any Indians?"

Lily shook her head. "They follow the buffalo, and . . ."

"And all the buffalo were shot by the men employed by the railroad," Elm finished for her.

"I wasn't here then," Lily said. "I—I don't know . . . there are some still who . . ." She trailed off. The story of the buffalo was not a pleasant one. "There is a tribe left," she said, changing the subject. "Kiowa. This valley used to be where they summered before . . . before the railroad men came through."

"And they let the white man drive them off?"

Lily shook her head. "There were some skirmishes. After the war, more soldiers came, along with a man from Washington who told the Indians this land wasn't theirs any more. He had papers that said so, but the Kiowa are not a people who put much faith in papers written by men in Washington."

"Since they wouldn't abide by the treaty, those men in Washington told the soldiers to move the tribe, didn't they? By force, if necessary."

"But they didn't need to. The Kiowa said they didn't want the land any more. They said we were welcome to it."

"Why is that?"

"The buffalo didn't come here anymore. The land wouldn't yield a good harvest. To them, the land had no value."

Elm recalled the conversation—or had it been a dream?—he had had with the Indian at the trading camp. "It's cursed," he said.

Lily stared at him. "Why do you say that?"

"I met an Indian—one of these Kiowa, I guess—a few days ago, at a trading camp east of here. He said the there is a sickness on this land that the white man ignores."

"What sickness?" Lily asked.

"He didn't say," Elm said. "Also, I met other men that day. Men who said they were from Fort Hollis. They said people needed protecting. They were concerned about Indian attacks."

"Concerned? But . . . the Kiowa are gone. What other Indians are there?" It was Lily's turn to look around. "I guess I don't understand . . ."

Elm gave her a rueful smile. "I don't either, Miss Harlstone. Hence my curiosity." He gaze fell on the broad door of the church. "This land is cursed," he said. He spoke quietly, almost as if he was reminding himself of something. "Tell me about the mine," he said. "I haven't heard that gold had been found in Kansas."

Lily let out a tiny laugh. "Does this look like a town where gold has been found?"

"No, it doesn't," Elm said. "Which is why I am curious. If it isn't gold, then what are they digging for?"

"I'm not sure they're digging for anything."

"What do you mean?"

"They've been digging for almost a year, and all they've found is dirt. Dirt that they have transported to another hole."

"I don't—I don't understand. Why would you fill a hole? Couldn't you use the dirt that came out of that hole in the first place?"

"No one knows how long that hole has been there, and no one knows who dug it—if anyone did."

Elm frowned. "How big is this hole?"

"It's not that big," Lily said. "But it doesn't appear to have a bottom. The Longspur Mining Company has been digging for more than a year, and it doesn't seem to have made any difference."

"Why are they trying to fill a . . . a bottomless hole? Couldn't you build a fence around it? If you are worried about people falling in or . . ." Elm's frown deepened. "How big *is* this hole?"

"It isn't the size that concerns Mr. Llewelyn. What aggravates him is that he cannot fill it," Lily said.

"I was very enigmatic last night," Llewelyn said. "I would like to apologize for my behavior. Your arrival caught me off-guard."

"I wasn't aware I needed to telegraph ahead," the Judge said as he refilled both Llewelyn's glass and his own.

"The world is a mysterious place, Judge Wallace," Llewelyn said. He punctuated his enigmatic pronouncement with a delicate sip from his glass. "No one really knows how mysterious it is, truly. And many—nay, most—are not willing to consider the scope of this mystery. In fact, they would rather live without knowing. It is as if they have spent their entire lives living in a dank cave. Then—imagine!—one day, a visitor appears in their cave. 'Come out of the cave,' he says. 'I want to show you everything outside these walls.' Do they listen? Do they venture out of darkness? No, they don't. They don't want to know what is out there. They don't want to know about the mystery."

"What little they know is hard enough," the Judge said. "Why would they want to make it harder?"

Llewelyn frowned. "The last time I was in Independence, I went to the largest church I could find. On Sunday, of course. For Mass. I dutifully listened to the sermon. I took communion. I nodded to those who greeted me and welcomed me. I wanted to be a part of that . . . that flock. But the whole time, I felt like . . . like I was the only one awake. It was like I had wandered into an immense crypt filled with coffins that had been nailed shut." He shook his head at the memory. "Those people . . . They sat obediently. They whispered the words without understanding what they were saying. They rushed to partake of the ceremonial sharing of the blood and the flesh, but none of them—not one!—truly believed. Oh, they were all very devout, of course—going to church would save them, after all—but they don't know what salvation is. They don't know the true meaning of sacrifice."

The Judge found a short-bladed knife in the basket. He cut several slices of cheese from a slab nestled next to a loaf of bread. He tore a hunk of bread from the loaf, before offering the bread to Llewelyn. He thought it prudent to keep the knife to himself. "You are I aren't different, aren't we?" he said to Llewelyn, letting the man know he was paying attention.

"We are," Llewelyn said. "We know about the Mystery. We know there are monsters. We know Heaven and Hell exist."

The Judge gazed out at the grass-covered landscape. "Here?" he asked.

Llewelyn frowned. "No. Not here."

"I suppose you might need to be a little more specific," the Judge said.

"It doesn't matter," Llewelyn said testily. "The conflict between the two is the important thing."

"Which conflict?"

"For our souls, of course, Judge Wallace."

"I see," said the Judge, though he did not. He took another bite of the bread and chewed it thoughtfully. "What of the combatants in this conflict?" he asked after he had swallowed. "Who are they? Who do they follow?" He waved his hand again. "Where are they?"

"They are right here," Llewelyn said savagely. "You and I. Here. Now."

"Ah," the Judge said. He raised his glass in acknowledgment of his apparent role in this charade. "And who are we fighting again?"

"Why, the Devil, of course."

The Judge pasted a polite smile on his face. "Of course."

"You don't believe me," Llewelyn said peevishly.

"Honestly, I think you're a lunatic," the Judge said. "But you pack a nice lunch, so please prattle on. I'll be investigating what other delights you might have in this—"

"Judge Wallace!" Llewelyn smacked his knee with the palm of his hand, and the Judge raised at eyebrow. When was the last time he had been admonished like that? He tried to recall such an occasion, and had a vague memory of when he was five or six . . .

"Why don't we drop the theatrics and get to the point of all this?" The Judge idly tested the edge of the small knife with his thumb. "Yes, I know the world is big and terrible, and there are awful things out there that beggar common sense. However, I do not have the temperament to sit through a bunch of poncy talk about how we are like Child Harolde. 'Where'er we tread 'tis haunted, holy ground,' or some such nonsense like that. Esoteric hand-wringing and specious twaddle bores an intelligent man—more so when he is treated like a prisoner. Especially in a dungeon guarded by half-wits and deluded madmen."

Llewelyn flinched at the Judge's words. His face reddened, and he gulped down the contents of his glass. "You are a charlatan, Mr. Wallace," he sputtered. "Your pathetic preening fools no none. Your sanctimonious arrogance is an ill-fitting jacket. Oh, yes, I am not some country simpleton easily fooled by a glib tongue and a flash of gold coin. I have no doubt you sat on a bench once upon a time, but you are out of your jurisdiction, sir. If you are a circuit judge, then I am the prince of Denmark." He regarded the Judge over the rim of his glass. "'Thus conscience does make cowards of us all.'" He raised an eyebrow, daring the Judge to acknowledge his quotation.

The Judge refused to play that game. He stared out the window of the coach. He felt a vague sense that the world was running in reverse. He was being taken back in time, back to a time and place in his history. What would he find there? Was he supposed to face some past action? Was he—older, wiser, more cynical—supposed to learn a lesson he had failed to understand the first time around? Was he, in fact, the popinjay Llewelyn was making him out to be? Was it true? What was his 'sanctimonious arrogance' hiding?

What are you afraid of?

The Judge grimaced and reached for the cheese. "Very well," he said, more to himself than to Llewelyn. He cut a thick slice and offered it to Llewelyn. A peace offering. "I will forestall further judgment. But put aside your flowery nonsense and your talk of mysticism. Get to the point, man. Just tell me what it is that you want of me."

"I want your help," Llewelyn said. "There is a breach that must be closed."

"What kind of breach?" The Judge forced the words out of his mouth.

"It's a doorway to Hell." A smug grin crossed Llewelyn's face. "Yes, I know what you think of me, Mr. Wallace, but it does not matter. Soon, you will see how foolish you have been. You claim to know something about the world, but you know so little about yourself. You work so hard to ignore what you are— what you are capable of. You refuse to consider the Mystery that created you. You were put on this earth for a very specific reason, Mr. Wallace. As am I. We have a duty to perform."

"And what duty is that?" the Judge asked, in spite of himself.

"Protecting mankind, of course. By sealing those breaches that give him power."

"Who?"

Llewelyn pursed his lips and tipped his head. His gaze made it clear he wasn't going to say a name, but he knew the Judge knew who he was referring to.

The Judge snorted, refusing to be caught in that snare.

"He has been walking this land for more than sixty years," Llewelyn said. "All the horrors of this century can be traced back to that night in December of 1811 when the ground shook and the rivers changed their course. The night when he escaped his eternal prison. He had roamed this land ever since, tainting the water and the trees and the people with his foul influence. Dear God, man, can you not see how the war between the states was caused by his pernicious touch? He turned families against one another. Brother slew brother on battlefields across this nation. We have spilled so much blood that—"

The Judge raised a hand, interrupting Llewelyn. "Stop," the Judge said. "I've heard enough. I cannot stomach the notion that the Devil is responsible for—"

"Of course he is," Llewelyn sputtered.

"And human greed and cruelty had nothing to do with it?"

"Those are hallmarks of his passage!" Llewelyn thundered. "Those are the stains left by his touch!"

"Naturally," the Judge said smoothly. "What else could they be?"

Llewelyn's face grew blotchy. "You still mock me," he snapped.

"It is hard not to," the Judge admitted.

Llewelyn struggled with his anger for a moment, and then he reached up and banged on the roof of the coach with his fist. "How much longer, Victor?" he shouted.

The coach driver's response was muffled, but it was enough to satisfy Llewelyn. "You'll see," he said to the Judge, waggling a finger. "Very soon. You shall see it with your own eyes, and then you will finally understand."

22

As he rode into Citrine Springs, Dixon found himself thinking about another town, in another time. Hidalgo was an unremarkable town less than a half-day's ride from the Rio Grande. A pair of saloons locked in an eternal death-struggle for customers dominated the dusty square, and nearby was a livery with badly shuttered windows, a general store that catered more to a transient population of Mexicans than the handful of ranchers who persisted on raising cattle that close to the border, a boarding house that had given up its dreams of becoming a real hotel, and a bank.

There had to be a bank. Why else would he and his men have bothered coming all the way down here otherwise?

For months, they had been hearing rumors of Spanish gold—snatches of story in every shady shack and decrepit drink hall—and these whispers had maddeningly lured them across half of Texas. Finally, in Austin, he heard something more substantial. Mexico had recently thrown off French rule and restored itself to an independent republic. This change was making ripples. Land changed hands. Families, suddenly finding themselves at the mercy of the people they had oppressed, were fleeing. Brides, payoffs, and all-out thievery was rampant. Coin was on the move.

Dixon didn't care where the gold came from. All that mattered was that it was moving north—across the river, into Texas.

His cadre—seven, counting himself—had been robbing banks across Texas for more than a year. They were quick and careful, though, and all the State Police knew was their number and a name hung on them by a newspaper man out of San Antonio. *The Red Rock Seven*, the newspaper man called them, and it wasn't until later that Dixon recalled that was the name of a town where they had pulled a job.

It hadn't been their first robbery. It was merely the first that the State Police (and the newspaper man) attributed to them. Truth be told, they hadn't gotten much out of the bank in Red Rock—Dixon hardly remembered how much (or how little) it had been. All he remembered was that Vash and Creel had brutalized a man during the robbery. The man had been someone other people cared enough about for a newspaper in San Antonio to write a story, and that had been the start of the narrative.

While the attention was unwelcome, the name became useful. People knew who they were when they stormed into a bank lobby, masks on and guns held high. People knew, and they made less fuss.

Until Hidalgo, when everything went to hell.

Dixon had heard the gold was going to be moved soon, and he hadn't wanted to assault a moving target. Not after the nonsense with the train a few months before, which was why, in fact, they were six now, instead of seven. *We're not chasing the gold,* he had told the others. *We take it now, and they can chase us.* And so, they rode into Hidalgo, where they discovered the gold was gone. It had been moved the week before.

All the bank had was a little more than three thousand dollars. Certainly not the haul the men were expecting. They had been angry. Words were spoken. Tempers had flared. Mouton blamed Dixon. Called him a liar and a fool. Vash had wanted to put a bullet in Dixon's head. *Maybe one isn't enough,* he had said. *Maybe what you need is a second ball, rattling around in there.*

Dixon reached the livery in Citrine Springs. He helped the Winslow kid take the saddle off his horse, and watched as the blonde-haired kid led the animal to one of the stalls and started to brush it. In his mind, however, he was still in Hidalgo, in the vault with Creel and Rooster. Waiting for the killing to start. Waiting for that first shot.

There it was: the thunder of Vash's shotgun, and, yes, this is how it always happened. He couldn't stop it. The bank manager took both barrels to the chest, the wall behind him glistening with the bright spatter of his blood and viscera. He heard Jenks, shouting at Vash, and Jack Mouton, yelling at Jenks to get out of the way.

At the time, the deputy had mysteriously appeared, but over time, as his brain replayed the day over and over again, Dixon grew to understand how the deputy had come to the bank. He hadn't been inside; rather, he had been nearby—at one of the saloons, no doubt. For some reason—Dixon still couldn't understand why—the man had come charging into the bank. Eyes wild, gun drawn, mouth stretched wide. So young and foolish.

Mouton shot first, and blood flew from the deputy's head. Dixon remembered thinking about a yearling, so recently calved. Blinking in the light. Wobbling on new legs. It was luck more than skill that the deputy returned fire. At the time, Dixon hadn't seen where the deputy's bullet went. He had been transfixed by what had happened next. Vash had reloaded, and both barrels of the shotgun lifted the deputy off his feet and threw him against the wall, splattering the brick with gore.

The deputy's errant round had struck Jack Mouton. By some stroke of luck—good or bad, it was hard to tell—it missed Mouton's spine. There were two holes, one on either side of Mouton's neck. He couldn't get his hands to cover the wounds, and he staggered around like a wounded chicken for a few moments, and then fell, face-down. His blood pooled on the floor.

A shaft of sunlight through a gap in the ceiling reflected off something shiny in the stable, and the sudden ray of light was a pin shoved into Dixon's left eye. He winced and ducked his head. Tears welled out of his eye, and he wiped at them angrily.

The headache wasn't going away. He had days like this. The throbbing started in the morning; it clawed at him during the day; if he was lucky, it didn't last through the night. The last time he had seen a doctor—some quack in Galveston whose rambling opinion had been as useful as a drunk coal miner's ideas about how to raise canaries—he had come to the realization that the piece of metal in his head would eventually kill him. One day, the headache wouldn't stop. It would get fiercer and fiercer, until something broke.

After the bloodbath in Hidalgo, he hoped to evade to the State Police long enough to spend what meager funds he had managed to squirrel away from those years of riding rough across Texas. Now, with those funds long gone, he wondered if any of it mattered. What he had stolen. Who he had killed. Who had died . . .

Through a veil of tears, he spotted a shape standing near the stable doors. Dixon stuck his thumb against his eye, and with his other eye, he peered up at the figure. It was Pete, one of the local men he had deputized.

"What?" he demanded. Pete's expression—while befuddled—suggested the man had something on his mind.

"Mr. Llewelyn came and got 'im," Pete said. "Like you said he would."

Dixon nodded absently. He was distracted by a red smear on his thumb. *Where had the blood come from?*

"Me 'n' Rufus are out some coin," Pete said. "We was wondering if—"

Dixon stared at the man. "What?" he said again.

"We lost" Pete said. "Playing cards with the Judge."

"You want to be paid?" Dixon wasn't following Pete's train of thought. "For what?"

"For what we lost," Pete said. His leg started to vibrate. "You know, to that Judge fellow."

"And why the fuck should I pay you?"

"Because we was watching him. And to do that properly, we had to—well, he started it, but what were we going to do? We had to keep him there. He wanted to play cards . . ."

Dixon was no longer listening. A glint of light stabbed him in the eye again. He brought up his hand to touch his cheek, and there was definitely wetness there. He slapped at the pockets of his coat, trying to find something he could use to wipe his face. To wipe off the dark stain on his fingers.

"Sheriff?" Pete's voice took on a plaintive note. "Are you all right, Sheriff?"

"I'm fine," he snapped, though he wasn't.

He was weeping tears of blood.

For the fourteenth time since she had returned to Harck's Emporium, Glory touched the gold coin hidden in her bodice, reassuring herself that it was still there. She had had customers lavish gifts on her before—there had been that fellow from Kansas City who had given her a number of fancy undergarments, for instance. Usually, she gave them over to Mr. Harck. That was the rule, after all. *It don't matter how they pay you*, he said, *you give it to me and I'll compensate you in coin.* After deducting the amounts he charged each girl for room and board, of course. And, in the case of the frilly silky things, well, what did she need of such things? Though, when she had seen Screamin' Ruby show them off to the other girls a few days later, it had taken her awhile to stop being angry. Which was why she had tucked the gold coin, given to her by the talkative white-haired gentleman, into a safe place. She wasn't going to give it up. Besides, *he* gave it to *her.*

He was a nice enough fellow. A bit peculiar in his tastes, but after a long summer of miners with dirty fingernails and dust on their skins, she hadn't minded. And he was definitely more pleasing company than the Longspur men, especially the buffalo hunters, Vash and Creel. Their tastes were . . . well, the girls didn't bother complaining to Mr. Harck any more. Not after what had happened with that one girl. Abbie said she had heard she was sucking off cowboys in Abilene—men fresh off the trail who didn't care that a girl couldn't use her legs. Though, how she had gotten to Abilene in the first place was a question unasked and unanswered, because it was best not to know, wasn't it? No one left Mr. Harck's employ because they were moving on to a better life. The trains didn't come to Citrine Springs anymore, and nothing came out of that hole in the hill but dirt.

A man like the Judge was akin to a miracle, and Glory wasn't about to share. If she showed the coin to anyone, she knew they would tattle on her. They would go scooting right on up to Mr. Harck's office on the second floor and breathlessly spill her secret. *It's a gold eagle, Mr. Harck, sir. Glory's man paid her in gold, and she's keeping it from you.* And then a cautious hand would stroke a thigh or a shoulder. *She isn't that special,* they would whisper. *I'm your special one. I don't keep secrets. Not like that one. Who knows what else she isn't telling you?*

Glory's hand strayed to the warm hardness pressing against her side. It was still there. No one knew. She was safe.

It was quiet in the main room at Harck's Emporium. Mr. Dennis had finished dusting the gaming tables and sweeping a little while ago, and now he was re-arranging the bottles behind the bar. In the evenings there was usually a man by the door with a shotgun loaded with rock salt, but with the room being empty, he wasn't needed and his chair was empty.

Ruby was doing something with a deck of cards at a table in the back. She spotted Glory and waved her over. "Let's play," she said.

Glory—her thoughts still circling the gold coin—begged off. She didn't feel like pretending to play one of those society lady parlor games the girls played while they were waiting for a man to notice them. Besides, there wasn't anyone else in the room.

"Where is everyone?" Glory asked. "Did they all . . . ?"

"Did you hear about the fire?" Ruby asked, her annoyance at Glory's refusal to play cards dissolving under the glee of sharing gossip. "Seven men died."

"Seven?" Mentally, Glory cut that number in half. Ruby always exaggerated. "Is everyone out there?"

"Oh, no, no. It was"—Ruby made a show of rolling her eyes around the room—"no one was here last night. Mr. Harck didn't want us to go. He said we'd just be in the way." Ruby held up her hands. "We're too delicate for such dirty work." She laughed, though there was no humor in her voice. "What about you?" she asked. "You were at the hotel, weren't you? Did you find a sweet fella? He let you stay with him all night?"

"Yeah," Glory said. "I met a fella."

Ruby appraised her. "He do nice things?"

Glory thought about what she had done in the tub with the Judge. Her foot, teasing the inside of his thigh, as she read to him from that book he had. The one about the fur trapper and the giant bear. "Nice enough," she admitted.

Ruby sighed. "He have a friend?"

Glory thought back on the evening. "He might," she said.

Ruby perked up. "Wouldn't that be something," she said. "Better than . . ." Ruby's eyes darted toward the end of the second-floor landing, where the larger rooms—the rooms for special guests—were located.

Glory raised her head and looked up. The doors to the guest rooms were all closed, and there was no one on the landing. She let her gaze roam around the room. Dennis had moved on to polishing glassware, and by the door, the deputy was openly snoring. "Who's up there?" she asked, returning her gaze to the second floor.

"He came just after dawn," Ruby said, her voice dropping to a whisper. "Covered in . . ." She shook her head. "He—"

She was interrupted by the front door, which swung open to reveal three men wearing Union blue. The one in front had silver emblems on his hat, and his stiff gait indicated he thought he was someone important. Glory recognized one of the two soldiers with the officer. She had laid down with him a few times, but she couldn't remember anything specific about his company.

The officer marched stiffly over to the bar. "Is he here?" he demanded.

"Who?" Mr. Dennis didn't have to work hard at appearing confused.

"Vash," the captain said. "Is he here?"

Dennis took too long to reply, and when the captain's gaze swept the room, he spotted Glory and Ruby. Glory, her hand instinctively covering the gold coin, put on a working smile. *Chin up, cheeks tight. Back straight, stomach in.*

Ruby, on the other hand, had gone pale. She was the one who looked up at the door to the special suite.

It was all the answer the Army man needed. He snapped his fingers, summoning his men. They stepped forward, suddenly aware that they might need their rifles.

23

They returned to the doctor's office, where Lily fussed over Willa, arranging and re-arranging the catatonic woman's blankets. Willa remained unaware of Lily's ministrations, but her forehead was cool. The fever was gone.

"Who is she?" Elm asked.

"One of the girls who works at Harck's," Lily said.

"The doctor sees girls from that place on a regular basis, doesn't he?"

It wasn't a question that required an answer. Elm had noticed Willa's bruises, and Lily had said something about the girls at Harck's the other night. She had also said something about the sheriff and the mining company. "The men who do this, they're protected by the company and the sheriff, aren't they. That is the rule of the law around here."

Lily started to respond, caught herself, and then firmed her lips against a reply. Elm, imagining the conversation that was occurring in her head, softened his tone. "I'm sorry. I don't mean to sound like the Judge. Quite often, he speaks without thinking—or, I suppose—he thinks and speaks without too much concern for the weight of his words. The bluntness of his diction can be off-putting, but there are times when his frankness cuts to the quick."

"Your frankness does not embarrass me." Lily found her voice. "Your thoughts are similar to thoughts I have had, but thoughts are not actions, and actions have other consequences."

"Yes, actions and their consequences," Elm said. "I saw a lot of terrible things during the war. I saw how we treated other men. I saw how we treated prisoners. How women and children—folk who played no part in the conflict between armies—were treated. The only law that mattered, time and again, was the law of violence. On and off the battlefield."

He shook his head. "Polite society, after participating in such a bloody conflict, was such an odd fabrication. A week prior, the men you faced, with musket and knife, were your enemy. You had to kill them before they killed you. And then, after the armistice, there was to be no aggression. We were to be friendly. To pass one another on the street. Comment on the weather. Talk about how lovely the peach harvest might be this year. We all pretended that we hadn't participated in killing."

"You are talking about sin, Mr. Stonebrook," Lily said. "Pastor Gleason talks about it often during his Sunday sermons. That we must all work very hard to scrub such a stain off our souls. That our salvation depends on our success."

"Does it?"

"Does it what?"

"Does it scrub off?"

Lily plucked at her dress. Her fingers were restless. "I'm not—I hesitate to speak knowingly of such matters," she admitted. "I like listening to the pastor's rhetoric. I like his earnestness, but . . ."

"But the girls keep showing up," Elm said. He nodded at Willa. "Like this one."

"Aye," Lily said. "Like this one."

"I have been dreaming—" Elm stopped himself. He struggled to compose his thoughts. If the Judge were here, he would be regarding Elm as if he had stumbled upon a mythical critter—a strange two-headed beast that could not only speak, but was eager to do so. It wasn't that Elm was reticent to speak; the Judge talked more than his share, and Elm was content to let the Judge yammer. But there was a pressure building and it needed some release. He worried what would happen if he didn't let it out.

He was also worried that, perhaps, he shouldn't let it out.

"During the war," he continued, trying to find the right words—walk the right path through a tangled wood. "I was part of a group of men who fought . . . some would say 'unpatriotically,' but there was nothing 'patriotic' about any of what we did during that time. If I did my job well, a man died quickly, without pain and often without even knowing that it was his time. It was . . . an act of kindness, I suppose. Regardless, I had to be numb to what I was doing. I had to . . . sequester part of myself from the man who was pulling the trigger on his rifle. That was a shadow part of me, if you will. He was the one who waited, the one who fired the weapon. He was responsible. Not me. And when the war was over, I put that part of me away. I wrapped it up in a leather cloth, and I went overseas, hoping that I might find a spot in some dark forest where I could bury it, once and for all. And I did, but . . . but I didn't. Not really. It's still there, lurking. Waiting."

"What is it waiting for?"

Elm ignored her question. *This was the wrong way*, he thought.

His tongue was dry, and the backs of his hands were starting to itch. If he were outside, he would be scanning the surrounding terrain, certain that someone was watching him. That special sense sharpshooters developed when they were within range of the enemy lines. If you had a shot, so did the enemy. He thought of the ridge at Forestal's trading post, of how he had known the sharpshooter was up there before he had taken his first shot.

"Men like Vash"—the man's name came out with a hiss—"Men like that learned something about themselves during the war. Things they did made them feel whole, and when it was over, they didn't want to go back to the way things where. They didn't want to let go of their shadows."

"It is not an easy path that God provides," Lily said quietly, "but it is the righteous path. It is the only path that leads to eternal light." Her voice got even softer. "A light without shadows.

Elm knew she was quoting something the pastor had said. *She is hiding behind his words,* he mused, *like she doesn't want me to see her private thoughts. Like she doesn't want to face her own thoughts.*

"In my dreams, I visit places that I know," Elm said. "Sometimes I meet my shadow there. Sometimes it is just a shadow; other times, it wears my face. It wants me to be afraid because that is how it grows stronger, how its voice gets louder. It wants to be heard outside my dreams. It wants me to listen to it."

Lily swallowed. "I suppose such dreams might be common among men who have seen what you have seen. They may even have shadows like yours. Hear voices like you do."

"I suppose they might."

"Perhaps that is what sermons like the ones Pastor Gleason give are for," she offered. "For men such as yourself to hear talk of redemption, of forgiveness. To hear that they are still loved. That there is still a place for them."

Elm started to pace. "Why is Longspur filling a hole?" he asked.

Lily was surprised by the shift in their conversation. "I . . . I don't know," she said, repeating what she had told Elm earlier.

"For the sake of our discussion, let us posit that all these dreams are about fear, about being afraid of the consequences of our actions, or about being afraid of actions we might yet take."

"Very well," Lily said. "Let us suppose that."

"Then, might it follow that what we do while awake might be to avoid these nocturnal thoughts? Might we strive to avoid the consequences of previous actions or—"

"Or act away from the course that we fear."

"Indeed. And is that not what the pastor instills in you every Sunday? Act as if God we're watching."

Lily gave Elm a knowing smile. "But He is, of course."

"Of course," Elm said smoothly. "But let us keep our focus on the things we fear and how we can avoid them."

"We avoid them by not facing them. By not giving them purchase in our minds. By—"

"By burying them."

Lily cocked her head and looked at Elm. "Literally *burying* them," she said.

"Aye. Literally." He stopped pacing. "So I ask this again: Why is Longspur filling a hole?"

The voice woke him up.

In the beginning, he had dismissed it as a nuisance, like one of those fat flies that droned back and forth across the ass of a cow during a hot summer day. The cow gave it no mind, because there would be a dozen more like it tomorrow. And a dozen more the day after that. And then, just as quickly as they had come, they would be gone, and the cow would go on, standing there like the dumb fucking animal that it was, staring at nothing and chewing the same chunk of grass over and over again.

He hated cows. In fact, he hated most things with four legs. They had big eyes, and the way they stared at you was like . . .

Get up. The voice cut through the haze in his skull. *It is time.*

Vash made a noise in his chest. It might have been an attempt to speak, but the words got lost somewhere along the way. It might have been the sort of cough a wounded bear makes when it realizes it is drowning in its own blood. He blinked and found himself looking at the slack face and staring eyes of a whore. She looked like a cow. He shoved her away from him, and he grunted as waves of pain lashed up his arms. The whore tumbled off the bed and made a heavy noise against the floor.

There was blood on the sheets. His hair was stiff with it, as was his beard. There was a terrible taste in his mouth. He stared at his hands. The skin was black and raw, almost as if he had been . . . had been burned.

The gun, the voice hissed. *Get the gun.*

He looked around. The bed was long and there were fancy bedposts. Framed pictures hung on the wall. Pictures of forests and trains and other stupid stuff that made the room gaudy and cheap. Vash struggled to recall how he had gotten here. His gaze fell on the bloody sheets again, and he tried to remember the face of the cow—the whore—he had pushed off the bed.

She's dead.

He flinched as his shattered memory turned over an image of a woman with an oil lantern. Raising it above her head. Screaming at him. Instinctively, his hands came up, trying to protect his face, but she vanished when he blinked. He ground his teeth together, feeling the muscles tighten in his jaw. Yes, that's it. That was how he had done it. A different image streaked through his brain. The town doctor. The sniveler who always looked like he was going to vomit, as if the sight of Vash made his stomach revolt. *Fuck him,* Vash thought. He leaned back against the warm feeling spreading across his shoulders. Easing his tight muscles. He grinned, showing his teeth. Feeling the stiffness of his beard. Remembering biting and gnawing and chewing. *Yes,* he thought. *That first taste.* When he felt the knot ease in his gut. When he felt the hunger lessen. And when the hunger eased, he heard the voice, didn't he?

Everything was easier when he listened to the voice. For a long time, he had ignored it. Once, a pale man in Denver dressed like he was playing at being a cowboy had laughed when Vash had told him about the voice. Vash bashed his skull in with a tin mug—*can't laugh if you don't have no face, can you?*—and the voice had starting purring, hadn't it? So warm and welcoming in his head.

It was always there, after that. *Oh, I have always been here,* it cooed. *You just didn't want to listen.* Sometimes it would get insistent, chattering at him like a wild bird, but when he did something violent with his bare hands, it calmed down. It never went away, but it did get quiet in his head.

But after Hidalgo, which had been bloody but ultimately unsatisfying—everything would have gone differently if Mouton hadn't been so fucking clumsy—the voice had gone away, and that had been a very bad time. He hadn't known how to bring the voice back. He had shouted at the night sky, howled with the nocturnal predators, and raged at everyone who came within shouting distance. *He would kill them,* he had shouted. Not just the people in that shit-hole town, but anyone that came after them. Even his own gang, if they couldn't keep their damn mouths shut. He would kill them all.

The thing that saved him was the buffalo. Or, rather, shooting the buffalo. They were big and dumb, like enormous furry cows. They didn't shoot back, which was slightly infuriating. But every time one of those shaggy monsters staggered and fell down—its brains blown out of its head by the heavy bullet from his long gun—he felt like there was an echo in his head. Like the voice might be coming back. He kept hunting. He kept shooting. The buffalo kept falling. And, finally—*finally*—the voice came back.

But then that bitch nearly took it away from him, didn't she? Howling at him like that. Smashing that lamp against his head. The oil, splashing on his skin. So very hot. And her rage—her screams—oh, they had drowned out the voice, hadn't they?

But he silenced her. Took her head in his hands and—

Get the gun. Get the fucking gun before it is too late.

"Shut up," Vash growled. He didn't like the way the voice was talking to him. It had been very pushy since it had come back. No one talked to him like that. Not Mouton. Not Dixon. Not Creel—the dumb fuck.

Vash had been several hundred yards away when Creel and those Army bastards had approached the trading post. Even at that distance, he had know those strangers had been trouble. What the fuck had Creel been thinking? And when that old man had popped out of that shitbox like he was some kind of kid's puppet—

"You, in there. Open the door!"

Vash focused on the shotgun on the floor. The voice simmered down, happy that he was focusing on the right thing. Happy that he was doing what he was supposed to do. *Get the gun*, it hummed.

Whoever was outside the room got tired of waiting and starting banging on the door. Vash grimaced as the sound echoed in his head. There was a second body on the floor as well, another one of the whores. He couldn't see her face—her head was turned away as if she was too shy to look at him, but he didn't remember any of them being shy. They had been—

The gun.

Shaking his head at both the pounding on the door and the tone of the voice in his head, Vash retrieved the shotgun. He breeched it to check that it was loaded—*of course it is loaded,* the voice chattered in his head. He snapped it closed and stood in front of the door, legs braced.

The door jumped in its frame as fists pounded against it. "Vash," someone shouted. "Open the door."

Gun, the voice said. Vash squinted. There was a pink light seeping around the door, and he dimly remembered a hole in the ground. He remembered the burn blackened woman too, and the man lying on the tracks who looked like he had been dragged behind a horse. He remembered the light coming out of the hole as he put them in it—the burned woman and the bloody man. But not before he had taken what was his. The hole had gulped them down, hadn't it? Swallowed them with such a hunger. He had felt that hunger too, and all that chewing and swallowing hadn't made the hunger go away, had it?

It must be fed, the voice said. Vash's lips moved, letting the voice use his throat. "The hole must be fed."

He pulled both triggers on the shotgun.

24

A serpent twisted in the Judge's guts, and at first, he attributed it to Llewelyn's talk of the Devil and monsters. Then he thought the source of the serpentine knotting might be the cheese. Eventually, he decided the true origin was neither the man nor his hospitality. Something was amiss in the very core of his being, in that place where he did not want to look. The hollow where the gold eagle was hidden. The secret place which he thought was his and his alone, but which he knew was not.

Llewelyn was distressed too—*maybe it* was *the cheese,* the Judge thought. When Victor brought the coach to a stop, Llewelyn roughly shoved the Judge back. "No, no, no, no," he babbled as he squeezed through the narrow door. In his rush, he had forgotten about the height of the coach, and with a squawk, he pitched out of the carriage.

In other circumstances, the Judge would have been amused by such a pratfall, but the humor of Llewelyn's tumble failed to cut through the tension in the Judge's gut. His ears were ringing with an angry buzzing noise. Like bees. Or snakes. Or both. Moving more cautiously, he dismounted from the coach.

There were hills in the distance, but the Judge knew they were farther away than they appeared. The steel rails of the trail track glowed in the afternoon sun, and when he looked back the way they had come, he could barely make out a pale smear of wood smoke drifting over Citrine Springs. An area near the track had been cleared of grass, as if the ground had been excavated and then put back, but like all digging projects, there was more dirt than space for it in the hole.

The curious item in the otherwise desolate landscape was an old wagon that looked like it had been abandoned but hours before.

As the Judge moved toward the wagon, the buzzing noise grew louder. Beyond the wagon, the ground was more rumpled, like the sort of disturbance you see when moles have been hard at work; though, judging by the amount of dirt, these were very large moles. The Judge caught sight of a depression in the ground—a nascent hole or a poorly filled in one.

Llewelyn scrambled to his feet. His hands were scratched, and the knees of his pants were flecked with dirt. "It can't be," he squeaked.

"What can't be?" The Judge asked.

"The hole. It's not sealed. How can it not be sealed?" He whirled toward the coach. "Victor," he snapped. "Go put the seal back on."

Victor, perched on the driver's seat like an ungainly vulture, shook his head.

"Victor!" Llewelyn stamped his foot. "You can't—I'm not—" He sputtered off, unable to complete either sentence.

The Judge chewed on his mustache for a moment, assessing Llewelyn's outrage. Was it more theatrics, or was the man genuinely vexed to a degree that he couldn't talk? The Judge looked at the dirt and the grass. *Was he yammering about that shadow?* the Judge wondered.

The Judge had seen hundreds of wagons like this one during his lifetime, and other than a disquieting stain in the back, this one was no different. The brake was set. The leads for the horse were unhitched. It was just a wagon. Hardly the sort of thing that should terrify a grown man.

The Judge started to turn. "There's nothing—"

Llewelyn was standing right behind him.

"Keep your distance," the Judge snorted, stumbling away from the ashen-faced man. "I am amused by such slapdash efforts to frighten me."

"I assure you there is nothing slapdash about this," Llewelyn muttered. He clambered clumsily into the back of the wagon, and from that height, eagerly scanned the surrounding terrain. "Where is it?" he muttered. "Where is the seal?"

"What are you talking about?" the Judge demanded.

Llewelyn stabbed a finger at the coach. "Victor," he shouted. "Get down from there. Find the seal!"

Victor might have replied, but the Judge couldn't have heard him over the surge of noise in his head. It was like being overwhelmed by a swarm of cicadas. The Judge staggered under the weight of the sound.

Llewelyn felt it too. He fell to one knee in the wagon.

The Judge tasted blood in his mouth; he had bitten his tongue. The taste was vile, and he turned his head to spit.

"No!" Llewelyn scrambled across the wagon, his hand outstretched, as if he could intercept whatever the Judge was spitting.

The Judge recoiled. *What the devil was the man trying to do?* He gagged on the foul taste. Afraid to swallow, he screwed up his face and jettisoned everything in his mouth.

The world stopped. It was as if the sun held its breath, freezing all the light in the sky. The Judge stared at his sputum, a frothy mix of saliva and blood—maybe a few morsels of bread that had been caught in his teeth. It was an elongated streak in mid-air, shining like a water-slick tadpole. He could—if he could actually move—reach out and touch it.

A presence made itself felt. The Judge imagined a broad hand fumbling at the shiny streak in the air, like a child, ankle-deep in scummy pond water, trying to catch minnows. The tiny fish were too quick, and the child's efforts merely made waves. Nearby, grass swayed and dust stirred on the ground. A shadow bloomed in the depression, and before a sudden snap in the air forced him to blink, the Judge saw a hole.

The glittering stream of blood and spit twitched. Its graceful arc from the Judge's mouth, a minuscule strand of saliva still clinging to his lip, changed. Instead of falling, it splintered into tiny shards. "What the devil . . . ?" The Judge had never seen anything move like that. His knees wobbled, and he leaned heavily against the wagon. His lip stung, as if a wasp had stabbed him before kicking off from its fleshy perch.

"That's what I've been trying to tell you," Llewelyn shrieked, and the Judge grimaced at the volume of the other man's voice. "There is no seal on the hole. It is open to the air and sky. It's open and awake. It knows we are here."

"What does?"

"The hole!" Llewelyn screamed.

"This is lunacy," the Judge said. He shook his head at Llewelyn. "You are mad, sir. You have lost your mind. I don't know what—"

"We have to seal it." The skin of his face was so tight the Judge could see the bones of the man's skull. "It is waking up. It wants to feed. We have to close the hole." He shivered, like a dog throwing water off its coat, and when he spoke again, his voice was more measured. More under control. "You don't understand," he said. "Evil dwells within the ground, and it will escape from this hole. It will come out and everyone will be damned. Everyone!"

The Judge wasn't fooled by the change in Llewelyn. He had presided over too many cases involving hysterics and court-room-filling drama to be lulled by a sympathetic mask hastily arranged by a cunning animal. Once you had seen behind the mask, the rest was broad theater, mugging for the fools in the cheap seats. The Judge was not one of those unwashed idiots.

Llewelyn snapped his fingers, trying to get the Judge's attention. For a brief second, a flicker of ruddy light sparked between his fingers. "You are touched," Llewelyn said. "I know you are. Like me. You were born after the Devil crawled free. You were born for the sole purpose of fighting him. You are one of His heavenly soldiers, sent here to destroy evil." He snapped his fingers again, and this time, when he opened his hand, a tiny flame danced on his palm. "Help me," Llewelyn begged. "Share your power with me. We can work together."

The Judge stared at the flame. His mouth was dry, and when he licked his lips, he tasted salt and iron. The buzz was an angry rattlesnake in his brain.

The flame wavered on Llewelyn's palm, guttering like it was about to go out. Spurred by that thought, the Judge lunged forward.

As soon as his flesh touched Llewelyn's, he felt as if he had been struck by lightning. The shock traveled up his arm, sparking and burning into his shoulder and then into his chest. It illuminated the inside of his skull. For an instant, he could see what was making the noise in his head—*so many rows of teeth!*—but the light shooting through him burned that image to ash. The shock arced into his groin, making him feel twenty—no, *forty!*—years younger, and it passed out of his body through the bottom of his feet. He gasped, and would have fallen to his knees if Llewelyn hadn't held him up.

He was blind to this world. What filled his field of view was someplace else, some world born of fever and nightmare. On his right: the steel rail was gone, swallowed up by a dark river. On the near bank, the ground roiled with crabs. On the far side, a wolf howled at the disc in the sky. But it wasn't the sun, it was the moon—a hundred times closer. He could almost reach out and touch it. If only he could move his hand. If only he could rip free of Llewelyn's grasp. But their palms were stuck together, bound by a flame that boiled and spat around their fingers. The Judge felt no pain, no heat, from the fire, but the flames were there nonetheless, crackling madly.

It wasn't real. It was a dream, imagined by something so vast and incomprehensible that his mind couldn't fathom the extent of it.

The Judge felt something shift inside him—in that secret place where the gold coin was hidden—and that subtle change was enough. The flames lessened, the shock passed, and the

Judge wrenched his hand free of Llewelyn's. He sagged, spent. His heart was making thunder in his chest, and his breath hissed in his throat. A thin plume of white smoke rose from his palm, and the air was heavy and thick with the threat of rain, even though there was no clouds in the sky.

Llewelyn was no better off. He was on his knees in the wagon, looking like he was going to be sick.

The ground shivered. At first, the Judge thought it was his own legs that were threatening to give up on him, but when he saw the stark terror on Llewelyn's face, he realized the other man felt the tremors as well. "What—" he started.

A sudden convulsion of the terrain threw the Judge against the wagon. He gripped the edge, trying to keep his balance. In the wagon, Llewelyn bounced like a child's top, and he let out a small cry when he landed heavily on his shoulder.

A black column erupted from the earth. It was thick and hard, like a pillar of basalt upthrust from deep under ground. The pillar rose, churning and straining into the sky. Would it reach the moon? Would it reach all the way to Heaven? The Judge was frightened by the immensity of these questions.

The black geyser reached the peak of its explosive surge, where it bloomed into a dark cloud. Something struck him in the head, and he yelped in surprise. More objects followed, and before he could duck under the wagon for cover, the cloud descended upon them with a palpable weight. It was like being caught in a furious rain squall.

But it wasn't water falling from the sky. The Judge stared at the black shapes hopping, twitching, and crawling all around him.

They were frogs. Slick, black frogs.

25

Private Jerold Sallie had been waiting for this day.

When he had volunteered in Topeka, the recruiter had been very enthusiastic. *There's no better way to serve your country, young man*, the recruiter had told him. *Keep its citizens safe. Help expand its border. You're going to part of something so much bigger.* Sallie had been eager, nodding his head so hard and fast that he felt like throwing up. But he didn't. He wasn't one of those vomited when they got dizzy. Or when he saw blood. No, he wasn't one of those who got all sweaty-palmed about violence and bloodshed.

He had almost told another recruits one boring afternoon while they had been on watch patrol, but he had managed to still his tongue at the last moment. Best to leave the past alone. Best to let it lie back there. He left for a reason, didn't he? Wasn't no reason to bring it up again. He volunteered to be part of something bigger, part of the future. The past was, well, *past*. Being a part of the Army got him out of Topeka, and hopefully, it would get him out of Kansas entirely. Maybe as far as Texas. Texas was where the action was, and that's where Sallie wanted to be.

Some day, he kept telling himself. After a few weeks of training, which hadn't instilled much in Sallie or any of the other dozen recruits, they had assigned to the Kansas Twentieth. *On the frontier*, they were told, *there will be all sorts of action.* And Fort Hollis was right there, wasn't it? But that hadn't been the case. So far, life in a frontier garrison was not much different than being in prison. Not that he knew anything about that— they couldn't jail what they couldn't find, after all. In the Army, stuck at a frontier fort where nothing changed, you spent all day doing pointless tasks. At night, you stared out at grass. *Grass!* As if grass was a danger to the United States. Horses ate it, for crying out loud. So did the buffalo—not that there were any of them anymore. Regardless of whether you were doing drills or moving rocks or staring at the grass, someone was always yelling at you. You couldn't leave the fort. You couldn't go into town without permission, and no one got permission.

It is no wonder then that Jerold Sallie's infatuation with the Army passed in the seventh or eighth month of his posting to Fort Hollis. His dislike of the uniform and the regulations and the constant belligerence from the senior offices was all that he had now. He cultivated these feelings, like he was some dirt farmer, trying to coax potatoes out of dry soil. Eventually—*soon*, he assured himself—these feelings would blossom. They would turn into something more satisfying. Something that would sustain him through the coming winter.

Because no one—especially that lying son of a bitch recruiter—had told him about the winter wind on the open prairie. It was always blowing, sneaking through gaps in the logs—and there were so many gaps, weren't there? Tickling a man on his backside, beneath the thin blankets—One to a man! *This ain't no fancy hotel for simps and weaklings! This is the United States Army, boy!*

Some days—more often as the nights got longer and colder—Sallie thought that if Fort Hollis was Hell, then Sergeant Marks was the Devil. He was a short man, with a short man's temper, and he relished heaping abuse on the soldiers in his command. *What sort of idiot complains about something that he volunteered for?* he would bark at them. *You wanted this. You signed up for this. You begged the United States Army to coddle you, you pathetic sacks of shit.*

The mood at Fort Hollis—on a normal day—was fairly bleak, and yesterday, when the cowboy and the man in black had showed up with the bodies of Bailey and Smith, the mood had gotten darker. After the pair left, Sallie heard that the others who had been out with Bailey and Smith—Sergeant Chilton and Billy Douglas—were dead too. Their bodies had been left at the trading post east of Citrine Springs.

This morning, Sallie had positioned himself near the front of the yard when Randall had told Sergeant Marks to send a squad and a wagon out to Forestal's trading post. Sallie tried not to look eager—Marks could always smell an over-eager recruit. He was already ready to crush a man's spirit. *But the Army doesn't coddle you like you wished your mothers had,* he would shout at them. *The Army doesn't play favorites.*

Marks looked right past Sallie—*twice!*—and picked four other soldiers.

Sallie knew better than to let Marks see that he cared. The one useful skill that he had learned during the ten and a half months he had been with the Kansas Twentieth was how to stare at nothing and to be nothing. *Yes, sir! I'll dig that trench. Yes, sir! I want another shift at gate duty. No, sir! My feet don't hurt. I can stand here all day.* You took in all the abuse and indifference and constant reminders of how you meant nothing to no one—*God won't miss you, you sorry shitstains!* You never let them see anything other than a totally obedient soldier.

On the inside, however, you could rage and seethe and kick up all manner of fuss. It's what helped keep you from doing something terrible. It stopped you from dreaming about sneaking into the officers' quarters at night and slitting their throats. It stopped you from thinking about what was under that tarp in the yard.

You knew it was there. You knew what it could do. Yes, you have all dreamed about it, haven't you?

And so when the bloodied man came staggering up to the gate at Fort Hollis, blabbering and wailing about a man eating other men—which sure sounded like the work of those rogue Indians they hadn't been able to drive off—Sallie found there was only one thought in his head: *It's about goddamned time.*

The two soldiers stomped up to the second-floor landing, and one of them banged on the door to the suite. There was no response, and urged on by his commanding officer, the soldier banged again. This time, he got a response. The double-barreled blast from the shotgun made a large hole in the door, and the soldier was flung back against the second-floor railing. Glory watched him topple over the railing—his arms and legs all floppy, like he was filled with rags and straw. The soldier bounced off a table, scattering cards and chips, and he left behind a dark red smear.

Ruby screamed, and the Army captain tried to shout over her. The other soldier fired his carbine at the broken door. Glory, knowing that all this screaming and shouting and shooting was only going to make things worse, dropped to her knees and scuttled for safety. She got turned around somehow, and instead of finding her way to the door, she found herself next to the upright piano, which was on the wrong side of the room. She panicked and pressed herself against the wall beside the upright instrument, trying to make herself small. If she was a mouse, she could slip into the tiny space between the base of the piano and the wall. She would be safe there.

The soldier stopped firing his rifle. Ruby crawled under one of the tables and sobbed hysterically. There was no sign of Mr. Dennis; like Glory, he had made himself scarce as soon as the shooting had started.

Revolver in hand, the Army captain approached the stairs. "Reload your weapon," he snapped at the soldier upstairs.

Against her better judgment, Glory peeked around the edge of the piano. The soldier was shoving cartridges into his rifle. He got one or two in before the damaged door of the suite swung open. The soldier brought up his rifle, but he wasn't fast enough. The shotgun sounded again, and the soldier's head disappeared in a spray of blood and brains.

The Army captain charged up the stairs, firing his revolver. The shotgun fired again, and the Army captain spun around. A dozen roses had bloomed on his arm. The captain missed a step, and he tried to catch himself as he fell, but all he did was tangle himself in the balusters of the stair.

Glory ducked back behind the piano. She squeezed her eyes shut and put her hands over her ears, as if not seeing and not listening would make her disappear. She started when the shotgun fired again—the sound was so *loud* and so *near* that her hands couldn't keep it out of her ears. The Army captain was dead. She bit her lip to keep from crying out and pressed her back firmly against the wall. *I'm not here*, she whispered to herself. She kept repeating the words, over and over again, wishing they would become true. *I'm not here. I'm not here.*

And someone hear her prayer, because the shotgun did not fire again.

Cautiously, Glory opened her eyes. There was no movement in the front room. She removed her hands from her ears. Yes, Ruby was still alive. The other woman was moaning and crying, but her distress less than it was. Glory listened intently for another sounds. Her fingers strayed to the gold coin tucked in her bodice. The gold was warm, and she sent a silent prayer of gratitude for whatever divine intervention had saved her.

Slowly, she edged forward and looked around the piano. The Army captain was still on the stairs, his arm caught between two of the balusters. His uniform and the stairs were stained with blood. The room smelled of black powder and death.

But of the monster that had emerged from the suite upstairs, there was no sign.

Rooster was behind the bar in the Bateman's public room, as Dixon expected him to be. Unlike Vash and Creel, Rooster didn't stray. You told him to stand in one place, he'd stand there, rooted like a tree, until you told him otherwise. You told him to follow a man, you knew damn well that man would be followed all day and night. Of the five who had come out of that bank in Hidalgo, Rooster was the only one who Dixon trusted to ride behind him. The others—Vash, Creel, and Jenks—they were marked by what they had done. It had eaten at Jenks until he was nothing more than a string of nervous tics and petulant complaints. Creel might have felt some remorse for gunning those folks down, but he drowned those feelings in whiskey before they had reached Oklahoma. And Vash? Well, Vash was Vash. You tried to keep the man pointed in the right direction.

Rooster poured Dixon a measure of whiskey without being asked. It didn't burn going down, which meant Rooster had found the barkeep's stash of the good stuff. Dixon finished the second pour before he turned to Rufus, who was slouching and glowering near the bar. "You played cards with him?" he asked the deputized local man. "Sat right where? Over by the window like a pair of fancy lads and made doe eyes at him while he whupped your hides?

Rufus scrunched up his face. "He put a gun in my ear," he whined.

Dixon turned to Rooster. "You play cards with the old man?"

Rooster uncorked the bottle and poured into Dixon's glass. "You said to watch him. Didn't say anything about being nice or polite." Rooster's voice was slow and methodical. He couldn't be rushed with his words. He didn't think beyond what he was told. None of the shit in Hidalgo would have happened if the gang had been filled with men like Rooster.

"Who put a gun in your ear?" Dixon asked. "The old man? Did he threaten to shoot you if you didn't play cards?"

"No, the other one."

"Which other one."

Pete joined the sulking game. "You didn't tell us about the other one," he said.

Dixon looked at Rooster. Solid, dependable Rooster, who would always be counted on to speak without making a fuss.

"Didn't realize they were together until he sat down," Rooster said. "You didn't say anything about a second man," he added, almost apologetically.

"Didn't know there was a second man," Dixon said.

"Rode in together, apparently," Rooster said.

"Put his gun in my ear," Rufus reminded them.

"And what? Forced you to play cards with the Judge?"

"No, it wasn't like that," Rufus said. "Before. When he was leaving."

"Before. After. A second man." The light in the room flared, and for a moment, everything got shiny and started to slide in strange ways. A scarlet aura glowed around Pete who was standing near the door. His mustache seemed to be on fire. Dixon pressed his thumb into the corner of his left eye, and the bright light went away. When he took his finger away, a fat tear slid out of his eye and oozed down his cheek. The pad of his thumb was smeared with blood.

"Boss . . . ?"

"It's—it's nothing." Dixon gestured for Rooster to fetch him a rag, which he used to wipe away the bloody tear sliding down his face. .

"Sure don't look like nothing," Rooster offered. It was a surprising contradiction to what the sheriff had just said.

"Who is this guy?" Dixon demanded. He felt like he was losing control. Like he was trying to gather a herd of cattle that had been spooked by thunder. "The one who stuck his dick in Pete and—"

"It wasn't Pete," Rufus corrected him. "It was his *gun* and it was my *ear*, and it weren't no—"

Rooster stiffened. He cocked his head to the side like his namesake, one eye more open than the other. "Did you hear that?"

Rufus and Pete looked at one another, like they shared a single set of ears. Dixon's headache came back all of a sudden, a vicious pounding in his skull. He felt like something was

trying to get out. Blood flowed freely from the corner of his left
eye. Dixon heard a series of muted pops, which he recognized
as rifle fire, and they all heard the muffled roar of a shotgun.
"It's starting," Rooster said, or at least Dixon thought Rooster
said it. Maybe he had. Either way, when he looked at Rooster,
Rooster wasn't there.

The man behind the bar was the deputy sheriff from Hidalgo.
The one who had come running into the bank when he had
heard Vash's shotgun.

"No," Dixon mumbled. "This can't be happening."

"Frogs?" Llewelyn was incredulous. "Where did these frogs
come from?"

The Judge kicked at a pair hopping near his boots. The tiny
black shapes were crawling and jumping in a chaotic frenzy,
but he did not like how they were crawling and jumping *toward*
him and the wagon. "They fell from the sky," he said. "But—ah,
get away, damn you—prior to that, they—"

"They came from the hole!" The wagon rocked as Llewelyn
struggled to his feet. "I told you we had to seal it. And now,
now look what has happened."

A dark shape leaped onto the Judge's coat, very nearly disappeared against the dark fabric, and the Judge flapped his coat
until the tiny frog flew off. "This might not be the best of
times to assign blame for matters that are clearly outside the
purview—"

"Mr. Llewelyn! Mr. Llewelyn!" Victor was standing on the
box seat of the coach, waving his arms. "Did you see it?" he
shouted. "Do you see them?"

"Yes," the Judge shouted back. "We see them, you fool.
They're all around us."

A few frogs had managed to reach the wagon, and one of
them leapt and clung to the fabric of Llewelyn's trousers. It
quivered and spat a glob of pale green mucus, which stuck to

the fabric. With a disgusted look on his face, Llewelyn swiped it off, along with the offending amphibian. His expression changed in an instant, and the acrid scent of burning meat assailed the Judge. Llewelyn frantically wiped his hand against his trousers, leaving a red smear on the fabric. "It burns," he shrieked. He frantically began stomping about in the wagon, trying to crush the black shapes beneath his boots. In another moment, his stomping turned into a one-legged dance, as he shouted and pointed at his right foot. The side of the wagon caught him behind the knee and he fell out of the wagon.

"For the love of God," the Judge muttered. *Though, God has little to do with this*, he thought, *unless it is one of those plagues, like the one Moses called down on the Egyptians*. He flicked away a frog which had managed to land on his jacket, and he half-expected the dark amphibian to burst when his finger touched it. But it flew away without popping, and he let out a sigh of relief.

On the other side of the wagon, Llewelyn popped up like a deranged child's toy, waving his arms and dancing about like a crazed marionette. There was blood on his cheek, and a patch of his hair was smoking. "Get them off me," Llewelyn shouted. "Get them off!"

Sidestepping the hopping amphibians, the Judge came around the wagon and grabbed Llewelyn by the collar of his coat. He shoved the man against the wooden frame. "Hold still," he snapped. There were frogs in Llewelyn's hair, and the Judge flicked them away before they could spit more green vomit. He brushed more off Llewelyn's coat. "We can't stay here," he snapped, shaking Llewelyn vigorously. He spun the man around and shoved him. "Get to the coach," he said.

"Yes, yes," Llewelyn stammered, nearly weeping with relief. "The coach." He waved his arms, nearly clouting the Judge in the face. "Victor," he shouted.

One of the horses snorted and surged in the harness. The coach rocked, and Victor, who was standing on the box seat, lost his balance. He flapped his arms, and the Judge wondered what was it about the men in Citrine Springs that they couldn't keep their feet about them. *Or perhaps he's being a dutiful manservant,* he thought, *falling on his face from an even greater height than his employer.*

The lefthand horse reared, kicking with its front legs, and Victor spun over the edge of the coach.

The Judge had seen enough. "Run, damn you," he snarled at Llewelyn.

Llewelyn did as he was told, and while he looked like he was trying to jostle something out of his trousers while simultaneously mimicking the wing motions of a whistling duck as it launched itself from the surface of a lake, he did make progress in the right direction.

The Judge, on the other hand, kept his wits about him. He strode swiftly and carefully, shaking frogs off his coat and batting away the occasional leaper. They were going to be all right. Just as soon as they got out of range of the frogs . . .

The horse continued to buck and kick. The other animal was starting to panic too, straining and pulling at the harness. The coach's brake was set, keeping the wheels from turning, but the horse was trying to pull the coach anyway. It eyes were wild, and it kept flinching from the black shapes darting around it. The coach wheels groaned as the wild-eyed horses started to drag it across the ground.

26

He didn't feel any pain. Everything below his wrist was numb. Like it was the flesh of a corpse. He could still move his remaining fingers—*yes, see? just like that*—but he didn't feel anything.

Ambrose had unwrapped the bandage for the soldiers. He showed them the ruin of his hand. Two fingers gone. As if chewed off by a savage animal. *No*, he had said. *A man did this to me. You have to stop him. He's hungry. He's going to eat. He's going to eat them all.*

He told them. Just like he had promised—well, he had promised to talk to the sheriff, but Vash and the sheriff were old friends, weren't they? It wouldn't have solved anything to talk to the sheriff. Why couldn't she see that? He had to tell someone else, someone more important. Someone who could do something about the violence. And yes, this way— revealing his blood-darkened hand with its missing fingers— they couldn't ignore him. They couldn't dismiss his warning.

He's going to eat them all.

The wagon bounced, and he shifted against the wooden crates. There wasn't much room in the wagon, and the soldiers had wanted to leave him at the fort, but he had insisted they bring him. He had to show them, after all. It wasn't just his hand they needed to see. It was the other ones too. All the bodies. He had to show them all the bodies.

Ambrose giggled at the image in his head. Just like he had seen on the battlefields during the war. That's what it was going to be like—no, that's what it *was*. He had gotten confused there for a moment. He was trying to prevent something terrible from happening. That is what he was doing. That is what the voice was telling him to do. *Do something*, it had whispered to him in the barn. *You must do something.*

And he was, wasn't he? He had gone to the fort and told them everything. He had showed them his hand. He had waited for them to load the crates onto the wagon. They had attached a team of horses and lined up in a neat formation behind the wagon. Eager to march into battle. Eager to save someone. That's all he had ever wanted. First, in the war; after, in Chicago; and even the fire—an accident, *oh dear God, yes, it had been an accident*—even then he had been trying to save people. That's all he wanted. That's all he's ever wanted.

Ambrose's giggle changed into a sob. The numbness was gone. He could feel everything again: his fingers, disappearing into that man's mouth; the tiny faces, pressed up against the metal bars; the whores from Harck's, battered and beaten. He could feel all of their pain and his own. He sobbed, knowing that he carried all their voices in him. They were down there, in the hole he could never fill.

But he had found a new voice, hadn't he? Out there on the prairie. It didn't accuse him of failure. It didn't sing songs of pain and suffering. No, this voice was kind. It wrapped itself around his hand, soothing the agony. It whispered away the dreadful memories. It sang and cooed, and Samuel Franklin Ambrose leaned back against the wooden crate of ammunition and let himself be swayed once again.

He was doing the right thing. That's what the voice said. Just like it had in the barn, when he had found the saw blade. *Feel it,* the voice had said. *So right in your hand, isn't it?* Ambrose had agreed. It was a much better tool than the saws he used for surgery. Those saws made his hand ache. Cutting bone was always so exhausting. But this new saw was better. Its teeth— and he couldn't help but flinch at that mental image—its teeth were sharper.

It had taken him a few strokes to learn how to use it. The first cut, done with his left hand, had made a mess of things. He had switched to his damaged hand, and even though he couldn't grip the saw very well, it had behaved better. He had learned how to hold it so it wouldn't twist out of his grip. How far to drag it back before reversing his stroke. How much pressure to apply as he cut. Knowing that once the blood started to flow, cutting would get easier.

He was a doctor, after all; he knew how to butcher people.

The sun was bright overhead, and he put up his hand to block the harsh light. A shadow fell across his face, he saw the flesh of his hand outlined in pink light. He fell out of himself—there was no other way to describe the feeling. The body of Samuel Franklin Ambrose was there, but he was . . . not *outside* his body, but *separate* from it. He was hearing everything, feeling everything (even the numb parts), and listening to all the thoughts, but they weren't his. If he tried to move his hand, the body didn't respond. If he tried to close his eyes, they didn't move. If he tried to scream, his lips wouldn't part. He was a spirit, trapped inside his flesh.

Nonsense, he thought. *There is no spirit. There is just the flesh. There is nothing that can detach itself. There is nothing else.*

"Nothing." The body's lips moved, freeing the word. And if he was nothing, than his actions amounted to nothing as well. There would be no consequences, either. Because nothing mattered. None of it. They were all going to die, anyway. Sooner than later. What mattered?

"Nothing," he croaked again.

He kept smiling. He felt as if there was a joke he was supposed to remember. But it didn't matter, because, in the end . . .

"Nothing," he said once more.

After killing the man in Union blues on the stair, Vash reloaded the double-barreled shotgun. It was a brutish weapon, meant for blasting birds or beasts when precision wasn't needed. When it was used indoors, it was noisy and messy. *Yes*, the voice sighed.

Vash closed the breech of the shotgun and crossed to the bar. Out of the corner of his eye, a flash of gold caught his attention. He turned, leading with the shotgun, but there was only the upright piano. He stared at the instrument. It posed no threat, and if he shot it, the piano couldn't play it later. Vash liked hearing the piano man play. It made him feel less like—

Gun.

"I have a gun," Vash growled. His finger tightened on one of the shotgun triggers. The light was wrong beside the piano, as if sunlight was reflecting off a mirror, but there was nothing there. Nothing but the piano.

Gun.

The voice nudged him again, and Vash turned away from the piano and the strange non-shadow next to it. He grabbed a bottle on the bar and thumbed the cork free. The whiskey was cool as it trickled down his burning throat. He drank more and still felt nothing. Cursing, he threw the bottle across the room. He noticed fresh blood on his arm, and dimly wondered when he had been shot.

Gun.

Vash banged the butt of the shotgun against the bar. He had a weapon. Why was the voice badgering him? Vash caught sight of a narrow-faced man cowering behind the bar. He pointed the shotgun at the man, who babbled and wept as he fled, his face a mess of tears and snot. As he knocked through the doors, the sudden glare of sunlight blinded Vash. He might have fired the shotgun. He didn't remember doing it, but his ears were ringing and there was smoke in the air.

Vash fired the shotgun again—yes, there was only one barrel left—and the sunlight dodged every single pellet of shot. Vash showed his teeth. The sun was laughing at him. That's what all that light was about. It was taunting him. His blood seething with frustration, Vash broke open the shotgun and pulled the spent shells. He fumbled in the pocket of his coat, distantly counting the remaining shells as he grabbed two.

The shotgun was the wrong gun. He had finally figured out what the voice was harping about. He had to go outside. He was done in here. He didn't need a shotgun anymore. He needed a better gun. A longer gun.

Yes, the voice purred. *The long gun. That is the gun that will strike down your enemies.*

The shotgun reloaded, Vash squinted and staggered toward the door. The light was too much and he made his eyes look away. *The long gun,* he thought.

The voice was happy to guide him. It told him where to go.

Dixon nearly ran into the pair as he rushed out of the hotel. It was the woman—Lily Harlstone, Doctor Ambrose's assistant—and an unfamiliar man. The stranger was tall and rugged, and he wore a heavy trail coat that had seen many days and nights outdoors, and he carried a revolver in a holster on his right hip. It was canted forward, butt-first. Cavalry-style. The man could draw his weapon while standing, sitting at a table, or in the saddle. In a flash, Dixon knew this was the man who had accosted Pete and Rufus earlier that morning.

Lily Harlstone was wearing a pale green dress that was open at the throat. He had seen her wear it a few times, mostly on Sunday when she was attending church. Her hair was tucked up under a flat-brimmed hat. Her eyes were wide and her cheeks were flushed. "Sheriff Dixon, are you—are you all right?" She was looking at his cheek.

"I'm fine," he replied. He had stopped in the doorway. Behind him, he heard Pete suck in a heavy breath.

"That's him," Pete said loudly. "That's the one who put his—"

"Shut up," Dixon snapped. "What are you doing here?" The question came harsher than he intended.

"We heard gunfire," the stranger said.

"What's going on?" Lily asked.

"I don't know," Dixon admitted. "But we might need the doctor. Where is he?"

"We haven't seen him," Lily said. She glanced at her companion. "He must be at the camp."

Dixon frowned. "He's at the camp?" Jenks hadn't said anything about the doctor when the sheriff and that annoying Army captain had been out there earlier.

"He was attending those who had been injured in the fire last night, including . . ." Her throat worked, but no more words came out.

"Vash," her companion said. There was something about his gaze that was all too familiar. Like he was looking straight through Dixon, both seeing him and not seeing him. All that mattered was the goal he had in mind.

"You a lawman?" Dixon asked. "Out of Texas?"

The man's eyes flicked over Dixon's shoulders, and he chided himself for what he had said. Rooster might not have been worrying about the law from Texas, but now that Dixon had said it, Rooster was definitely thinking it. Which meant—

The man's hand dipped and came back up with his revolver. He pointed it past the sheriff.

Lily gasped. Pete let out a tiny shriek. Dixon put up a hand, in a vain effort to forestall any further complications. "My mistake," he said in the tense silence that followed the stranger's quick-handed draw. "If you were a Texan lawman, you would have shown me the courtesy of stopping by my office earlier and introducing yourself."

Behind him, Dixon heard Pete shuffling his feet. The sheriff assumed Rooster had pulled his own sidearm. Pete was trying to get out of the line of fire.

"That's right," the stranger said. "I would have stopped by and said hello."

"And since you didn't, it would follow that you aren't the law."

The stranger's gaze brushed across Dixon's face, and there was a tiny challenge in the man's eyes. "I'm not the law," the man said. In other circumstances, Dixon might have taken offense at the subtle accusation hidden in the man's words, but this wasn't the time to get all worked up about something that was probably nothing.

"How about we put the guns away," Dixon suggested. "Maybe have a bit of a palaver so that we can learn what—"

Lily caught sight of something off to the sheriff's left. Her head turned and her eyes widened.

The stranger moved his arm, fired twice, and then swept Lily behind him. Dixon was dazed by both the report of the revolver and the swiftness of the man's action. As he tried to recover his senses, he heard another weapon discharge, and he was overwhelmed by a swarm of stinging wasps.

27

The coach could reasonably hold four—the Judge had ridden from Baton Rouge to New Orleans in a conveyance about this size, and the trip had been tolerable—but these two men overwhelmed the available space with their presences. Every time Victor squirmed, the coach rocked. Llewelyn moaned and fussed, and somewhat reluctantly, the Judge had given him one of the bottles of whiskey. Llewelyn had poured himself a full glass and he sipped at it religiously.

The Judge, trying his best to ignore both men, drank straight from the bottle.

A tiny black shape landed on the sill of the window, and Llewelyn contorted in a spasm of panic. The Judge clacked his tongue—at Llewelyn's reaction, not the frog's arrival—and he flicked the intrusive amphibian away before it could jump again.

"My God, how can you dare touch them?" Llewelyn gasped.

The Judge showed Llewelyn his teeth as he sat back. He took another swig from the bottle and stared out the coach window.

Maybe unhooking the horses hadn't been such a good idea, he thought. Both animals had frogs on them when he had reached the coach, and even if he brushed all the black spots off them, more were going to leap on. And once they started spitting . . .

The Judge felt like he had no choice. He had pulled the pins on the harness and unwrapped the reins from the brake. He had nearly been pulled off his feet as the horses surged away from the coach. He couldn't blame them; if he could run like they could, he'd have done the same.

The frogs couldn't get into the coach. Occasionally, one would manage an extraordinary leap—like the one that had just landed on the sill—but it was easy to dispatch them. They were safe as long as the food and drink in the hamper lasted.

Once the whiskey ran out, however, the Judge would be forced to pay attention to Llewelyn's playhouse dramatics and to suffer Victor's incessant squirming. *My God, the man was worse that a six-year old child forced to wait for a plate of cookies to cool.* The Judge summoned up a mental image of the young woman who had kept him company last night. Imagining her sliding and squirming on the leather seat was much better entertainment than Llewelyn's pallid manservant. He raised the bottle to his lips and sucked at the remaining drops. Thoughts of Glory's naked body, however, made him grumpy, and as Elm liked to point out, a grumpy Judge was a restless and short-tempered Judge. Trouble, in a word.

The Judge didn't care for that word. He preferred "decisive." *A decisive man is a man who neither frets nor overthinks,* he'd say. *A man of action is a man in motion,* he'd say. He might even go so far as to invent some aphorism, dress it up with a bit of Latin, and attribute it to Cicero or Seneca or Herodotus— one of those ancient Roman philosophers. And then Elm would point out that Herodotus had been Greek—more of a historian than a philosopher, in fact—which would ruin the whole thing. And then he'd be right back where he started: grumpy, annoyed, and—

The Judge raised his bottle to his lips and nothing came out. —*And out of whiskey,* he thought sourly.

Another frog landed on the sill, and the Judge clobbered it with the whiskey bottle. Fearing what might be smeared on the bottle, the Judge tossed it out of the coach. "Well, I don't want to grow old and die in the company of you two," he said.

"What?" Llewelyn stared at him.

"I am reminded of an opinion our great American poet Walt Whitman once expressed about God. What was it?" The Judge cocked his head to one side. "Ah, yes. Only a mean-spirited bully obsessed with revenge would take such delight in the continual failure of His children to live to His immaculate standards."

"What? What are you talking about?"

"God isn't interested in saving us, you fatuous flesh-monger."

Beside him, Victor let out a mean laugh, and the Judge noticed the look that passed between Victor and Llewelyn. Llewelyn looked like he was about to burst.

Like one of those frogs, the Judge thought, and that thought gave birth to an idea.

"All your fretting about the Devil. Look where it has left us," Victor said.

"Victor!" Llewellyn swelled up even more.

"He's right." Victor tried to point, but all he managed to do was dig his elbow in the Judge's side. "Who is going to save us?" Victor slithered on the seat until he was pressed against the outside wall of the coach. "He's afraid of frogs," he said, nodding toward Llewelyn.

"I am not," Llewelyn protested.

"You are," Victor said. "I saw you in the wagon."

"This is preposterous," Llewelyn snapped. "How dare you speak in such an uncivil manner, Victor. I am your employer. I—"

"Frogs," the Judge said. "Little bitty frogs."

Llewelyn glared at the two men; they stared back. For a blessed moment, Victor remained still. And in the silence of the coach, the Judge could finally heard a distant sound. A slow thump. Not quite a heartbeat. It reminded him more of the sound waves made as they crashed and ebbed against a rocky shore. It was the sound of something swallowing, over and over.

The Judge felt his throat tighten and he fought the urge to swallow himself, fearing that he might fall into rhythm with that disturbing reverberation. "You're afraid of tiny frogs," he said, his tongue dry in his mouth.

"I—" Llewelyn thought about protesting more, but when he gulped, a flicker of something flashed through his eyes, as if he had become cognizant of the sound the Judge was hearing. "I—when I was a child, one crawled into my mouth when I was sleeping," Llewelyn said. "It—I nearly choked to death." Llewelyn breathed heavily from his mouth. "I can—I can still taste its foul flesh on my tongue."

The Judge rubbed his temples, as if he could relieve the weight in his head. As if physical ministrations to the outside of his skull could quicken germination within. The idea was there. If only it would sprout faster. "Frogs," he said.

"Yes, frogs!" Llewelyn raised his voice, overreacting to the Judge's response. "I hate frogs. They have a . . . a chthonic grittiness to them. Like they have the dirt of the grave stuck to their feet."

"Chthonic," the Judge said.

"And the way they stare at you! They are waiting for an opportune moment to leap into your mouth."

The Judge stared morosely at the bottle he had unceremoniously thrown out of the coach. It lay on the ground, undisturbed and unnoticed by the frogs. The idea—that tiny seed laid in dark soil—finally pushed out a tiny leaf. The Judge's gaze went the wooden window frame, where he had smacked the frog. The wood was unmarked. There was no smear of frog guts. No sign at all that he had struck the frog. He glanced at the back of his hand where one of the frogs had landed. He had briefly felt its touch, felt the burn of its ichor, before he had flicked it off. And yet, there was no mark on his hand.

He looked at Victor. "What about you?" he asked. "Are you afraid of amphibians?

Victor looked at him like he was daft. "No, sir," he said. "I am not."

"Are you injured?"

Victor squirmed. "I have bruised myself," he admitted. "When I fell off the coach."

"I don't care about that," the Judge said. "I'm more interested in the frogs. Did any of them expectorate on you?"

"Did they what?"

"Spit on you, man. Did any of these hellspawn spit on you?"

Victor's face squeezed into a fist. "Why would I let one of these damn things do that?"

"Indeed," the Judge said. He reached over and plucked the remaining bottle from between Llewelyn's legs. He raised it to his lips and let whiskey fill his mouth. He held it for a minute, feeling the hardy spirit inflame the flesh of his cheeks and tongue, and when he swallowed, the hot spirit was like a warm rain falling on that tiny sproutling in his mind. The Judge looked at Llewelyn. "Why would anyone let a frog spit on them?"

"Yes, fine. Yes, they spit on me." Llewelyn thrashed his legs, and it took the Judge a moment to understand that Llewelyn wasn't trying to get out of the coach, but rather find something on his pant leg. "There," Llewelyn said, pointing with a shaking finger. "Do you see what they did."

The Judge peered at the fabric. "That might be blood," he suggested. "Or it might be dirt."

"It is blood," Llewelyn snapped. He was not amused by the Judge's apparent thick-headedness. He showed the Judge and Victor the palm of his hand, which was marbled with streaks of dried blood and what seemed like ash. "This is where that blood came from." He felt at his face, searching for a streak on his cheek. "And here," he said. He continued his enumeration. "And here. And here. And my hair here. And here."

A frog landed on the sill. The Judge watched as it wiggled its dark body along the wood, moving toward Llewelyn. Just before it jumped, the Judge reached over and closed his hand over it.

"What is that?" Llewelyn shouted. "Did you catch one? Why are you—no, get it away from me!"

The frog wiggled in the Judge's hand. When he tightened his fist, the frog's movements grew frantic. The Judge set his teeth, waiting for the frog to spit. Waiting for the pain that would follow as the amphibian's ichor ate at his skin.

Llewelyn drew his feet up on the bench, trying to put as much room between him and the Judge's fist. "Don't let it get free," he wailed. "Don't let it touch me!"

Mean-spirited and pugnacious, the Judge thought. He had been out of sorts since the riverboat, since he and Elm had faced the monster on the river. In the weeks following, he had spent many nights in a drunken stupor, trying to forget, trying to erase, what he had seen. A line of poetry surfaced in his mind. *Not Whitman,* he thought. *That other one. Wordsworth.* In one of his poems, Wordsworth had been wagging prolix about sunbeams and flowers and bees, but, amidst all that talk, he had said—what was it? The Judge tried to remember the line. *Something about creating and seeing,* he thought. *That his mind had dreamed an equal portion of what he saw.*

The frog squirmed in his fist. He felt the knot in his guts— the knot that had been there since the riverboat. The knot that had been winding tighter and tighter. He didn't know much tighter it could go, or how much more he could take. *Revenge,* he thought, returning to Whitman, *like an insane bully obsessed with imagined slights.*

The Judge didn't like bullies.

He turned his hand over, and Llewelyn shrieked as the Judge opened his fist. He stretched his fingers out so that his palm was wide and flat. There, in the middle of his hand, rested a solitary black frog. Llewelyn made incoherent mewling noises, and the frog hopped and turned until it was facing Llewelyn.

The Judge brought his other hand down on his open palm. Hard.

Victor jumped. Llewelyn let out a blood-curdling shriek.

The Judge felt only the sting of flesh against flesh. When he parted his hands, a puff of greasy smoke drifted away. There was nothing else between his palms.

The frog was gone.

28

Their conversation in the doctor's office had been interrupted by the dog. When the animal started barking outside, Elm had crossed quickly to the door and opened it. He paid no attention to the dog. Instead, he looked up the street, his body taut. A change had come over him. The laconic stranger prone to quoting Shakespeare and pretending to enjoy a dull tour of a dull town had been pushed aside by a man of fierce intensity.

Distantly, Lily heard repeated pops, followed by a heavy pop. She suspected it was gunfire, but she had no idea what sort of guns were firing. *He knows*, she thought, watching Elm.

Without waiting for her, he started off toward the hotel. Lily hurried after him, and the dog followed her. She caught up with him as they reached the hotel, and they were both surprised when the doors to the public room swung open. The sheriff had been surprised as well. Behind him were Rufus and Pete, the pair who had been in the hotel last night, and behind them was one of the sheriff's deputies. A sleepy-eyed man named Rooster.

The conversation on the porch had been tense and it got tenser when the sheriff mentioned Texas. Guns were drawn, and Lily watched Pete try to sidle out of the conversation. She couldn't blame him. This was no conversation for a lady, and as Sheriff Dixon tried to calm the situation, she looked down the porch, considering her route away from the group.

That was how she saw Vash before any of the rest of them.

The Bateman faced two roads, and its wide porch wrapped around the front of the building. Lily looked toward the curve of the porch, and her eyes widened as a figure out of her night-mares came around the corner. His beard and hair were black, stained with blood and ash, and his eyes—she couldn't believe his eyes. They were rolled back in his head. Only the whites were showing. And when he stretched back his lips, showing his large teeth, all she could think was that she was looking at Death. Elm—not a lazy cowboy, anymore, no, he was a coiled serpent, eager to strike—moved with great speed. He shoved her aside as he brought up his gun. He fired twice, each report like a thunderclap, and the man with the death's head staggered.

As Vash returned fire, Elm pushed her again, and she tumbled off the porch. She fell, and as she struggled to stand, someone grabbed her arm and bodily hauled her upright. She stumbled and flailed, feeling like she had fallen in deep water and her clothes were hindering her movements. She heard Elm's gun firing, and she had a brief glimpse of the street before she was pulled into the narrow gap between the general store and the doctor's office. She fell against the wall and tried to catch her breath. Her ankle hurt when she put her full weight on it, but she could walk. Elm leaned against the wall next to her. His fingers were expertly replacing cartridges in the gun's cylinder while his attention was on the street. When he finished reloading his gun, he spared a glance in her direction. She gasped when she saw the bloody streaks on his face and neck.

"You've been shot," she exclaimed needlessly.

"So were you," he said, and Lily finally noticed the dark holes in the sleeve of her dress.

"They just broke the skin," Elm said, reading her horrified expression. "Shot disperses quickly. We were far enough away." His lips twisted in a rueful smile. "Nothing that can't be picked out with a pair of tweezers and a steady hand."

Overwhelmed, Lily pressed herself against the wall as the street and sky threatened to switch places. She would have collapsed if Elm hadn't grabbed her hand.

"You'll be all right," he said. "We were lucky."

"What about—what about the others?"

Elm shook his head. "I don't know." He gave her hand a squeeze. "I'm going to look."

She was reluctant to let go. "Be careful."

"Always," he said.

"I've been shot!"

Dixon stumbled against the bar. The left side of his face burned, and it felt like wild animals were gnawing on his shoulder and back. He tried to wipe the blood out of his eye. Objects were doubling in his field of vision and there was a pink haze everywhere.

They had been standing on the porch: Lily and the stranger, he and his men. And then, something—*someone*—had fired on them. From the left. His bad side. The side which had been weeping blood all day. *It was a warning,* he thought. That's what it had been. The headaches. The bloody tears. The vision he had seen in the hotel, where Rooster had been replaced by the man from Hidalgo. The deputy who had come into the bank. The first victim—

No, he corrected himself. *The second one.* The first one had been the bank manager. It had been his death that had summoned the deputy.

And then he remembered the sound: the resolute thunder of a double-barreled shotgun. The sound heard at the beginning, God coughing and separating light from dark.

Sheriff Dixon swiped at the blood on his face as he put his back to the bar. He didn't see Rufus and Pete; he assumed they were hiding behind the bar. Rooster stood near the door. His gun was in his hand and he was cocking his head from side to side. "Sheriff?"

"Whazzthhhduuu." What was wrong with his voice? Dixon felt the lower half of his face, making sure it was all there.

Rooster gave him a one-eyed stare. He didn't understand what the sheriff was trying to say.

The public room door opened.

Rooster brought up his gun, but he didn't fire. "Vash?" Dixon could read Rooster's confusion. The man stayed true to the gang. Where the gang went, Rooster followed. What the gang did, Rooster did as well. They were family. They stood by one another.

Vash grinned as he emptied a shotgun barrel into Rooster's belly. Dixon tried to draw his own weapon, but his fingers kept slipping on the butt of the gun. Vash came into the public room, stinking of powder and death. His eyes were white— Dixon didn't understand how the man could see with his eyes all messed up like that—but he walked unerringly over to Dixon.

Vash clamped his hand over Dixon's. "Gun." The word came out through clenched teeth. Dixon wasn't sure who had spoken. It could have been him or Vash.

Dixon struggled to pull his hand free. But when Vash opened his mouth, Dixon was transfixed by the dark hole. It consumed Vash's face. A wave of vertigo swept over him, and if it wasn't for the reassuring touch of the bar against his lower back, he would have thought he was falling. The hole got bigger— darker—and then Vash's teeth loomed.

Dixon screamed as Vash's mouth closed over his ear.

"They aren't real," the Judge said. He showed Llewelyn his unmarked palm.

"No, no," Llewelyn moaned. "You did something. Some parlor trick. A . . . a sleight of hand."

"I squashed it." The Judge indicated his palm. "You saw it. It was right there. And then"—he brought his hands together again—"I squashed it flat. How can you sit there, you sniveling pustule, and tell me you didn't see it?"

"Look—look at me," Llewelyn wailed. "I am bleeding. Why am I bleeding?"

"My God, man. You bleed because you are alive. That's the simple truth of it. You bleed because you are frightened of . . . of frogs, for Christ's sake." The Judge shook his head disgustedly. "How can you prattle on about a crusade against the Devil when little frogs make you run and shriek like a snot-faced child?"

"You—you will not malign my efforts." Llewelyn shook a finger at the Judge. "That—that hole out there. I am the only one who knows what it is. I am the only one who has done anything to stop it. This land would be ruined—*ruined!*—if it weren't for me. All the work I have done." He punctuated his sentence by turning his finger and jabbing it at his chest. "I am not afraid of the Devil, Mr. Wallace."

"Well, be sure to tell him so when you see him." The Judge tried to navigate around Victor.

"What are you doing, Wallace?" The note of panic was back in Llewelyn's voice.

"I'm getting out of the coach," the Judge said. "I have had enough of your hysteria and blather."

Victor eagerly squeezed out of the Judge's way as he opened the door and jumped down to the ground. There were frogs everywhere, but none of them were under his boots when he landed. When he took a quick step, the frogs scattered away from his boot.

The buzzing noise that had been plaguing him wasn't gone, but it was markedly less in his ears. As was the tension in his belly. The pressure had eased. Though, he acknowledged, it would be foolish to say that it had lessened. Merely that it had receded. It was still there, and in fact, there was a hint of urgency to it now, an aggressiveness that hummed just below the surface. It brought to mind being stalked by a mountain lion that knew it had been spotted but wasn't about to give up on its prey.

The Judge turned in a slow circle, his head cocked as if he was listening intently. He swayed back and forth, like a compass needle flickering. "All right," he said when he felt confident about where the noise was coming from. "Let's see this hole."

"No, wait!"

The coach shook as Llewellyn fumbled to the door. He thrust himself out of coach, but he didn't come down. The swarming frogs made him pause. Finally, with an expression like he was about to drink a glass of spoiled milk, he carefully lowered one leg toward the ground. If he could have levitated, he would have. He shut his eyes tightly as his boot neared the ground.

The frogs swarmed, drawn like eager moths to a bright flame. For a moment, the Judge watched the mass of frogs transform into a pair of dark hands, reaching for Llewelyn's feet. But then there was an exhalation of fetid air, and the frogs were gone.

Cautiously, Llewelyn opened one eye. "Are they . . . ?"

"They have returned to whatever dank dream that spawned them," the Judge said. He turned away from the coach and its passengers.

He saw the shadow on the ground. The hole Llewelyn was so deathly afraid of. He understood the noise in his head now. It was the noise a rattlesnake makes, a warning that you were getting too close. *Stay away,* it sang. *I will be the death of you. Stay away.*

The Judge smiled grimly. "I hear your song," he said. "But I don't care for the tune." He took a step toward the hole.

29

Vash gave himself over to the voice. It was easy, and part of him wondered why he had waited. Why he hadn't made this decision years ago. Like that day in Hidalgo, for instance, when it had shouted and raged in his head. *Kill them. Kill them all.* The voice had been loud and insistent, but there had been other voices too, other voices that confused him. They made it all so complicated. Dixon, yelling that he was out of his mind. Jenks, shouting about all the blood. The customers in the bank were screaming—he had been happy to shut them up. *Kill them!* And he had.

But he had stopped listening to the voice in his head. He had let Dixon convince him that they needed to run. That they couldn't stay and fight everyone. *It won't just be the sheriff and his deputies,* Dixon said. *Soon it'll be those lawmen from Texas and then the Army. We can't fight them all. We can't win.*

The voice had argued otherwise, but Vash had been afraid. He remembered Antietam, Gettysburg, and Vicksburg, and he didn't want to feel like that again. And so he had stopped listening to the voice that day.

Now, though, there was only the one voice in his head. It chanted loudly—"Gun! Gun! Gun!"—and he listened. He was unaware of anything else. The voice got louder when he got closer—it was telling him where to go—and when he killed someone, it broke off from its chant to cheer. To congratulate him. To tell him he was a good boy. *You are a very good boy.*

No one had ever said that to him, and while he was old enough to bristle at being called "boy," at the same time, the words made his stomach warm. His stomach was never warm. It was always cold, and empty. It needed filling. Just like the hole. *You must keep filling the hole.*

Vash ran his tongue around in his mouth. He could still taste the sheriff.

Dixon had screamed when Vash had bitten his ear. Just like those people in the bank. All that fearful caterwauling. He had shot Dixon—one time—with the gun he had taken from him, and the sheriff stopped making all that noise. Vash could hear the voice again. *Gun. Gun. Gun.*

What gun was it talking about? Vash angrily shot a man cowering behind the bar, as if to say to the voice: *I have a gun. What more do you want from me?*

Gun, the voice whispered. It drew out the word, making it longer, and Vash remembered why he had left the Emporium. *My long gun,* he thought. He turned, looking sightlessly toward the mining camp. His rifle had been in the camp house, and he hadn't seen it since then. He didn't even know if it had survived the fire.

Too far, the voice whispered. *Closer.*

Vash lifted his face toward the ceiling of the public room. His nostrils flared, as if he searching for a scent. *Yes*, the voice said. *Closer. Upstairs.*

There was a long gun in the hotel. Vash knew this was true, because the voice wouldn't lie to him.

Such a good boy, the voice sang.

Vash decided he didn't like it when the voice said that. He liked it better when it talked about the gun. *Upstairs*, it whispered.

Elm saw no movement at the Bateman. Dixon and the others had gone inside, and there was no sign of Vash. They had traded fire—one barrel from Vash's shotgun, two shots from Elm's revolver. At least one had hit Vash. The other four shots he had fired, while dragging Lily to safety across the street, had been covering fire. He hadn't expected to hit anything. They had been to keep Vash from pulling another weapon.

He hadn't been worried about the other barrel of the shotgun. His weatherproofed leather coat had protected him from the first barrel, though it was likely ruined from all the shot embedded in it. A few pieces had hit him in the head and neck—a shotgun blast was not particularly specific in its spread. It was meant to shred in the blast radius. They had been lucky.

In his mind, Elm saw a black-haired woman in a white dress running across the yard at the trading post. Vash had been several hundred yards away, and he had put a bullet in the woman's head. He was a very good marksman. It was only the limited range of the shotgun which had saved them. If Vash had managed to get closer, he would have killed them all with a single barrel.

There were people on the street. The gunfire was drawing a crowd. People wanted to see what was going on. Were they in danger? Were they under attack? Elm wanted to shout at them. *Why are you coming out and looking? You are in great danger!* He heard horses, and he looked toward the church, wondering—hoping—that the newcomers weren't more earnest citizens, eager to see some sort of spectacle.

The riders wore blue, and a wagon trailed behind the group of horsemen. In the wagon was a large tarp-covered object.

"The Army," Lily said. "It's the Army."

She stepped out of the alley before he could stop her, and he spared a quick look at the hotel, fearful that the doors would burst open and gunmen would come rushing out. Nothing happened, and with a final glance at the upper-floor windows, Elm hustled after Lily.

The soldiers stopped their horses in the middle of the street, and a short, pinched-face man with three stripes on his jacket dismounted. "What's going on here?" he demanded.

"Oh, thank God you've come," Lily said. "There's a man—"

"This woman is injured," the corporal said to the other men. "Where's the medic? Goddamn it, Private. What kind of moron are you? This woman needs medical attention."

More soldiers dismounted, and one of them hurried over to Lily. He had a kit with him, and he fumbled with a wad of gauze. Lily brushed him aside. "I don't medical help," she snapped. "I'm am Doctor Ambrose's assistant. There are others that need more help than—"

Her words were cut off by a heavy clap of sound. Concurrent with the report from the long gun, the sergeant's head exploded.

Before she could react to the horrific death of the soldier, Lily was thrown to the ground and someone lay heavily on top of her. She couldn't see anything but boots and hooves, and they were engaged in a chaotic dance. Men started shouting. Rifles were fired. There was another boom from the long gun, and a second soldier fell down. A horse stumbled on the body, and it fell as well. Lily stared fearfully at the animal as it thrashed on the ground, trying to get back up. Its eyes were wide with terror.

"Lie still." Elm's voice in her ear had a calming effect. She stopped struggling, realizing that it was his weight holding her down. She tried to see what was going in all the pandemonium as the soldiers, directionless and corporal-less, argued about whether they should shoot back or run.

And while they argued, the sharpshooter kept firing.

The spire of the church rose up in Ambrose's field of view, and he was mesmerized by its slow revelation. He wasn't as devoted to attending Sunday service as his assistant Lily. Crowding into the tiny church to watch Pastor Gleason shake his Bible and rail about the perils of sinful living wasn't an activity Ambrose looked forward to. And yes, he knew there was more to going to service than the lecture, but Ambrose had left his faith in

Chicago. No white-haired, brimstone preacher was going to bring it back to him.

Ambrose leaned against the crates in the back of the wagon and stared at the spire. It was crooked—though maybe that was his own perspective—but it mesmerized him nonetheless. He stroked his bandaged hand, and for a time, his thoughts were at rest. He wasn't joyous. He wasn't sad. He was strangely contemplative—at peace, perhaps, if he allowed that sort of foolish thinking to find purchase in his mind. "Nothing," he whispered, trying to remember why that word was important, but he couldn't.

The wagon bounced its way into Citrine Springs. Ambrose found himself looking backward, at the church, as the wagon and troop detachment made their way down the center of the street. A tiny smile worked its way onto his face. The expression felt strange, and he raised his uninjured hand to his lips to touch the skin around his mouth.

The wagon lurched to a stop, and Ambrose heard a voice he recognized. It was Lily's, and he struggled to stand in the wagon. He wanted to see her, to let her know that everyone was going to be all right. His hand hurt, but that would heal. He would have a scar, but wasn't a man's life measured by the scars he wore?

He couldn't see around the tarp-covered object in the wagon, and he climbed onto one of the boxes to get a better view. He was frustrated by the confusion of men and horses, but, yes, there she was. He raised his hand to wave, but stopped when he realized he was raising his bandaged hand. Suddenly embarrassed by his injury—*it's more than a scar*, the voice in his head chided, *you've lost two fingers*—he lowered his hand. He was about to call out when a gunshot shattered the afternoon sky.

Ambrose stared as the head of a soldier burst. He had seen such traumatic death before, and in a flash, he was back on the battlefield, listening to the whistle of Minié balls and hearing the crump of cannons. The scene in the street was just like that, in fact: horses in a panic, rifles firing indiscriminately, men shouting and screaming and whimpering.

Above it all was the long gun, thundering with deadly precision. Each time it sounded, another man fell. Ambrose couldn't watch. He couldn't bear to listen. He recoiled and slipped, tangling himself in the tarp. He struggled to get free, pulling the tarp with him. It was heavy, well-cured against the weather, and once it started to move, it kept sliding, like an avalanche scraping down the side of a mountain.

Ambrose stared at the weapon the Army had brought to town. It had six barrels, banded and clustered in a circular design. A heavy crank was attached to a metallic case, and sticking out of the top of the case was a long shaft was filled with brass objects. Ambrose had heard of such a weapon, invented late in the war when everyone had forgotten why the conflict had started and all that mattered anymore was the killing.

Gun, whispered a voice in his head.

30

It was a beautiful rifle, a truly elegant weapon compared to the stubby Springfield Armory-finished carbine that Vash owned. Technically, his was also a Sharps rifle, even though it had been converted from a percussion musket to fire modern cartridges. The forend only had two bands around it, versus the three wrapping the longer barrel of the Model 1859 he had found. His rifle had a rear sight marked for 700 yards, though he had never scored a hit at that distance. Vash lovingly ran a hand along the length of the barrel of the Model 1859, imaging what a bullet from this gun could do to a man at 700 yards.

He went to the window. It had only been a few minutes since he had entered the hotel, and while he expected to see a crowd outside the hotel, he was surprised to see horsemen wearing Union blue. Soldiers, from the fort. How had they come so quickly? Vash wondered how much time had passed since he had been dragged from his stupor at the whorehouse.

Gun, the voice whispered, bringing his attention back to what he had in his hands.

Yes, he thought. *Gun*. He grabbed the satchel he had found along with the rifle and dumped its contents on the floor. The voice had guided him upstairs, and in the third room from the landing, he had found a long oilskin wrap. Inside was a well-used and well-maintained sharpshooter's weapon. This was the weapon that would speak for him. This is the song that the world would hear. Vash let out a deep sigh as he closed the breech on the rifle. This was what he had been waiting for. He pushed up the window sash and rested the barrel of the rifle on the window sill. He didn't even need the rear sight. The soldiers were so close. "Gun," he whispered as he pulled the trigger on the rifle.

They were exposed, lying in the street, but Elm knew that, in the chaotic churn of frightened soldiers and panicked horses, a sharpshooter would only see the moving targets. Until he assessed and dealt with those threats, a marksman wouldn't concern himself with bodies on the ground. He wouldn't have time to check if they were truly dead. He put his mouth close to Lily's ear and told her to lie still, and during the cacophony that followed as the soldiers tried to hide in plain sight and return fire, she trembled beneath him.

Elm watched as the sharpshooter killed two more soldiers. It had to be Vash. There was no one else who knew how to fire a Sharps rifle with such precision. *He is using my rifle*, Elm thought grimly. He knew which room was his in the hotel, and he saw wisps of smoke drift out the third window after each shot was fired.

The soldiers returned fire, but Elm knew they weren't going to hit Vash. The sharpshooter was kneeling and resting the barrel of the rifle on the window sill. He was protected by the wall of the hotel. It would be a lucky shot that would penetrate the wood, and a luckier shot altogether that would fly through the open window and graze the top of Vash's skull. *I have to get inside*, he thought. *That's the only way to bring him down.*

He gathered Lily to him, surprised by his own urge for human contact, and pressed his lips against the side of her head. She felt his brush of affection and reached out a hand as he scrambled for a carbine lying nearby. "Elm," she called out, but he didn't look back.

Elm rose to his feet and strode toward the hotel. He pressed the butt of the carbine—a lever-action Spencer rifle—against his shoulder. He cocked the hammer, sighted past the iron sight, and pulled the trigger. The hammer fell on an empty chamber. He cursed the lax skills of the man who had held the gun before him as he levered the rifle's action, loading a cartridge into the chamber. He cocked, sighted, and pulled the trigger again. This time the rifle fired, and wood splintered from the far side of the window frame. He adjusted his aim as he levered, cocked, and fired again. The muscles in his belly were tight, anticipating return fire from the hotel window, but as long as he kept levering, cocking, and firing, the sharp-shooter might not risk taking a shot. Even with all motions necessary to fire the Spencer rifle, he managed to put five bullets through the window by the time he got to the porch, where the roof put him out of sight.

When he worked the lever action a sixth time, he could tell the magazine was empty. He discarded the useless rifle as he bounded up the steps to the porch. Behind him, he heard a bark of alarm from Laelaps, followed by an incongruous and ominous clatter of metal.

Lily watched Elm walk toward the hotel. He had one of the army's carbines, and he was shot it quickly and proficiently as he walked. She marveled at his poise, at how unperturbed he was by the chaos around him. He moved with an economy of motion and a confidence that said he was utterly focused on the task at hand: get to the porch.

The soldiers from Fort Hollis were a flock of unruly chickens. They were not well trained, and what meager training they had relied on a distinct chain of command. The commanding officer, the one who had spoken to her earlier, had been the first to die, and none of the other solders were eager to assume the mantle of leadership. They milled about, they fired their weapons, they fell off their horses or tried to hide behind them. It would be farcical to watch if it wasn't for the fact that avoiding command meant more men dying.

Someone pulled the heavy tarp off the object in the wagon, and Lily got her first glimpse of the weapon the Army had brought with them.

Of course it was a weapon. The Army was not know for hauling medical supplies or protective barricades with them.

The weapon looked like someone had bound six rifle barrels together. At one end, there was a brass box topped with a metal rod. A heavy crank protruded from the box, and as Lily stared, a man stood up behind the weapon and reached for the crank. It was the white bandage wrapped around his hand that made her gasp. It was Doctor Ambrose! What was he doing on the Army wagon?

The barrels rotated as Ambrose turned the crank, and each fired as it passed a hammer inside the metal box. The gun was mounted on a swivel, and as Ambrose cranked the Gatling gun, it swung back and forth. The noise the gun made was worse than the most terrible thunderstorm she had witnessed.

Men died. Horses died. On the porch, Elm dived for the door as bullets from the Gatling gun blew holes in the walls of the hotel.

Lily curled up on the ground, covering her ears. She sobbed uncontrollably, unable to watch as the doctor indiscriminately savaged everything in the path of the Army's terrible weapon. She had seen the doctor's face. His cheeks were flush with joy, and there was a savage light in his eyes. She didn't know who he thought he was killing, but the joy of doing it was overwhelming.

Vash dropped prone. Bullets from the Gatling punched through the wall, showering him with splinters of wood. What had the Army brought with them? He stared at one of the holes. It was bigger than his thumb, like one of the holes the Sharps rifle made. And this weapon was firing how many rounds a minute? It made his long gun seem like a peashooter.

"Gun," he growled. He crawled to the window and carefully peeked over the sill. The man was still cranking the weapon, but the barrels had stopped firing. A slender magazine mounted to the top of the brass box at the back of the housing had run out of ammo. Vash frowned as he peered at the man. He wasn't wearing Union blue. In fact, he looked like that doctor fellow who Harck sent his girls to. That fellow who had come out to the mine after the fire.

He grabbed a loose cartridge from the floor and quickly inserted it into the rifle. He raised himself to one knee and let the rifle's barrel rest on the window sill.

Gun, the voice sang in his head.

"Shut up," Vash growled. It had lied to him. All the hard work he had done. Shooting. Biting. And now, abandoned while someone else—someone so less worthy than himself— was given the power. *I fed you,* Vash thought, sighting down the rifle. *I bled for you. I killed so many for you.*

The voice was quiet in his head, and the silence was sudden and vast. Vash was reminded of the open prairie, the endless expanse of grass. There was life on the plain, but it was hidden. If you didn't know how to listen for it, all you heard was the wind, sighing through stalks. Vash had always hated that empty sound, and hearing it now in his head was more than he could bear.

He pulled the trigger on the rifle, and reveled in the noise it made. *Gun,* he thought. This was the true voice, the only voice. The voice that was his.

During the storm season in Baton Rouge, the winds became showed their true power. Raging and howling, they would push trees over. They would flatten small buildings. They would get behind a wagon and push it as far as the road would allow, and then they would smash it to kindling. The Judge had been in his share of Louisiana storms, and if he leaned in the wind, he felt like the power of the weather would not let him fall. Each step he took toward the hole in the ground was like walking into one of those tremendous storm winds, even though the Kansas sky was clear. Each step was a struggle, but he was moving.

The Judge had lost track of how many times he had been in the presence of evil (a lie, by the way, as the Judge knew full well the count was at least sixteen, and, all things considered, there were five more that were, at the very least, *adjacent* to evil, if he could be allowed such nit-picking). He wasn't a God-fearing man, and, yes, there was a Bible in his saddlebags, but there were also books by Homer, Seneca, an early edition of Whitman's opus, and even a copy of that trashy novel by whatshisname. He wasn't an expert in anything but his own opinions about the law. Matters more demonic, if you insisted on using that word, were matters in which he had personal experience. From those experiences, he knew it was difficult to kill what you couldn't see. A hole filled with darkness? Well, maybe Llewelyn was right: the only way to seal it was to fill it.

Fill it.

The Judge wavered, a fine sweat dampening his brow.

He had definitely heard an echo, but he couldn't fathom where it had come from. There was nothing out here but tall grass and blue sky.

The Judge slid his foot forward, edging a step closer.

A rifle cracked behind him, and he flinched, expecting to feel a bloom of pain somewhere. He ran his hands down the front of his jacket as he inhaled, and he decided he hadn't been struck by a bullet. It had been a warning shot.

"Judge Wallace," Llewelyn shouted. "You are wandering off."

The Judge looked over his shoulder. Llewelyn was walking with exaggerated care, lifting his entire leg with each stride as if he was stepping in and out of gopher holes. He was wearing a gunbelt—the Judge's belt, in fact—and he was carrying a Winchester rifle.

"Where did you get that?" the Judge asked.

"Victor packed more than a picnic lunch."

"Victor's very thorough," the Judge groused. He turned around so that he was facing Llewelyn, and he waited for Llewelyn to come closer.

"Where are you going?" Llewelyn asked.

"We came all the way out here to look at a hole . . ."

"Not look," Llewelyn said. "Seal."

The Judge made a production of scanning the surrounding landscape. "Yes," he said. "That's what we were looking for, wasn't it? Some kind of cover. How big did you say it was?"

"I didn't," Llewelyn said.

Something in Llewelyn's voice brought the Judge's attention back to the master of the mining company. "Ah, you have played me, haven't you, sir?"

Llewelyn feigned embarrassment. "I might have," he admitted. "I know you can feel it, Judge Wallace. It doesn't want us here. It knows that we have the power to banish it. It is trying to push us away. If there were others nearby, it would influence them. It would infect their minds with its vile lies. It would seduce them with terrible fantasies."

The Judge frowned. "And how would it do that?"

"What do you mean?"

"How would a hole in the ground seduce me?" The Judge leaned back, idly marveling at how the air supported him. If he relaxed his body, the pressure against his back might move him. Like a leaf. He dropped a hand in the outer pocket of his coat, and his fingers touched the blade of the small knife he had pocketed earlier. Carefully—so as to not nick himself on the blade—he plucked at the knife until he found the handle.

"Oh, your arrogance is so insufferable," Llewelyn said. "You pretend to be a fool. You stick your tongue in your cheek and prattle like one of those idiots at a country fair. You say you don't believe in the Devil, but you ignore what we have just witnessed. That rain of frogs. Their acidic touch. From whence did they come but from the bosom of evil."

"Well, I wouldn't go so far as to 'whence' about them, and I even hesitate to ascribe attributes more befitting a comely wench—"

"Enough," Llewelyn said, raising the rifle. "Your tongue is tiresome, and I am done listening to it."

The Judge turned his body slightly and dropped his hips, letting his entire body rest against the invisible hand pressing against him. He drew his hand out of his pocket, the paring knife pressed against his palm.

"How are you going to seal the hole?" he asked, curious in spite of the threat of Llewelyn's rifle.

"By forcing it to swallow what it doesn't want."

"I beg your pardon?"

"You saw how it rejected your blood," Llewelyn said. "When you spat earlier. Before it vomited all those frogs. It has a voracious appetite, and it will devour anything you feed it. Anything, except . . ."

"The blood of the innocent?"

"Hardly," Llewelyn snorted. "You are anathema to the Devil, Judge Wallace. Your blood is too pure for it."

"Ah, so that is how you mean to seal the hole," the Judge said. "And here I thought you were eager to make my acquaintance because you were starved for some intelligent conversation. But no, all you want is my sacrifice."

"I do," Llewelyn said. "You are the only one who is strong enough."

The Judge jumped. He wasn't trying to imitate one of the devil frogs. He was merely taking his feet off the ground, and once he was free of the earth, he was at the mercy of the weight pressing against him. Llewelyn gasped at the Judge's sudden levitation, and before he could fire the rifle, the Judge slammed into him.

31

A percussive hammering brought Dixon back from unconsciousness. He groaned as his headache made itself felt, and he raised a hand to his head, sure that he would find that his skull had burst. When his fingers brushed the side of his head, he yelped in surprise and jerked his head. More pain bloomed, but not in his head. In his gut.

He dragged his eyes open and tried to make sense of his surroundings. He was in the public room at the Bateman, but the room looked as if had been the target of a sustained assault by an infantry company. Holes peppered the wall, and shafts of sunlight speared into the room. There was blood all over the floor, and Dixon's breath hissed in his throat when he caught sight of Rooster. The man was sprawled on his back, his gaze fixed on the ceiling. A beam of sunlight lanced one of his open eyes, and Rooster did not blink. "Goddamn it," Dixon moaned.

Some of the blood was his. It was coming from a hole in his belly. Dixon reached up to touch his ear again, clenching his teeth against the pain he knew was coming.

"It's gone," a voice said.

Dixon looked up. His eyes were watering and he was having trouble focusing. The man's face was blurry, but he recognized the long coat. "You," he croaked.

Miss Harlstone's stranger crouched in front of him. He pushed Dixon's hand down. "Looks like a wild animal chewed on you," he said. "Stop fussing with it."

"I wasn't fussing with it," Dixon complained. His other hand slipped on his bloody thigh. "I've—I've been shot," he said.

The stranger gave him a grim smile, a twitch of his lips that spoke of companionship, of knowledge shared about pain and misery. "I have been too," he said. "Once or twice."

Dixon's head lolled back, and he squinted as one of the sun's beams passed across his face. "What's happening?"

"Terrible things," the man said.

Dixon let his tongue slide across his lip. "You're a awful storyteller," he said.

"So I've been told." The man removed his sidearm from its holster. He broke it open and checked that it was fully loaded. "Here's a different story," he said. "A few days ago, a man in your employ killed an Indian woman. A Kiowa."

"Where," Dixon asked.

"A trading post, east of here. Run by a man named Forestal. You know the place?"

Dixon swallowed and let out the breath he had been holding. "Was Vash by himself?"

The stranger shook his head. "I never saw him, but I did see a man named Creel, along with a handful of soldiers from Fort Hollis."

"What happened?"

"A friend and I were getting supplies from the trader when a trio of Indians showed up. Forestal didn't mind. We didn't mind. But the Army men and Creel?"

Forestal had a native woman living with him. The Army wasn't thrilled with it, but Dixon hadn't cared. If Forestal was on speaking terms with the Kiowa, then maybe they would trade. And while they traded, maybe they talked. Dixon bought whiskey and information from the fat trader, and the trader always had a goodly share of both. It was how he kept tabs on Creel and Vash. The pair had gotten restless after Longspur had stopped paying them to kill buffalo. They had to find other ways to stave off their boredom.

Slowly, grudgingly, Dixon understood what had happened a few days prior, what had brought the Army captain into his office earlier this morning, what might have precipitated the fire at the mine. *All of this,* he thought. *All of this over . . .*

"They minded," Dixon said. He groaned as pain bloomed in his belly. "And Vash?" he asked once he had his breath back.

"Vash was on the ridge." The man paused and raised his head. He looked like he was listening. "Where you'd expect a sharpshooter to be," he said after a moment.

A rifle fired overhead, punctuating his statement. Reminding them of who was upstairs.

The stranger stood, his gun held loosely in his hands. Dixon stared at the weapon, and his hand wandered to his own holster, which he found empty. *Vash,* he thought. Vash had taken his gun. And the following thought: *he shot me with my own gun.*

"What?" the stranger said.

"He shot me with my own gun," Dixon said, pointing at the hole in his belly.

"I can't help you with that."

Dixon looked over at Rooster. "Give me his," he said, flinging out his hand to point at Rooster's weapon. "I don't want to die without a gun in my hand."

"There's no absolution in that," the stranger said.

Dixon laughed, even though it hurt. "Fuck absolution," he wheezed. "I'm already damned. I just want a chance to shoot the bastard myself."

The stranger nodded. "I'll grant you that." He walked over to the corpse and retrieved Rooster's gun. He came back to Dixon and crouched again, offering the sheriff the revolver. "You rode with him," he said.

"Rooster?" Dixon nodded as he took the gun. "Yeah, we rode together."

"And Vash?"

Dixon hesitated and then nodded. "And Vash," he said.

The stranger stared at him, and Dixon felt like the man was reading his entire history, all the way back to Hidalgo and the decisions made that day in the vault. "All right," the man said, and that was all the judgment he passed. "Don't miss if you get the chance."

"I won't," Dixon said. *Not this time,* he thought.

The Judge knocked Llewelyn's rifle aside and slashed at the man's arm with the knife that had appeared in his hand. Llewelyn pulled the trigger on the rifle, and the Judge was blinded and deafened by the weapon's roar. He dropped the knife, and as he shoved away from Llewelyn, his hands scrabbled for the butt of the revolver in the holster hanging against Llewelyn's thigh.

Leaning against the pressure from the hole, the Judge did a little dance to get his feet under him. He was too old for that sort of athletic frippery, and he managed a stumbling step or two before he tangled his legs. He went down, face-first, and his mouth was filled with dirt. He spat, and his spittle danced and glittered as it left his lips. The hole flicked it away. The malevolence lurking in the shadowed depth of the hole wanted no part of him. The Judge couldn't blame it. He didn't want any part of that in his mouth either.

A shadow eclipsed him. The Judge rolled onto his side, hiding his right hand from Llewelyn. His grip tightened on the smooth handle of his revolver.

"You are a clumsy old man." Llewelyn shook his head. "I shouldn't have even bothered. This is my burden. I know that. I've always know it. I was a fool to think that you and I were simpatico."

"Simpatico?" The Judge frowned. "About what? You want to throw me in that hole. Why would I agree with you about that?"

"About the privilege we have been given. The gift."

"You mean that trick where you sweat a lot and make a little 'pfft' with a candle?" The Judge made a farting noise with his lips. "I've seen dogs do better tricks."

Llewelyn flushed. The rifle, which had been pointed at a spot above the Judge's head, drifted down. "Not only are you a clumsy oaf, old man, but you are rude as well."

"Perhaps," the Judge said. He rolled onto his back. "But I'm definitely much more clever than you." His pistol was pointed at Llewelyn's belly. The Judge made a noise with his tongue when Llewelyn's hand tightened on the rifle. "Careful," he said. He lowered the tip of the revolver. "I'll shoot your balls off."

"You wouldn't," Llewelyn said.

"You've got two," the Judge said. He wiggled the barrel of the revolver. "You only need one."

Llewelyn's knuckles whitened on the stock of his rifle. "This is foolish, Mr. Wallace," he said. "If we shoot each other, the Devil wins. Our blood will stain this ground here, which will make no difference. Other there"—he tilted his head to the left—"we can achieve something extraordinary."

"By jumping in together?" The Judge shook his head. "No thank you, sir. We are not—as the good playwright once said—a pair of star-crossed lovers." He dredged up the beginning of the English playwright's classic story. "How does that go? Ah, yes. 'From ancient grudge break to new mutiny, where civil blood makes civil hands unclean.'"

Llewelyn stared uncomprehendingly.

"It's from a play," the Judge said. "By William Shakespeare."

Llewelyn's expression didn't change.

"*Romeo and Juliet*. No?" The Judge made a noise similar to the one he had made moments ago. "Two lovers. Their families are at war. But love doesn't care and—oh, for the love of God, how can you not know this play?"

"I've—it's been a very long time," Llewelyn said. He pursed his lips. "And I don't understand what a story about two teenagers has to do with us."

"I'm just saying that we're not going to jump into that hole like—oh, never mind."

The Judge pulled the trigger of his revolver.

His aim was a little off. But not by much.

Llewelyn shrieked and danced wildly, like a man who had—well, like a man who had just been shot in the balls. His eyes murderous with rage, Llewelyn swung his rifle toward the Judge.

As Llewelyn fired, the Judge rolled out of the way.

Vash crept to the window sill and looked down on the carnage in the street. He had shot a handful of men. Oh, the Sharps was a marvelous tool; there was much he could do with it. But bullet for bullet, it paled in comparison to the destruction the Gatling could do. He had shot the man behind the gun, and as he watched, a woman rushed to the wagon and pawed at the body. What was a woman doing out there?

A tiny worm wiggled in his brain and he wondered at the gaps in his memory. There was the woman in white. It had been a difficult shot, but he had gauged her intent correctly. And then there had been the broken one, the one who came at him with fire in her eyes. He had dealt with her too. He hadn't needed a rifle. He had used his hands. Vash frowned. There were more, weren't there? More that he had used his hands on.

Vash went to grab another cartridge, but they were all out of reach. Cradling the rifle in his arms, he scooted across the floor and gathered several. He loaded one into the rifle and dully stared at the rest in his hand. He couldn't hold the cartridges and fire the rifle at the same time. As he shoved the cartridges into the pocket of his coat, he thought about the Gatling. It had a proper magazine. You didn't have to scrabble around like a rat for ammunition. It was held at the ready.

Vash tapped his fingers against the wooden floor. He had better things to do with his hands than chase ammunition. He opened and closed his hand, watching the skin stretch across his knuckles. "Gun," he whispered.

Maybe the voice hadn't lied. Maybe he didn't truly understand the complications of the world. Hadn't the doctor cleared the way for him? The gun was downstairs. No one could stop him. *Yes*, he thought. *I will take the gun.*

Vash left the room. He heard voices downstairs, and when he reached the banister, he spotted two men in the public room below. He recognized them both, but they were from different points in his past. The man on the floor, his lower extremities soaked in blood, was the sheriff. Vash vaguely recalled a deeper history with the man than what was symbolized by the tin star on his coat, but he didn't have time to ruminate about what had gone before. The other man was the man from the trading post. The one who had known he was on the ridge.

Vash's grip tightened on the rifle he had found in the room. The Sharps Model 1859. A true sharpshooter's weapon. *No!* he thought. *It is mine. My gun. My—*

The sheriff, a man who had looked away for so long that he was going blind in one eye, lifted his head and spotted Vash. With a grim smile, he raised the revolver in his hand.

32

As Dixon raised his weapon, Elm swung around, bringing his own gun to bear on the figure at the upstairs balustrade. Dixon's gun spoke first, but Elm's spoke several times. Vash staggered and leaned against the railing. He snuffled and huffed like a wounded bear. He left a bloody handprint on the wood as he struggled to stand upright. He grimaced, waved at something Elm couldn't see, and then tumbled over the railing. He landed with a resounding thud on the floor of the public room.

Dixon's gun clattered to the floor. "And that's done," the sheriff sighed.

Elm waited a few seconds. He wasn't as sure as the sheriff, and when Vash didn't move, he made to put his gun away. Unexpected movement danced at the corner of his vision, and he whirled, raising his weapon again.

The man named Pete was standing behind the bar. His hands were up, and he looked even more miserable than he usually did. "Don't—" he squeaked. He pinched his eyes shut so that he wouldn't see Elm pull the trigger.

Elm moved his finger away and lowered his revolver.

Dixon stirred. "Is that—?" He coughed and groaned. "Pete? Are you still alive?"

"Yes—yes sir." Pete opened his eyes, and a look of great relief washed over his face. "I'm still alive, sir."

Dixon coughed. Or maybe he laughed. "Of course you are." He squinted up at Elm. "And Vash?"

Elm looked over at the shape on the floor. "Dead," he pronounced.

"Good." It took the sheriff several tries to get Rooster's gun into his holster, and when he had accomplished that task, he rested. "Pete," he said after getting his breath back. "Come help me."

Pete hurried around the bar. He recoiled on seeing all the blood, but the sheriff snapped his fingers, getting his attention. "It's not all mine," he said. "And I don't want to die sitting in it, so do something useful once in your life and help me up."

Pete crouched next to the sheriff and gingerly put the sheriff's arm over his shoulder. The sheriff waved his other hand at Elm, who holstered his weapon and lent his support. The sheriff cursed loudly when they helped him stand.

"I had a gang once," the sheriff said. "We robbed a train, down in Texas. Didn't kill anyone. Just took their money. That was enough, though, enough that they would have hung us if they caught us. Funny how that changes a man. Rob one train. Rob ten trains. Rob twenty banks." He wheezed out a painful laugh. "They can only hang you once, and so you stop worrying about how many times you break the law. Once is all it takes."

He let Pete and Elm assist him, and they made slow progress toward the door. When they reached it, Pete let go, and the sheriff leaned heavily against Elm. "I never liked the decor," he said, eying the holes in the wall made by the Army's weapon. "Decent enough place to die, though. Better than—"

As Pete swung the door open, the Gatling began firing.

For a very brief moment, Private Sallie felt something close to joy. It was the happiest he'd felt since he had joined the Army. His elation sprang from witnessing what a heavy bullet did to Sergeant Marks's head, but his joy was swiftly transformed into guilt and horror as he was spattered by the sergeant's blood and brain matter. As he tried to wipe his face off, someone knocked him down. During the ensuing confusion, a horse stepped on his shoulder. After that, Sallie stayed down, pawing at his face. Trying to get the sergeant off him.

The recruiter hadn't told him about all of this. The United States Army was the greatest army in the world. No one would shoot at them, because they would shoot back, and they had more guns than anyone else. They had a Gatling gun, in fact. One of the most devastating weapons ever made. Sallie had assisted in test-firing it when the gun had been delivered from Chicago. They put up a bunch of wooden targets on the plain, and what had taken them three hours to set up, the Gatling had reduced to splinters in less than a minute.

And when it started firing in the street of Citrine Springs, Sallie knew everyone was going to die. He cowered on the ground, mouth stretched in a frantic scream. Horses and men fell all around him.

When it stopped, Sallie looked up, and he couldn't believe what he saw. The man behind the gun was the one who had come to the fort. The doctor fellow who had been wailing and shrieking about an Indian attack in town. Filled with frantic fantasies, he had convinced Sergeant Marks to march from the fort. Marks had ordered them to bring the Gatling. Just in case. They were the United States Army, after all. They had a duty to show their strength. A damn near patriotic duty.

Sallie staggered to his feet as the doctor smacked the Gatling with his hands. *He doesn't know how to reload it*, Sallie thought. He stumbled toward the wagon, intending to wrestle with the doctor. But before Sallie could reach the wagon, the sharp-shooter fired, and once again, Sallie watched as a man died from an calamitous impact with a .50-70 caliber bullet.

The doctor collapsed, and the woman who had met the Army when they had arrived, rushed over to the wagon. She tried to climb into the wagon, as if she could provide some aid to the doctor. Hadn't she said something about being his assistant? Sallie couldn't remember. It hadn't been all that important at the time, and certainly wasn't now.

He stared at the empty magazine sticking out of the Gatling. Unlike the doctor, he knew how to swap it out for a fresh one. That's what were in all the crates they had brought wit the gun. A mighty weapon like the Gatling gun needed to be fed—it was so very hungry, wasn't it?—and Sallie knew what to do. He hauled himself into the wagon and pushed past the woman and the very dead doctor.

Sallie retrieved a full magazine from a crate. He slotted it into the case at the back of the Gatling. Satisfied that it was properly set, he grabbed the crank and felt it catch as the first round chambered. Remembering one of the lessons the Army had pounded into him, he checked his field of fire. Not only could he sweep the weapon from side to side, he could also elevate and lower the barrels. The doctor—either through incompetence or evil intent—had tilted the front of the gun down, and the initial rotations of the barrels had blasted those standing in front of the wagon. Sallie wasn't going to make the same mistake.

He pointed the barrels at the hotel, tightened his grip on the crank handle, and waited for a sign. And when the hotel door started to open, Sallie wet his lips. "Gun" was the word that suddenly popped into his head, that was suddenly on his lips like a lover's kiss. This was the gun of the United States Army. As Sallie turned the crank and fired the Gatling, he thought he would feel like he was finally a part of something great. Part of the greatest army in the world.

But when the woman hit him in the face with the empty magazine he had tossed aside, all he felt was pain. Pain and emptiness. Like he had been used up and cast aside.

Llewelyn's expression was equal parts incredulity, rage, and indignation. "You shot me," he shrieked at the Judge.

"You shot my hat." The Judge was half-reclining on the ground not far from where Llewelyn had sat down. He had retrieved his hat after it had fallen off his head, and he stuck a finger through the one of the holes in the crown. The rifle bullet had gone straight through. If the hat had been firmly seated, the bullet would have gone into his skull instead.

"That's—that's a hat. This—" Llewelyn took his hands away from his groin so the Judge could get a good look at his injury. The Judge didn't need to examine the wound. He knew what a bullet did to a man's anatomy. Besides, he had missed emasculating Llewelyn, which wasn't much consolation at the moment . . .

The Judge smacked some of the dust off his hat and put it back on his head. "This was never going to work," he said.

Llewelyn's face was caked with dust, tears, and blood. "Wh—why?"

"Your plan doesn't make any sense," the Judge said. He tapped his fingers against his chest. "If—and this is merely a general speculation, I'm not saying that I actually believe anything you've been blathering about—but if your nonsense is true, then why should we sacrifice one of the most righteous of God's soldiers? Hmm? If that hole is leaking Devil-stuff, and if it takes some of our—our *stuff*—to drive it from this world, then why would we waste it? Shouldn't we be thinking about the war, instead of just this battle?"

"What—what do you mean?"

The Judge watched rivulets of Llewelyn's blood crawl across the ground. The hole was pushing the holy blood away, but it was having less success than it had with mere spittle.

"I'm older than you," the Judge said. "And meaner, frankly. Why should I go into the hole?"

"But—but—"

"Is the Devil walking this earth? I don't know about that. But I've seen evil, and yes, I'll grant you the semantic handwaving that equates one with the other, that the taint of one comes from the touch of the other. Regardless of all that, let us focus on what lies before us."

He waved a hand at the shivering strands of blood. "Is this all this fetid pit can do?"

Llewelyn flapped his mouth, but the Judge didn't wait for him to speak.

"Oh, yes. The frogs. How could I forget the frogs? Ah, but they were caused by your own fear. But as soon as I demonstrated to you how phantasmal they were, they lost their power. If we stand before this hole, armored with the awareness afforded by our wits and our own constitutions, then what power does this hole have?" The Judge shrugged. "So again, I ask: why should I jump in?"

"Some—someone has to," Llewelyn sobbed.

"Aye," the Judge said. "Someone has to. That is, if you believe what it is that you've been yammering about."

Llewelyn groaned. He looked at his hands. "My blood," he whispered. He drew a finger through the crawling lines of blood, mixing them into the dirt. "It's afraid of my blood." He shook his head at the thoughts rising in his brain.

The Judge held his tongue, knowing better than to interrupt a man when he was arguing with his own faith. He eyed the crimson mess of Llewelyn's hip and groin. The wet strands of blood, shivering across the ground. He thought of Wordsworth and of lines written about an old stone abbey. *We make as much as we see*, he thought, *and eventually, we stop seeing. All that remains is what we make.*

Finally, Llewelyn raised his head, and there was a bright gleam in his eye. "Show me," he said, his voice earnest and desperate. "Show me your gift."

The Judge chewed on the inside of his cheek as he considered Llewelyn's request. *All that remains is what we make,* he thought again. With a sigh, he shifted onto his knees. "Very well," he said. He lifted his hands, and without being clever or disingenuous or deceitful, he brought forth the gold eagle.

The ground shivered beneath him as the hole reacted to his special trick.

Llewelyn's face softened. He looked like a small child who had just received a puppy for his birthday. "I knew it," he whispered. He leaned forward, trying to touch the coin in the Judge's hand. His bloody fingers brushed the Judge's, and then they faltered.

Llewelyn collapsed on his side, his outstretched hand curling like a flower closing at night.

The Judge rolled Llewelyn over. The mining master was still alive. *But not for long*, the Judge thought. He knelt beside Llewelyn and tucked the gold eagle into the front pocket of the Llewelyn's coat. He tried to sit the unconscious man up, but as soon as he let go, the hole pushed the body over.

The Judge shaded his eyes and looked at the coach, trying to discern if Victor was still hiding inside. He yelled for the manservant and got no response. The Judge couldn't fault him. He would have jack-rabbited too, given the opportunity.

"Just you and me," he said to the body beside him. "Two old men who aren't right for this world." With a sigh, he pulled Llewelyn upright again and leaned the slack body against his leg. "For what it's worth, I'm sorry about this. It's not very dignified." He grabbed Llewelyn by the collar of his coat and dragged him toward the hole.

It took a long time, and the Judge wasn't sure how much blood Llewelyn had left when he finally reached the hole. There was a long trail behind them, and he couldn't tell if Llewelyn was still breathing.

Only one way to find out, he thought.

Elm sat on the floor of the Bateman hotel. There were even more holes in the wall, and one of the hinges of the door had been blown off in the recent fusillade from the Gatling. Part of Pete lay inside the hotel. The rest of him was outside. Elm wasn't sure the halves were fully connected, and he was too tired to crawl over and check.

Beside him, Dixon lay supine. The sheriff's hand were pressed over the wound in his belly.

Neither man had been hit by the fusillade from the Gatling. Nor was either man in a rush to poke any portion of their anatomy out of the hotel.

They had done enough. The Army could come to them when they were sure there was no one else to gun down. Elm didn't know how long that would take. He glanced down at Dixon. The sheriff didn't look like he was worried about any plans he might have had for the rest of the day.

The sheriff's eyes danced back and forth. His tongue touched the corner of his mouth. "A little parched," he whispered. "Wouldn't mind some whiskey."

Elm nodded and got to his feet. Avoiding the windows—what was left of them, anyway—he made his way to the bar, where he found Rufus. The man had been shot in the back. Elm figured it had happened shortly after Vash had shot the sheriff. He stepped around the dead man and found a bottle that had escaped the gunfire.

He brought it back to the sheriff, but the sheriff was no longer thirsty.

Elm raised the bottle to his lips, but his hand faltered as he noticed something else was missing from the room.

Vash's body was gone.

33

The Judge was tired of walking. The day had gone on without him, and the sun was now an orange slash across the horizon. The sky was the color of the bruises he knew he'd find when he finally got back to Citrine Springs and managed to get these damn clothes off. They were stiff with blood and dirt, and he was going to have to get a new suit. The prospects of a decent tailor in town were slim, and the idea of wearing the sort of rough-and-ready clothing like Elm did was almost too much to bear. Hadn't he suffered enough today already?

He hadn't seen any sign of Victor, nor the horses he had freed from the coach. He had hoped they would come back, somehow sensing his need and returning to transport him to town. He had saved them, after all, hadn't he? From devil frogs that would have—well, spectral amphibians that were phantasmal manifestations of Llewelyn's own insecurities—but that was beside the point. He had saved them. They should come back and thank him.

There had been some noise earlier, the sort of distant *pop-pop-pop* that was either fireworks or gunfire, and given the dour mood adopted by everyone in this town, the Judge suspected it was the latter. He wondered what he was missing, and for awhile entertained the idea that it had something to do with Llewelyn's hole, which had sealed itself up shortly after he had rolled the company man into it—*nice and tidy, thank you very much.* But it was more likely, he decided, that Elm had done something foolish, which was prone to happen when he wasn't around.

Since then, the day had stretched out like a luxurious woman who wouldn't let you touch her. To break the monotony of his journey, he selected landmarks and tried to guess how many steps it would take to reach them. The first one—an angry little bush with upraised branches—had vanished when he thought he had reached it. Or maybe he had misguided what he had thought he had seen.

The second landmark—a solitary tree blasted by lightning a few years back—was easier to track. Other trees—if there had been other trees, once upon a time—had run off when this one had caught fire. It was all alone now. Sticking up out of the endless grass like a shriveled finger.

The Judge knew how it felt.

Anyway, he was confident that he had guessed correctly as he neared the tree. Only twenty or so paces more and—

The Judge stopped, not quite sure of what he was seeing.

There were two shriveled black things. One—yes, that one— was the tree, and the other one was . . . well, it was moving, whatever it was.

Fortunately, the Judge wasn't carrying Llewelyn's rifle because he needed something to do with his hands. He checked that the weapon was ready to fire and waited. After a few minutes, he decided that waiting was even duller than walking. He began to close the distance between himself and the staggering shape.

It was a man. A giant hairy man, wearing a long coat. He looked worse than the Judge felt, which the Judge hadn't thought possible until he got close enough to the figure to take its measure, and he was carrying a long rifle. When the Judge recognized the rifle, he stopped, braced his feet, and raised Llewelyn's rifle. "That's far enough," he called out.

The Judge wasn't surprised that the man didn't react. Maybe he hadn't heard the Judge or made he didn't think the Judge was serious. Either way, the Judge had given due diligence to his fellow man, and he started to squeeze the trigger.

At the last second, he held off, because the man wasn't alone.

There was something in the grass. Several *somethings*. Trailing behind him. Circling him. When the man finally noticed he wasn't alone, they closed in. The Judge watched as a pair of Indians appeared out of the grass. They were carrying long strips of ragged cloth. At first, the Judge thought he was witnessing some sort of crazy Indian ritual where they marked their enemy without harming him. The man slowed, unsure of what was happening. The Indians wrapped his legs, and when he tried to walk, he stumbled. The grass thrashed where he had fallen, and then it went still.

The Judge, curious in spite of himself, lowered his rifle and came forward to investigate.

When one of the Indians stood up, the Judge nearly pulled the trigger. Calming himself, the Judge tucked the rifle into the crook of his arm, barrel pointed at the sky. "Good evening," he said amiably, as if there was nothing unusual about what he had witnessed.

"There are many traditional greetings one offers when strangers meet on the plain." The Indian spoke surprisingly passable English. "Most of them speak admirably about the other's horse. But you have no horse."

"I do not," the Judge said.

"Have you lost it?"

"I—" The Judge shook his head. "We parted accidentally."

The Indian inclined his head. "You and this horse are separated often."

"Well, I wouldn't go that far," the Judge said.

The Indian smiled, and the Judge felt like he was missing something. "Have we met?" he asked.

"You are the companion of the small dog and the quiet one," the Indian said.

"Yes," the Judge said. "I guess I am." He recognized the Indian. "You were at the trading post. You and your friends." He snapped his fingers. "You were the one who took on that soldier, weren't you? My God, man, I have never seen anything like that. How did you accomplish such a feat?"

The Indian shrugged like the Judge had asked him about something so inconsequential that it required no answer.

"What was your name?" The Judge snapped his fingers again. "Scarlet . . . No, no. Red. Red Eagle. That's it."

"That is the name Fat Bear gave me," said the Indian.

"What are you and your friend doing out here?" The Judge looked toward the spot in the grass where the man had been taken down. Some of the stalks were still quivering. "You have trussed up that man like a giant baby. Is that another tradition out here on the plains?"

"You were going to shoot him," Red Eagle said.

The Judge considering denying the Indian's statement, but he was tired and he had lost his enthusiasm for being contrary. "I was," he said.

"You can't spill his blood," Red Eagle said. "Not here."

"Why not?"

"He's too close. His blood will find its way back. Your sacrifice will be undone."

A chill went up the Judge's spine, and he found his throat constricting when he swallowed. "Is that so?" he said, trying to sound like this was the sort of thing he heard every day.

"It is," Red Eagle said. "No part of him can return to the earth. That is the only way the darkness can be truly purged."

The Judge recalled a fire he and Elm had made earlier that summer, when they had burned something that had no place in this world. "Aye," the Judge said quietly. "I suppose that is the way."

Red Eagle raised an arm and pointed at the lonely tree, blasted by lightning. Fire from Heaven. "We must burn him."

"We?"

Red Eagle nodded. "You say you know the way it must be done," he said. "All that remains is the spark. As I told your friend."

The Judge didn't know what the Indian was talking about, but he had seen Llewelyn's parlor trick. The way the man's face had lit up when he had concentrated. The way he had stared so intently at the candle. All that effort. And yet, he had made a tiny flame. The candle had been lit.

The Judge was older than Llewelyn. By nearly three months. And, by his own account, *meaner*.

"Aye," the Judge said, acquiescing to what was being asked of him. Knowing that he could no longer feign ignorance about the matters that had consumed Llewelyn. There was a burden—a responsibility, even—a burden that, in accordance with some supernatural accounting, he had been born to bear. "I can provide that spark."

34

Elm leaned against the bar. A ragged groove ran across the dusty surface next to the glass he had been drinking from. He tried not to think about how close the bullet that had made this groove had come to hitting him. It was chilly in the Bateman's public room—understandably so, given the broken windows, the holes in the wall, and the way the door wouldn't close all the way. Still, the mood in the room was festive and merry, filled with the raucous noise that survivors found great delight in making.

A black hat fell onto the bar, covering part of the bullet groove. There was a hole in the crown of the hat, evidence that someone else had been close to a moving bullet.

"Did I miss anything?" the Judge asked. He reached for the whiskey bottle nearby and splashed an inch into Elm's glass.

"No more so than usual," Elm said as he watched the Judge pick up the glass and drain its contents. "I was—" He noticed that the Judge had leaned a long object against the bar.

"You left it out in the yard," the Judge said. He refilled the glass. "I know how you get about your things."

The Judge's face was smudged with dirt and ash. He looked haggard—*more so than usual*, Elm thought—and there was a haunted gleam in his eye. "Is that all?" he asked.

The Judge paused for a moment before downing another shot of whiskey. "There was a man that needed killing," he said. "And a hole that needed filling."

Elm eyed the Judge's clothing. His jacket and waistcoat were dark, which hid a lot of sins, but given the heavy stains on the Judge's shirt, it was likely the rest of the Judge's clothes were equally stained. "It must have been a pretty deep hole," Elm said, deciding nothing more needed to be said about the former.

The Judge looked at something that wasn't on the wall behind the bar. "It was," he said. Shaking himself out of his reverie, he poured a third shot into the glass. This time, he pushed the glass toward Elm. "You sure I didn't miss anything?"

Elm eyed the glass. He knew if he didn't claim it, the Judge would, and he wasn't that much of a fool. "There was a bit of trouble," he said, "but it's over now."

The Judge turned around and surveyed the room. His gaze didn't linger on the broken chairs or the holes in the walls or the stains that hadn't been scrubbed out entirely. He looked at the people who were talking loudly and drinking madly and carrying on with all the delight that those who know they are going to see another sunrise do. "Yes," he said. "Yes, it is." He looked at Elm, and there was a knowing look in his eye. "They'll blame this on us, you know."

"I do," Elm said.

"Probably tomorrow. The day after, at the latest."

"Aye," Elm said. "At the latest."

The Judge caught sight of a familiar redhead in the crowd and a wolfish grin made its way across his face. He picked up his hat and crammed it on his head. "Tonight, I intend to get in a tub with that young lady over there and splash about until the water runs all over the floor." Fumbling in his jacket, he found something and slapped it against Elm's chest. As Elm took what the Judge was giving him, the old man nodded toward one of the tables by the broken windows. "You should do the same."

He pushed away from the bar, whistling loudly as he pushed his way into the crowd. "Glory," he cried, making himself heard over the noise. "These old bones cry out for your sweet solace, dear lady."

Elm glanced down at what the Judge had given him. It was the paperback book from Forestal's trading post. The one written by Meriweather Vance. It was decidedly more tattered than it had been the last time he had seen it.

Elm picked up his glass from the bar and walked over to the table where Lily Harlstone was sitting. "Miss Harlstone," he said.

She made an effort to smile, and very nearly succeeded. "Mr. Stonebrook," she said. He had only seen her briefly when all the shooting had ended, before she had been swept away by the needs of the wounded. With the doctor dead, she was now the sole medical practitioner in town. Shortly before the Judge had arrived, he had noticed her sitting by the window.

"May I join you?" he asked.

"You may," she said. "On one condition, though."

"And that is?"

"Call me Lily."

He set his glass and the book on the leaning table. "All right, Miss Lily," he said. "I can manage that." He drew out the chair and sat down.

She shook her head at his stubbornness, but it came with a smile. "What is that?" She asked, indicating the tattered book.

"It's not Shakespeare. That's for certain."

"I didn't think it was."

"It is a book about a man who hunts a bear, and—"

"Oh, is that the one you mentioned the other night, when we first . . ." She trailed off and he understood the look in her eye. It did seem like so long ago.

"Aye," Elm said, not letting himself get pulled into a well of lamentable melancholy. "It is."

She reached for the book. "*Ferret Finnegan and the Black Bear of*—The rest is gone. I'm afraid we don't know the origin of the bear." She traced a finger along the ragged edge of the cover. "The beast is also missing its head."

"Some stories are like that," Elm said.

Her smile faded, and it took her a moment to summon it back. "I—I am not sure I want to be a party to a story like that," she said.

"Nor do I," Elm said. "This one, though, I am confident this one has a satisfying ending."

She looked at him carefully, a wistfulness in her gaze. "I would like a tale with a satisfying ending."

"As would I," Elm said.

She looked across the room and watched as the Judge found Glory. She threw her arms around his neck, and the old man looked like he was spry enough—or at least, enthusiastic enough—to carry her upstairs.

"I do not think he is interested in reading tonight."

"I do not think he is," Elm said.

They watched the Judge stagger up the stairs. He almost fell twice, but he persevered, elevated by the jeers and cheers from the assembled crowd watching them. When he reached the landing, he put Glory down and they turned and accepted the room's adulation.

And while everyone's attention was on the Judge, Lily reached across the table and took Elm's hand. She looked him in the eye, communicated a desire to him without words, and he nodded in agreement. Hand in hand, and with much less fanfare, they left the Bateman through the door that did not quite close.

Laelaps was the only one who noticed their departure, and being the good watchdog that he was, he did not bark. He merely wagged his tail in approval.

EPILOGUE

The days got colder and shorter, but the sun never wavered. Every day, it spilled its light across the plains, and every day, the land below was delighted to reflect this light back. It was all white, these days, from the great and lazy curls of the Mississippi nearly all the way to the Rocky Mountains. Oh, there were a few dark spots on the prairie. Places where the sun would poke around, chasing after shadows, hoping to find holes without bottom.

And the one near the train tracks in Kansas? That one was gone. It had puckered like the back end of a scrawny little dog, as the sun had heard an old man with a bushy beard speak of it months ago. At first, the sun had been sad. It hadn't ever seen the bottom of that hole; now, it never would. Ah, but the sun's sorrow didn't last. It never did. It was easily distracted, after all.

It saw the lonely tree, of course, but the black and twisted thing that hung from it never moved.

And then, one day, as the sun coursed across the winter landscape, a coach departed from Citrine Springs. Curious, the sun followed it, wondering if the coach was going to a new hole. But it wasn't. It only went as far as the tree. The sun waited for awhile, but it couldn't wait long, and soon, it had to be on its way.

The coach sat by the tree for awhile. Eventually, one of the occupants called out to the coachman, and he got down from the box seat and brought around a wooden stool to the door.

Lily Harlstone, wearing a heavy winter cloak and a beaver-lined hat, got out of the coach. She waited beside the stair, and a second woman got out of the coach. If the sun were still staring down at the coach, it would have marveled at the color of her hair, so much like its own fiery crown. The second woman wore a heavy coat as well, and she moved as if she were still unused to wearing such mundane attire. The third woman, who was timid and unsteady as she stepped down, wore a cloak that was too big for her. Her head was a tiny bump that stuck up like an early sprout from the bunched collar, and when she stepped off the stool, the coat dragged on the ground. Her hair was wild and unruly about her head. Her face was no longer swollen, and she had the use of both eyes.

Lily and Glory and Willa walked to the lonely tree. They looked at the black and twisted shape. It looked as if it was bound to the wood, but there were no ropes and no chains. It was burned as badly as the tree trunk—*worse*, Lily hoped— and it looked like there wasn't much left of it but bones. The skull was bent forward, as if it was crying, but Lily found it more reassuring to think that it was admitting defeat.

"I—I don't think I want to do this," Willa said.

"Yes, you do," Lily said. She brought out the mallet she had been holding under her cloak. She had borrowed it from the farrier in town. He used it to shape horseshoes and other bits of iron as needed by farmers and travelers. She offered it to Willa, who stared at it as if might be too heavy for her to lift.

It wasn't. Perhaps Willa was stronger than she realized. Perhaps the weight was reassuring and it gave her purpose to swing it. Perhaps it sang to her, a song without words but with rhythm and meaning nonetheless.

Willa looked at Glory, who gave her a nod, and Willa walked toward the lonely tree and the charred skeleton. Her step quickened as she got close, and when she reached the tree, she did not hesitate. She raised the mallet and brought it down on the leg of the skeleton.

Black dust stirred—a minor acknowledgment of her action. But Willa had the song of the iron mallet in her now, and she swung it again. This time, Lily heard old bones crack. Will grunted with her third swing, and Lily thought: *Yes, that's it. That's the way to do it.*

As Willa beat and broke the burned skeleton of the man who had hurt her, Lily looked at Glory, who nodded in return. *Never again*, Lily thought.

And she was right.

Elm and the Judge shall return.

About the Author

Mark Teppo lives in the Pacific Northwest, where he writes, reads, and sells books. Every once in a while, he goes out into the woods. His favorite tarot card is the Moon.

You may find him on the web at www.markteppo.com, as well as on Instagram @mark.teppo and Twitter @markteppo.

In addition to frontier stories with monsters, he also writes stories about conspiracy theories and esoteric mysteries, dark fantasy stories, the occasional bit of science fiction, and books about writing. He also writes sun-soaked Southern California noir under the name Harry Bryant.